Tм

Books 1 – 3

Katrina Kahler

Copyright © KC Global Enterprises Pty Ltd

Table of Contents

Book 1

Swapped

PROLOGUE

Ali

The throb of my pulse quickened as I raced up the hill. Something was wrong. I had no idea what, but I felt my anxiety deepen with each step. The crest of the hill was so close yet so far. The muscles in my legs burned. If I stopped, I would probably fall over and not reach the top. I pushed through the uncomfortable cramps in my legs and abruptly stopped at the edge of the steep incline. I leaned over, catching my breath as my worst fears were realized.

The car pulled out of the lot. The girl in the backseat turned her head. She had the exact same profile as me. Where was she going? Why was she leaving? And now what was I supposed to do without her?

CHAPTER ONE

Casey

One week earlier...

I rolled over in bed and blinked a few times until the red numbers on the clock on my bedside table formed. I blinked some more, the numbers not moving. But they didn't make sense. It couldn't be that late—

The animated voice of my brother, Lucas, could be heard from the kitchen down the hall.

I jolted awake. Lucas was never up before me. Normally, Mom had to drag him out of bed. I looked at the clock again, and it all made sense.

Oh my gosh! The time wasn't wrong. I was terribly late!

Jumping out onto the floor, I sprinted down the hall to the kitchen. Lucas had his action figures on the table and was making them stomp all over the cereal box while exaggerated explosion sounds poured from his mouth.

Mom was dressed in a pants suit and her hair was slicked back into a bun. She was pulling out file folders from her bag and placing them on the table. She had a meeting that morning. She always got up early for her meetings, why didn't she bother to wake me?

"It's about time you were up," she said without

looking at me.

"Mom! You were supposed to wake me up earlier!"

"That's what an alarm clock is for," she said, continuing to organize the file folders on the table.

I placed my hands on my hips. "I forgot to set it, I was up last night finishing the paper for Mrs. Halliday's class."

She turned around to look at me, her brown eyes wide and unconcerned. "Well, that will teach you about responsibility."

I ground my teeth together. I wanted to argue more, but I didn't even have enough time for that. Instead, I grumbled loudly enough for her to hear and ran back to my room. I only had ten minutes before the bus was scheduled to arrive. When I looked in my full-length mirror I could have screamed. My hair was a tangled brown mess atop my head, and my eyes were still sleepy. I resembled a zombie. I opened my dresser drawer and pulled out a random outfit for the day. Anything would have to do. I couldn't be late for school. Not after staying up until eleven-thirty the night before finishing off my paper. The paper was half my grade for the semester, and Mrs. Halliday didn't give excuses for late work.

After dressing, I brushed my teeth and combed my hair. It was a good thing I decided to shower the night before. My hair was something I never had to worry about. It obeyed with the stroke of a brush, smoothing down into glossy waves over my shoulders.

I finished with enough time to grab a granola bar and water. Then I rushed out of the house to the bus stop. Lucas was already there with his dorky friends.

I took a breath as the bus appeared down the road. I'd made it! I smiled and knew that today would be okay.

At least I thought so until a short while later. We were on the last stop before school and I remembered the one thing I'd forgotten. The only thing that mattered all week. I saw the five-page paper in my mind's eye, sitting on my desk where I placed it after I printed it the night before.

No, no, no!

My stomach twisted, and my throat tightened. How could I forget the most important thing? I'd been so concerned with how I looked that I forgot to put the assignment in my bag. I shoved my fingers through my hair, lifting the tresses from my suddenly hot neck.

Gripping the top of the seat in front of me, I wanted to propel myself down the aisle, off the bus and race home. I'd never make it to school on time, but at least I'd have my paper. Being late would be better than my paper not in Mrs. Halliday's hands by the end of the day.

"No standing!" Mr. Chambers, the bus driver, shouted at me. His eyes looked at me in the mirror above his head.

A few kids glanced towards me, and I slumped down in my seat. Could this day get any worse?

I used the school's front office phone to call Mom's cell. She didn't pick up so I had to leave a message.

"Mom, I forgot my paper on my desk. It's crucial for my grade. Please drop it by the school office after you get this..." I trailed off then hung up. I knew she wouldn't leave whatever meeting she had, once she got to work. Her job was so important to her, more than her daughter. Why did Mom wake Lucas and not me? Our bedrooms were right next to each other. Once again I was an afterthought. Now I had to go to class without my paper and probably get a stern lecture from Mrs. Halliday and a failing grade.

A tear slipped from my eye, and I wiped it away. I glanced at the clock, realizing I only had two minutes to get to class.

I thanked the secretary for letting me use the phone and tried to ignore the pitying look on her face.

The final bell rang when I reached the top of the stairs. I ran down the hallway and arrived at the classroom too late. The door was closed, and all of my classmates were looking at the front of the room. I placed my hand on the knob and slowly turned it, trying not to make a peep. I expected all eyes to be on me, but this was not the case. Everyone listened with rapt attention as Mrs. Halliday spoke. She moved, and I saw a girl next to her at the front of the room.

I gasped lightly and wondered if I were still dreaming, the girl in front of the classroom looked exactly like me. I pinched my arm and bit down on my lip from the pain. I was definitely awake. I looked down at my clothes and realized we were wearing different outfits. Maybe I was still sleepy and seeing things. There were plenty of brown-haired girls in the world, she was just another one.

"Take a seat, Casey," Mrs. Halliday said with a smile, showing a smear of lipstick on her front teeth. "Class, I want to introduce our newest transfer student."

I found my seat and dropped my bag next to it before sitting. Whenever anyone was late for class, Mrs. Halliday always made an example out of them. I supposed I had the new girl to thank.

"OMG!" my best friend, Brianna, Brie for short, whispered in my ear. "She looks just like you!"

Brie sat in the seat behind me, and I waved her off. "No, she doesn't."

Though I knew deep down, I was only fooling myself. I looked at the new girl again, and I felt as if I were looking into a mirror. The only differences being her long braid cascading down her back and her shy expression. Her pretty top complemented her dark eyes and olive complexion. The same color eyes and complexion that strangers complimented me on all the time.

I pinched myself again to be certain I wasn't dreaming.

"This is Ali Jackson," Mrs. Halliday announced to the class. "I'd like you all to make her feel welcome."

The class chorused, "Hello, Ali."

Her eyes darted around the room, and she gave a small smile and a wave. "Hi, everyone."

I narrowed my eyes, inspecting every detail of the girl, desperate to find more differences. Though with Brie's confirmation of what I saw, I was almost sure that I wouldn't find any. How the heck was this possible?

"You can take the empty chair next to Grace," Mrs. Halliday said while pointing to the back of the room.

"Thank you." Ali started down my aisle, and I turned my head, allowing my hair to cover my face when she passed.

Mrs. Halliday went to her desk to take attendance.

A few moments later I glanced behind me. Ali had her hands clasped together on the desk, and just as I turned, she looked in my direction.

Her eyes flicked to mine, and her eyebrows shot up in surprise. She stared at me and I could see that she was as startled as I was.

I whipped around, embarrassed at being caught. Who did this girl think she was anyway? Out of the thousands of schools in the country, she had to come to mine? And look like me nonetheless. This entire day was shaping up to be the worst of my life. I didn't want to fathom what else could go wrong.

"Alright class," Mrs. Halliday said, brushing her hands over her knit skirt. She didn't have the best fashion sense for, but she was my favorite teacher. I wondered if she would give me a break since I was never late with assignments. With my luck so far that day I doubted it.

"Let's all turn to page fifty-four in your books," she continued.

I pulled the book out of my bag and placed it on my desk. While going to the appropriate page, I glanced behind me once more.

My cheeks heated up when my crush, Jake Hanley, turned in his seat and offered to share his book with Ali.

She smiled at him and moved closer. He leaned forward to say something to her, but I couldn't quite make out what he said. She covered her mouth and quietly laughed.

Of course she did! He was the cutest boy in our grade! Jake rarely talked to me, and now he was chatting away with someone who looked exactly like me? So unfair!

I whirled around in my seat, fuming. I could imagine their conversation. Her with her flirty eyes—my exact eyes—and him getting to know her instead of him getting to know me. I'd tried all year to get him to notice me, and she walks in here on her first day and catches his attention right away.

Ugh!

While Mrs. Halliday rambled on about something in the book, I found I couldn't take my eyes away from Jake. Ali was following the text on the page, and he was staring at her. How come he never looked at me that way?

It was clear Ali and I looked a lot alike, even though I disliked her for that. Maybe it was because Jake and I had gone to school together since kindergarten that he didn't see me in the same way. The new kids who came into the school were always popular, but soon enough she would be ordinary like the rest of us. I hoped so, anyway!

"Casey," Mrs. Halliday said.

Ali's eyes met mine again while Jake continued to watch her.

I turned around in my seat to meet Mrs. Halliday's gaze.

"Pay attention please," she said.

"S-sorry," I said and slunk down in my chair.

Mrs. Halliday continued with the lesson, and I struggled to concentrate. I wanted to look back again to see if Jake and Ali were getting closer than we ever had, but I didn't want to risk being caught out. Instead, I stared at the clock, counting down the minutes until the next bell.

CHAPTER TWO

Brie and I walked outside together for recess. We put our bags down at the designated spot by the stairs and started for the benches on the far end of the lot. A few kids already were sitting there, but there were enough spots for the two of us. We squished together on the end of the bench just as Ali came outside. The seat was cold and still damp from the night before, the sharp feeling under me added to my annoyance.

My chest tightened as I watched her. She was alone for two seconds before Jake and his friends welcomed her into their group.

"It's so unfair," I said to Brie.

"Tell me about it," she said. "If I didn't know any better I'd say you were sisters. Twins, even."

"Really?" I said and squinted my eyes. From that distance, Ali could be any other girl. But then I remembered seeing her up close where the resemblance was uncanny.

"Yeah, actually," Brie said. "Unbraid her hair and she's basically you. You have the same brown eyes, same nose, same chin…"

"Chin?" I asked, touching my own. I didn't realize it was unique enough to compare to others.

Brie shrugged. "You know what I mean. You have the same facial features and skin tone. It's odd actually."

"Really odd." *Nauseatingly odd.*

Brie turned to me, her leg bumping into mine. "I read this article once that said everyone has a look-alike somewhere in the world. Most of the time they aren't related. Something with genetics or whatever. That's crazy, right? Maybe Ali is your look-a-like."

Across the way, Ali was laughing with Jake and his friends. I silently wished she was across the world, and I'd never discovered her.

"People always say that Adam looks like Daniel Radcliffe."

I turned to her. "Your little brother, Adam?"

"It's so annoying," Brie continued. "People come up to him all the time in the grocery store, the mall, wherever! Now he's starting to believe it. I can't go into any room in the house without finding a wand. And he always insists on wearing my dad's robe which is way too big for him. And to make matters worse, he says he wants to be a famous actor someday."

I laughed. "As a Harry Potter look-a-like?" Letting out my laughter made the tightness in my shoulders loosen.

Brie groaned. "Probably! I can't even watch the movies in the house now without him reciting the entire thing!"

Adam did look like Harry Potter, I had made the assumption before since those books were my ultimate favorites. I'd even said it to Adam a few times, myself. I hated being one of the ones to annoy Brie. I made a mental note to keep those thoughts to myself from now on, even though the likeness was definitely there!

While Brie's attempt to make things better had

helped, I still felt uneasy about Ali. I couldn't quite put my finger on it. I'd never felt so strange about a person before. It was as if I had some new supernatural sense, but only about Ali. Besides that, I was the only person in my class with someone who looked like me. It was just weird!

Brie chatted on about something else. I tried to pay attention, but I couldn't think of anything besides Ali. I tried to find some more differences between us as the day wore on but I couldn't. I'd never been more excited for school to be over so I could go home and get the day over with.

I tossed and turned the whole night dreaming that I was being chased by hundreds of look-a-likes. It was terrifying!

For the first time ever, I was happy when my alarm clock went off. I set it for an extra half-hour early so I wouldn't be rushed like I was the day before. Mrs. Halliday had been in a good mood the previous afternoon and gave me a second chance to hand in the paper that I'd left at home. She said everyone was allowed to have an off-day. And what a day it had been!

I made sure to place the paper in my backpack and leave it by the door so I wouldn't forget. I was ready for school with fifteen minutes to spare. Plopping down on the couch, I flipped on the television, dreading going into school and seeing Ali. My dreams from the night before still haunted me, but there wasn't anything I could do about the new girl. Secretly, I hoped whatever made her move to our town would change and she could leave. Though I doubted that would happen. That would be a miracle indeed!

Lucas bounded into the room, full of energy. I wasn't sure where he got it all from that early in the morning. As usual, he was wearing his favorite yellow hat. I swore he must even wear it to bed, I never saw him without it on his head.

"How come you're watching T.V. before school?" he asked, scrambling to get his arm into his shirt.

"I got up early."

"Mom!" Lucas called. "Is Casey allowed to watch television?"

I swatted at him, but he jumped back with a goofy grin on his face.

Mom strode into the room, already dressed and perfectly presented for another meeting. Twice in one week wasn't common. She smoothed her hand over her hair and rolled her eyes. "I don't have time for this bickering. Lucas, finish your breakfast."

I smirked at him. At least she didn't tell me I had to turn the television off. Mom's uncaring attitude had finally worked in my favor.

Switching my gaze back to the T.V. my thoughts returned to the new girl at school and my uneasy feelings about the day ahead.

CHAPTER THREE

During gym class, Mr. Pavoni our gym teacher announced that he was splitting the class into pairs for volleyball and we were to practice bumping the ball to each other. Brie and I moved closer together and I grabbed her arm, hoping Mr. Pavoni would get the hint that we wanted to be partners. He gave us a look but then nodded his head in agreement. Brie and I jumped up and down with excitement. I jogged to the bag of volleyballs and picked one out for us.

Over the past few weeks in class, I'd become really good at volleyball. I wasn't normally the sporty type but volleyball seemed to come naturally to me.

Brie, on the other hand, struggled with the concept of hand-eye coordination. She either missed it entirely or hit the ball over our heads. I was happy to be her partner and help her get better, but I was pretty sure volleyball wasn't her sport. At least she could laugh at her attempts. It helped smooth the knot in my stomach over Ali's presence.

Halfway through class, Mr. Pavoni asked us to switch partners to practice serving.

I immediately looked at Jake. My nerves jumped, and I wondered how cool it would be for Mr. Pavoni to pick me as Jake's partner.

Mr. Pavoni had sorted most of the class before he

came to me. "Casey, since you're doing well, how about you help out our new student. And Grace can work with Brie."

My body froze. I looked to my right where Ali stood next to Grace. Grace moved over to Brie's side, and I reluctantly stepped closer to Ali.

Mr. Pavoni was completely oblivious to the fact that Ali and I looked alike. After he finished swapping everyone. He blew his whistle, and everyone started to practice serving.

I handed Ali the ball, and she held it in her hands as if she were handling a foreign object. She gnawed on the inside of her cheek, avoiding my eyes.

"Here," I said, taking the ball from her. "You hold it in the palm of your hand like this and then put your other hand into a fist and swing it back." I showed her each motion.

Her eyebrows furrowed.

Geez, even Brie wasn't this clueless. Why did Mr. Pavoni have to stick me with her? I was happy he noticed my progress with the sport, but I needed to be challenged, not brought down to her level.

"I'll show you," I said taking the ball from her.

Ali dropped her hands to her sides. Did she not realize she was supposed to return my serve?

"Put your hands in front of you in the bumping stance."

She looked even more confused than she already had.

Oh well, she'd learn soon enough.

I walked backward, distancing myself from her. "Ready?"

I could have sworn I heard her say no, but I served it anyway. Hard.

The ball soared over her head, and she ducked. She actually ducked!

Ali looked behind her as our ball rolled away then she looked back at me, her eyes wide with confusion.

I grumbled. "Go get it!"

She nodded and ran for it. When she finally reached it, she walked slowly back to face me. At this rate, the class would be over before I had another turn.

Ali positioned her hands all wrong and barely hit the ball. It plopped a few feet in front of her and rolled the rest of the way to me. I glanced at the clock, needing for the class to be over so I could get away from this Casey-imposter.

I picked up the ball, twirled it in my hands and served it again.

Once again, the ball soared over her head, and I couldn't help a small smile when she missed it completely and had to go running after it again.

Brie was looking at me, and I smiled towards her. Her smile faded when she watched Ali run after the ball.

I looked over, and my stomach dropped. The ball had rolled right to Jake's feet.

He bent over to pick it up and handed it to Ali. Their hands brushed, and my cheeks flushed.

He grinned at her and said something to make her smile.

I had the worst luck!

Ali came back to her spot and tried to serve again. And like before, it bounced a few feet in front of her then rolled to me.

"Oops," she said.

She didn't even seem like she was trying. She was probably one of those girls who pretended to be bad at sports so the boys would help her. I was so not that girl. My anger built up inside me as I pictured her with Jake. I served the ball again and like before she didn't even try to go for it. It flew over her head, and she even let out a girly squeal as the ball zipped by.

A loud whistle made me turn around.

Mr. Pavoni came to my side with a stern expression on his face. "That was too hard, Casey. I'm disappointed that you're not trying to help Ali. I think you should sit on the bleachers for a little while and think about what you've been doing."

"But, Mr.—"

"No buts, go." He pointed to the bleachers, and I shuffled towards them, plopping on the bottom bleacher and crossing my arms, fuming.

Mr. Pavoni had taken Ali over to Jake and his partner, Mark, to join in with them.

I sat up straighter, watching them. They threw Ali the ball so lightly a child could hit it. And she still missed! Though instead of complaining, the guys clapped for her and said she did a good job.

My heart raced in my chest. This wasn't supposed to happen! I wanted to show off how bad she was at the game to bring her down a notch, not make her get closer to Jake!

Jake had moved to Ali's side and showed her how to hold the ball. She did as he said and nailed her next serve.

Ali jumped up and down, cheering.

I had shown her the exact same way to serve, and she had been hopeless. Why was it different with Jake? Probably because he was gorgeous and she wanted to show-off for him.

I watched them play, and Ali began to get better within a few serves.

I didn't realize Mr. Pavoni had come over until he stood directly in front of me.

"Casey, you can play again now if you want. We're going to practice serving a little more before doing a scrimmage."

I stood up, not wanting to miss out on the practice game.

I beelined it towards Ali while Mr. Pavoni called for Mark to be my partner. My heart sank as Mark jogged awkwardly in my direction, then stood waiting for me to pass the ball, a huge grin on his face.

His glasses slid down his nose, and he had to keep pushing them up. I turned around, picking my ball up from the ground. I didn't want to get in trouble again, so I gave him an easy serve. I didn't need to learn a lesson twice in one class. Besides, I had the practice game to show off my skills to Jake, he would be impressed then, and Ali would be ancient history.

Even with the easy serve, Mark managed to miss each one. And on his wild serves, I had to run after every single ball since they either went over my head or nearly knocked out my other classmates. At least with Ali, I didn't need to move to get the ball.

I was relieved when Mr. Pavoni split the class into teams. I made my way over to Brie but then we were told to count off by twos which meant that she was on the other team. All the twos went to the opposite side of the net. With the luck I was having I wasn't sure why I was surprised. I was sorely disappointed that Ali and Jake were on Brie's team as well.

I looked around at my team which was made up of Mark, his only other friend, Kenneth, and some of the girly-girls in my class. Needless to say, we didn't do very well. I had to carry the whole team, and the only points we got were from my impressive serves. Too bad Jake wasn't watching when I served, he was too preoccupied with Ali. At the end of the game, they even high-fived! What I wouldn't give to be her at that moment.

Mr. Pavoni dismissed the class, and we went into the locker rooms to change back into our regular clothes.

Some of the more popular girls attached themselves to Ali so they could talk to her.

I'd never felt so invisible. It wouldn't be as annoying if she looked different to me. I began to think it wasn't my looks that were the problem. Maybe it was my personality.

When I told this to Brie, she reassured me there wasn't anything wrong with my personality.

I knew she was trying to make me feel better, but I couldn't shake the uncomfortable feeling inside of me when I thought of Ali.

When the bell rang for lunch, we all left the locker room in one large group. Brie and I walked in front. I couldn't stand to be in the room with Ali any longer.

My body flushed when I saw Jake outside the locker room, leaning against the wall with one foot propped up against it. He looked like a model straight out of a magazine.

When our eyes met, he gave me a broad smile.

I smiled back, my stomach doing somersaults.

The group of popular girls and Ali went over to Jake. He did a double-take from me to Ali and then shifted that adorable smile to her.

He had mistaken me for Ali!

"Want to sit with us at lunch?" Jake asked Ali.

She agreed, and they all walked away.

My shoulders slumped and suddenly I wasn't too thrilled about eating at all. In fact, all I wanted to do right then was go home.

CHAPTER FOUR

After another restless night of sleep, I woke up early to study for my Math exam. All of the numbers in my textbook mushed together in my vision. I skimmed over the equations, confident that I would do fine. I loved Math and tended to do well on assignments and exams. During breakfast, I allowed my mind to wander to Ali. It was disturbing enough that she had the same face, but that uncomfortable feeling I had about her deep inside still hadn't gone away. Thankfully though, it disappeared during the bus ride as I attempted to review the material for the exam.

But when I entered the classroom, the weird sensation became stronger than ever. Then I spotted Ali and Jake at the back of the room, talking. Jake looked really good, especially his messy dark hair. I shook my head and sat in my seat, turning my back to them, but at the same time, I couldn't help straining to hear their conversation. They were speaking too low to hear anything important, but I cringed every time she giggled. I *so* did not laugh like her.

I was grateful when Mrs. Halliday started class, and I didn't have to hear their voices chatting together any longer.

I breezed through the exam and felt a warmth inside me. Then I looked around and noticed I was the first to finish. I turned over my paper and smiled smugly. Mrs. Halliday always encouraged those who finished early to check their work, but I didn't think it was necessary. I knew I had aced the exam.

Glancing over my shoulder, I saw Ali with her neck

bent toward her desk, chewing on the eraser part of her pencil. She looked worried, and I knew, this time, she would not come out on top.

When the time was up, Mrs. Halliday asked us to swap papers with the person to our left. I handed my paper along.

Brie leaned forward, her face close to my shoulder. "I don't think I did that well. How do you think you went?"

"Pretty good I think."

Brie scoffed. "You actually like Math, though."

I smiled at her. "I'm sure you did fine."

"Doubt it," she mumbled and sat back in her seat.

I decided to go over the exam with her later and make sure she did better on the next one. Besides, what were friends for?

"Alright, everyone," Mrs. Halliday said. "Mark only the incorrect answers on the papers in front of you."

I looked at Holly Steadman's paper and saw that she had different answers to mine.

My fingers tightened over my pencil as that uncomfortable feeling returned to my stomach.

Mrs. Halliday went over the answers to each question, and I saw that Connor Peters had marked several wrong answers on my sheet. That couldn't be right! Holly only had one wrong answer so far, and I couldn't remember what I'd written down for each.

My mouth went dry, and I had trouble swallowing. I leaned over in my chair to see how many marks Connor had made on my paper. Why didn't I review my answers? My brain was so distracted by Ali that I was about to fail my first Math exam!

There was nothing I could do about the exam now. I turned to Holly's paper and ground my teeth together, concentrating on grading her paper.

After Mrs. Halliday had gone through all the answers, she asked that we pass our tests forward. I didn't bother to see my grade. I was too embarrassed.

She flipped through the sheets and picked several from the pile.

I sunk down in my chair, hoping she wouldn't want the people with bad grades to stay after class. I was humiliated enough for getting such terrible marks on a subject I was good at. I didn't need everyone else to know how badly I had done.

"Wow!" Mrs. Halliday exclaimed. "Apparently, I'm doing my job right, most of you did marvelously."

Except for me. Her comment made me feel even worse.

Mrs. Halliday held up one paper and waved it. "And we have one person who got all of the answers correct. Great job, Ali!"

Jake whooped and clapped his hands. "Go, Ali!"

Since he had so many friends, a couple of other kids applauded too.

I turned in my seat to see Ali beaming. She pretended to be embarrassed, but I knew she was proud.

My chin trembled, and I turned around to face the front of the room. Even though we had the same face, Ali was the clear winner in many aspects. She'd caught the attention of Jake, learned to be great at volleyball in one period, and got high marks in class. She appeared to be the better version of me. And it was only a matter of time before I knew I had to accept that.

On the way to lunch, three people asked if Ali and I were related.

"I swear you could be sisters!" Melissa Friedrich said.

"We're not," I snapped.

Melissa didn't sense my attitude and ran off to introduce herself to Ali.

Ali walked a few feet in front of us. And of course Jake was next to her. I wanted to scream, but on the other hand, I couldn't help watching her interact with *my* classmates. Something about her drew me in. Maybe that's what the other kids were feeling. She was strangely captivating. Annoyingly so.

Ali got into the hot lunch line. I really wanted the chicken tenders, but I didn't want to be near her. Instead, I went toward the sandwich line.

"You're passing on the chicken?" Brie asked, following me.

"Yes."

"You never pass on the chicken," she said.

"I know, but I don't want to be around Ali right now. I swear if one more person tells me we look-alike I'm going to scream."

Brie shifted on her feet. "You don't look that much alike. I mean there are similarities, but she wears her hair *way* different. And her style choices are more preppy while you tend to go for casual."

I knew she was trying to make me feel better, it just wasn't working. If Ali took her hair out of the braid and swapped clothes with me, then she would look exactly like me.

"And I think her teeth are a little crooked…" Brie said, trailing off.

I patted her on the arm. "Thanks."

Brie offered a smile then stepped forward to choose her sandwich, allowing me another stolen second to watch Ali. I didn't want to, but I had to accept that Ali was going to be in all my classes. I promised myself to work harder to prove I was the better look-a-like.

CHAPTER FIVE

Later that afternoon when I arrived home, I looked for my mom. I needed an outsider's opinion on the Ali situation. I'd even snapped a picture of her when we were in the library during study hall so I could have photographic proof for her. She almost caught me, but I managed to hide my phone just in time. That would definitely have been embarrassing.

I went to Mom's office and knocked on the door. There was no answer.

"Mom!" I called, knocking again. I knew she was working, but this was important.

I turned the knob and slowly opened the door, calling for her once more.

Inside the room, she was at her desk talking on the phone, which was why she couldn't hear me.

"Mom?" I asked, firmly. I knew I shouldn't interrupt, but I needed to talk to her.

She held up a finger and continued talking.

After what seemed like hours, she finally turned around. "Hon, when my door's closed, I'm working. You know that."

I stepped into the room. "I know, but I have to talk to you about something."

"And it can't wait?"

I was about to say it couldn't, but I stopped myself. If Mom knew I just wanted to talk about school drama, she'd become annoyed with me for disturbing her important work. And I needed her on my side. "I guess it can wait."

"Well, you've already interrupted me," she sighed. "Tell me the problem."

She continued to type while I quickly told her about Ali and how we look alike and how weird it is at school. I was midway through talking about the Math exam when I realized she was barely paying attention.

I stopped speaking, and she turned around to face me a few moments later. "It doesn't matter if you look similar. It's what's on the inside that counts. Work hard and be the best you can be. I'm sure this girl has flaws too."

"We don't just look *similar*," I said, but she had already turned her attention back to the computer screen. Thinking how quickly she'd shrugged off the conversation, I wondered if I was reading too much into it.

"Is there anything else?" she asked with a slight edge to her voice.

"No," I said dejectedly and started for the door.

"Oh by the way," Mom said. "I'm going away tomorrow for a work trip. Grandma Ann will be watching you."

"You're leaving tomorrow?" I couldn't believe it. She could at least have warned us in advance.

It wasn't the first time she'd done this to us. In fact, she'd gone on more trips this year than we'd ever been on as a family, ever.

"It was a last minute trip, hon. Money is tight now and with these trips, I have the opportunity to bring in a lot more revenue."

"Aren't these trips *costing* money?"

"They are tax-deductible."

I didn't know anything about taxes except that Mom had to deal with them at the beginning of every year. From what I understood is that she had to shell out the money first before seeing any benefits.

From her pinched expression, I knew not to push her further. She was the parent, though most of the time I felt I took over that role. Especially when Grandma Ann was "in charge". I knew I'd be taking care of Lucas who was a handful on regular days. Grandma Ann let him do whatever he wanted, which usually meant that I was left to clean up the mess before Mom returned home.

"Listen, why don't you and Grandma Ann go shopping tomorrow while Lucas is at school?"

I raised an eyebrow. "Skip school to go shopping?" That wasn't something I'd ever imagine Mom saying.

Mom smiled. "It will be fun. Give you two a chance for some alone time."

"But *we* were supposed to do that, remember? I need stuff for school camp next week."

"Casey, please. You're being very difficult. I have to run this household, and we need money to do that. I'm going on the trip, it's up to you if you want to go shopping."

I frowned. As much as I preferred to go shopping with Mom, I could use a break from school for a day to clear my head about Ali. And I did have a growing list of things to get for the school camp trip the following week. It wasn't an ideal situation but the need to be away from Ali had won.

"Okay," I said.

"Grandma Ann will help you get everything you need, hon. I'm sorry I can't go with you. And think of the bright side, you only have a few days here until your trip. I promise it will go by in a flash."

I seriously doubted that. "I'll let you get back to work."

I left the room and headed for the kitchen. I grabbed a box of cookies from the cabinet and selected a few to take with me to my bedroom. Lucas would be home at any minute and would probably destroy something on the way. I went to my room and closed the door, then sat down on my bed and ate the cookies. The chocolate melted in my mouth, and I began to relax. At least if I was taking the following day off, I didn't have to rush through all my homework. That idea quickly disappeared. I'd have to try double as hard on my homework to make sure each answer was correct. I didn't want a repeat of the Math exam.

Sighing, I opened my backpack, tossing my books beside me. I organized them by subject and started with my English assignment. Thoughts of Ali filtered through my head, but I was able to push them away for the time being. As the next day was Friday, I wouldn't have to see her until the following week, and I wasn't going to have annoying thoughts of her ruin my day off. Maybe when I returned to school, it would all be better.

I could only hope.

CHAPTER SIX

As much as I dreaded spending the entire day alone with Grandma Ann, it turned out to be the best day I'd had in a while. And the idea of taking the day off school made it so much more fun! Grandma Ann was not normally very generous when it came to spending money, but she wanted to spoil me. So in addition to getting all the essentials for camp, she even bought me a new outfit for Ronnie's birthday sleepover on the weekend.

That night, after the delicious home-cooked lasagna that Grandma Ann made for our dinner, I tried on my new clothes. The black and white top with capped sleeves perfectly matched the white flared skirt. I pulled my black converse high tops from my closet, and they completed the outfit. I couldn't wait to hear all the compliments from the girls! As I twirled around my room I became more and more excited for the party. I could hardly wait.

The following night, Grandma Ann dropped me off at the party. I jumped out of the car and smoothed down my top and skirt wanting to look flawless. I said goodbye to her and headed down the drive towards the front door.

Ronnie opened the door to welcome me and wrapped me in a hug. "Thanks so much for coming, Casey!"

I handed her a glittering gift box containing a pretty charm bracelet that I'd bought a few weeks earlier. I knew she was going to love it. "Happy Birthday, Ronnie!"

"Thanks, Casey," she beamed at me while at the same time taking in my outfit. "Oh my goodness! I love what you're wearing!"

"Thanks!" I said, smiling back at her. "And I love your denim skirt, Ronnie. It looks so good on you!"

Smiling in return, Ronnie beckoned me to follow her. "Come inside," she said, pointing to the living room. "A few people are here already."

We entered the living room, and I could see that Brie had already arrived as well. She jumped up and came to my side. "Is that your new outfit? It looks awesome on you!"

I'd called her the night before to talk about my shopping trip with Grandma Ann. She seemed just as excited as I was.

I waved to Lacey Gordon who sat on the couch. But then I froze when I realized Ali was sitting next to her. She smiled at me but I turned away in shock, quickly grabbing Brie and dragging her from the room.

"Brie, can show me where to put my bag?" I asked loudly enough for the others to hear. I had to get out of that room.

Brie took me to Ronnie's bedroom and I dropped my bag near the other girl's brightly colored overnight bags.

Then, whirling on her, I could not contain myself any longer, "What is Ali doing here? She just started school, and she's already invited to a sleepover?"

Brie sighed and avoided my eyes. "Well, yesterday in class we had to do a group project. And since you weren't there, Mrs. Halliday asked Ali to join our team. She's actually really nice, and we ended up hanging out during recess and lunch. When Emily Masters told Ronnie she couldn't make the party, Ronnie invited Ali to come instead. And she accepted."

I crossed my arms, my neck burning with heat. Even when I wasn't in school, Ali was ruining my life. "I can't believe this!"

"I didn't want to tell you because I knew you'd be upset. And I was worried that you might not even come, so I decided not to mention it."

I frowned back at her, clearly unhappy.

"I know it's weird that she looks like you, but seriously, Casey, I think you should give her a chance. I really think you'd get along with her."

That was the last thing I wanted to do and Brie could obviously see from my expression, exactly how I felt.

Chewing on her lip, she shrugged her shoulders, not really sure what else to say. "I guess, we should probably head back in there, Casey. They'll be wondering where we are."

"Yeah," I said reluctantly, as I followed her back to the living room.

After finding a spot on the couch next to Ronnie, I tried to put on a happy face, though it was hard, especially with Ali in the room. I glanced at her every so often.

She had merged into the group so easily and after only one day of my absence! She looked so good in what she was wearing. Her outfit was so cool.

It took me a minute, and then I recognized the top she had on. I'd seen it the day before at one of the boutique shops at the mall. It was the exact one I would have loved to wear but when I saw the price tag through the window, I felt bad asking Grandma Ann to buy it as it was so overpriced. I'd been thinking about it ever since and seeing it on Ali proved how nice it would have looked on me.

Ali's family must have a lot of money to afford that top. I added that to the list of things I didn't like about her. If only I hadn't been selfish and gone shopping with Grandma Ann, I could have been in the class group instead of Ali and she would never have been invited. It would have cost me my new outfit but at that point, I didn't care.

Just then the doorbell rang, and Ronnie got up from the couch to answer it. It gave me another opportunity to watch Ali unnoticed. She had turned to face Lacey, and they were chatting away about something. What could they possibly have in common? Lacey was always the girl that I had trouble getting to know as she was so shy, but somehow Ali had managed to befriend her in only a few days.

When all the guests arrived, Ronnie suggested we play some games while we waited for the pizza to be delivered. Placing a few sheets of paper on a nearby table, she explained, "Here are the lists for the scavenger hunt. The first team to find everything will win a prize! And it's a good one too," Ronnie said, grinning widely.

I moved to Brie's side so we could be on the same team.

"I want to be on Ali's team!" Lacey said, jumping up from the floor and moving to stand by her.

"Me too!" Ronnie said, folding her arms adamantly. "I'm the birthday girl, so I get dibs!"

Holly was visibly disappointed that she couldn't be on Ali's team.

"Holly, we can be on the same team for the next game," Ali reassured the girl.

My hands clenched into fists. I felt as if the world had flipped on its side. Sure, Brie and I were always on the same team, but no one had ever fought to be on my team before. And here was Ali, the new girl who fit in better than I did.

My shoulders slumped. What I thought would be a fun night had quickly turned into a disaster, and it was all Ali's fault!

Just to add to my frustration, Ali, Ronnie, and Lacey's team won the scavenger hunt. They even made up a fun dance to celebrate. Holly and Brie wanted to learn the dance too. They both gathered around Ali who was teaching them the moves.

I was not in a dancing mood. Instead, I sat on the couch with my arms crossed.

"Why aren't you dancing with us?" Holly asked with an encouraging grin.

Each of the girls looked at me, and I felt embarrassed. I stood up and mustered a smile while I attempted to copy the moves. All of their attention returned to Ali.

"What's the next game?" I asked Ronnie a few minutes later.

She was too busy with Ali to hear me. I nibbled on my lip and moved away from the group, needing a second to myself. This time, no one seemed to notice my absence. Heat prickled behind my eyes, but I was determined not to cry.

Later in the evening, after games, pizza, cake and ice cream, we set up our sleeping bags in the living room on top of mattresses. I made sure I was on the edge next to Brie, so I could be as far from Ali as possible. I wanted to go to sleep and then go home so I could enjoy what was left of my Ali-free weekend.

I grabbed my toothbrush and headed for the bathroom. The door was ajar so I pushed through and came face-to-face with Ali.

"Oh, sorry," I said, turning away. "I didn't think anyone was in here."

"You can stay. There's plenty of room," she said.

I hesitated. It would be weird if I left after she'd said that. But I really didn't want to be alone with her. In the end, I decided to stay.

Ali moved away from the sink and slid her toiletry bag closer to her, making room for mine.

I put it down and dug through it for my toothbrush and paste. I smeared the paste on the toothbrush and brushed my teeth as quickly as I could.

"This party is so much fun," Ali said.

"Mmhmm," I said, still brushing.

"I've never been to a sleepover birthday before. It's a cool idea."

I nodded and continued to brush.

"Everyone has been so kind to me this week. It made the change to your school so much easier."

"That's good," I said and rinsed the foamy toothpaste

43

from my mouth.

Ali smiled and pulled the elastic from her braid, working her fingers through her hair.

I watched as the only big difference in our looks faded into oblivion. She brushed her long locks into soft waves over her shoulders. The exact same way I always wore my hair!

We stared at each other through the mirror for a few seconds before Ali looked away. She continued to brush her hair while I finished up. The effect was striking and this time, I found it hard not to gape at the girl. We really did look like the same person. The effect was even more so with her change in hair style. Her brown eyes followed the strokes of the brush, up and down, up and down.

I fiddled in my bag for something, not wanting to leave yet. I just had to know.

I turned to her at the same time as she turned to me. "Why do you have my face?" we asked simultaneously.

CHAPTER SEVEN

Ali

Our words hung in the air between us. We looked in the mirror again, and then back at each other. "You look just like me," we said at the same time.

How was this happening? I still couldn't believe that I'd moved to a new school where this girl, Casey, looked exactly like me. And now we were speaking the same words at the same time. Talk about freaky!

Casey's mouth tugged down into a frown, and I felt my lips doing the same. I looked in the mirror at her. Was she as confused as I was? We had the same facial expression so I guessed she was. I didn't know what to say. My hands had the urge to do something so I picked up my brush again and started pulling it through my hair. I hoped Casey would leave, but at the same time, I wanted to know more about why she looked like me.

I moved my hair to the other shoulder and started brushing that side.

"What is that?" Casey asked.

"What is what?" I asked.

"That." She pointed at my shoulder.

I placed my hand over the blemish on my shoulder. "It's a birthmark."

Casey looked at me strangely.

I chuckled lightly. "When I was a kid, I used to try and scrub it off each time I took a bath. Even though my mom told me it was permanent, I always thought it was dirt under my skin."

Casey still said nothing.

My body flushed with embarrassment. I was always protective of that spot and typically wouldn't have shown it, but I felt comfortable about sharing it with Casey for some reason. "I don't mind it now. I think it looks like a heart. Sort of like a tattoo, you know?"

"Yeah," Casey said. "I have a birthmark too." She lifted one leg of her pants and revealed a circular birthmark on her left ankle.

"Birthmarks are common," I said. I was slightly relieved that she didn't have a matching heart-shaped birthmark on her shoulder. That would have taken our same looks to a whole other level.

"When you first came to school," Casey stated, "I thought it was really strange how we looked so similar. Brie told me she'd heard that everyone has a look-alike somewhere in the world. I wonder how many people actually get to meet their look-a-like."

"Probably not many."

"It's a freaky coincidence that we're at the same school."

"Totally."

We laughed. I thought it was more lucky than freaky that we did end up meeting each other. Most people would go through their lives not meeting their look-a-like at all. It was a very cool idea and even though we weren't close, I liked being around Casey.

"Where are you from originally?" Casey asked.

"I was born in Springfield, Missouri."

She nodded. "How come you moved?"

I winced. It was the question everyone wanted to know. And the one I most feared to answer. I told everyone who asked that it was for my mom's job. That was only part of the truth. The move had been for my mom, but not for a job. For her life. Casey's ability to put me at ease made me feel comfortable opening up to her completely.

"I don't tell a lot of people this," I said. "But my mom is very sick with cancer."

"Oh no, I'm so sorry," Casey said, her eyes filling with concern.

"Thanks." I hesitated a moment before continuing. "We had to move here for her to get the best treatment possible. She's in a trial for a new medicine, and it's our last hope."

"Ali, that's awful," Casey said, touching my arm.

Her touch made me feel as if a weight had been lifted from my shoulders. It felt good to talk to someone about what was going on in my life. The move was scary for many reasons, but on the top of the list was Mom's health.

Tears welled in my eyes. "I don't know what we're going to do without her. It would just be my dad and me. I can't imagine her dying. She's like my best friend." My voice cracked, and tears burst from my eyes.

Casey pulled me into a hug, and I cried into her

shoulder. "Ali," she said. "It will be okay. I have no idea what you must be going through, but I know it must be terrible. I'd feel the same way if it were my mom."

A sharp knock at the door made us both jump. Ronnie poked her head through the opening.

"Hurry up you two, we're going to start the movie now. You don't want to miss the beginning."

"We'll be out in a minute," Casey said.

I turned my head to the side to make sure Ronnie didn't see that I was upset. I didn't want to answer any questions about why I was crying.

"Okay, be quick!" Ronnie replied as she headed back to the living room.

Casey took my hands in hers. "It's going to be okay. You can talk to me anytime about this."

I nodded in response, a feeling of relief flooding through me.

"Now," she continued. "Let's go out there and try to have fun. Forget about all your worries for one night and enjoy the party."

I swallowed and nodded, wiping the streaks of tears from my cheeks. Following along behind her, I had the overwhelming feeling that somehow we had been destined to meet.

CHAPTER EIGHT

Casey

Ali and I entered the room where we could see all the girls splayed out comfortably on the floor ready to watch the movie. The opening credits to the film were playing on the television screen.

"Whoa," Lacey said, staring towards us.

Every pair of eyes turned in our direction.

I looked at Ali then back to the girls, each of them now staring openly. "What?"

Holly's mouth gaped open. "Did you two do this on purpose?"

Ali shrugged. "Do what?"

Brie chimed in. "This is freaky. You two looked similar before but now with Ali's hair down and wearing almost the same color pink pajamas, you could be identical twins!"

Ali smiled at me, and I smiled back. She was so much nicer than I'd initially thought and it felt great that she'd confided in me, trusting me enough with her secret. She was going through a lot with her mom so I couldn't fault her for trying to make new friends, especially at a new school. She was braver than me.

I would have been devastated if my mom was sick

like hers. She hid it well, but I knew deep down she was hurting. I made a promise to myself to take it easy on her from now on.

"It's starting!" Ronnie exclaimed.

All of the girls settled into their sleeping bags to watch the movie.

Ali headed to her spot across the room. I watched her go and didn't sit down until she did.

Brie nudged me after I settled in my spot alongside her. "I see you two are getting along now?"

"Yeah," I said. "She's not so bad."

"I told you. It's kinda cool you two look the same *and* are friends."

"Yeah, it is." Until Brie said it, I didn't believe we were friends, but friends told each other secrets. And Ali had chosen to share a big one with me.

The others, including Ali, were fully immersed in the movie. While I usually love watching fantasy films, I couldn't help thinking about the exchange between Ali and myself in the bathroom. As quickly as my life had shifted when she arrived at school, another change seemed to have taken place the moment she shared her innermost secrets with me. And the fact that we seemed to speak the same thoughts at the same time made my skin prickle.

I struggled to pay attention to the movie but continued to find myself distracted by Ali and our likeness in appearance.

I was relieved when the movie finally ended and everyone began chatting. At last, I could escape my thoughts for a little while.

"That was so good! I can't wait for the sequel," Brie said to the group.

"And how hot is the guy who plays David?" Holly said.

Holly and Ronnie pretended to swoon, falling back on their mattresses. All of the girls giggled at their play-acting.

"It was alright," Ali said. "I don't think any book-to-movie series can compare with Harry Potter."

I sucked in a breath.

"No way!" Lacey said. "Harry Potter is too violent. I love the romance in this series."

Holly and Ronnie agreed with Lacey.

I met Ali's eyes for a brief moment before I spoke. "Ali is right. Nothing compares with Harry Potter."

"I wouldn't argue with her," Brie said, warning the group. "Casey is a serious hardcore Harry Potter fan."

"Well I'm the birthday girl, so I win this conversation!" Ronnie said with a grin.

Then everyone began chatting about their favorite parts of the movie we'd just watched. I listened to the conversation since I hadn't paid much attention to the movie itself. My brain had been too preoccupied with thoughts of my lookalike.

Lacey grabbed her phone. "Who wrote the books? I want to read them since the movies are so good."

The name of the author popped into my head, even though I hadn't read the books either.

"H.W. Knowles," I said at the exact same time that Ali did.

Everyone looked at Ali and me.

"That was really weird!" Ronnie said.

"Yeah," Brie agreed. "You two look alike, like the same things, and say the same things at the same time. Very freaky!"

"Are you sure you're not twins?" Holly grinned. "That would actually make a lot of sense."

Holly stared at us for a moment longer, waiting for an answer.

I grinned and waved my hand dismissively. I didn't want to entertain the idea of us being twins. It was impossible. I grew up with my mom and Lucas, while Ali was across the country with her parents. That was that.

"I can't hold it in any longer!" Ali declared, a curious expression on her face.

Her outburst made me jump. "Hold what in?" I asked.

She hesitated and looked me straight in the eyes. "I think there might be a possibility we're twins since...I'm adopted."

All of the girls, including me, gasped at the news.

Then the room exploded in noise. Everyone began to talk at once.

Brie grabbed my shoulders. "Oh my goodness! Imagine you *are* twins and you were separated at birth. It sounds like a movie plot. A really juicy one. Can you imagine that you were adopted by your mom, and no one ever told you?"

I couldn't imagine it. I didn't want to. As much as my mother wasn't around too much, she was my mom. I'd hate it if I found out she'd lied to me all these years. But I really wanted to know more from Ali about her adoption.

Ronnie's mom came into the room. She was in an oversized t-shirt and sweatpants. I'd never seen her without makeup before. She looked as if we'd woken her up. "What is all this racket? It's getting late, time for bed girls."

Ronnie stood up, her eyes wide. "Fifteen more minutes, please Mom?"

Ronnie's mom sighed. "Fifteen minutes then lights out. Don't make me come back out here."

Ronnie shooed her mom out of the room then sat back down on her sleeping bag. "Ali, spill."

Ali's shoulders were tucked under her ears, the attention from all the girls overwhelming. I could almost feel her reluctance to share her story, but there was obviously no turning back now.

"Well," she started. "My parents told me when I was younger that I was adopted. But they never shared anything about my birth mother."

"Did you ask?" Brie questioned.

Ali nodded. "Many times. I love my parents, but I wanted to know more about my real mother; what she was like, and who she was and all that."

"And your parents didn't tell you?" Lacey asked.

Ali sighed. "All they said was that my mom was very young when she had me and she didn't have enough money to take care of a baby. That's pretty much it."

"I would push my mom to tell me everything," Ronnie interrupted.

"It seems to upset her when I ask," Ali said sadly.

I didn't know how long Ali's mother had been sick for, but I could imagine how upsetting it would be for her if Ali continued asking about her real mother. I didn't voice my thoughts since it wasn't my place to tell everyone about her mom's health.

"Did your parents ever tell you where you came from?" Brie asked.

Ali shook her head. "No. I don't think they want me to know too much about it."

"There's something fishy about this situation," Brie said.

I could see her mind ticking over as she contemplated all the details. "Ali?" She asked, "When is your birthday?"

"Tenth of October," Ali replied, her eyes darting towards me.

"OMG!" Brie exclaimed. "The same day as Casey's! That has to be more than coincidence!"

Brie pushing for answers made me feel a little uncomfortable, and I just wished she would stop. Although finding out that Ali and I shared the same birth date was freakier than ever.

"That's it! I agree with Brie," Holly said. "I think you are twins, and someone has been lying."

They all looked at me for confirmation.

"My mom didn't give birth to twins," I said. "It's not possible."

"How do you know?" Brie asked.

"Because I do!" I stated firmly, my cheeks flushing red-hot. "I think we need to get off this topic and go to bed before we get into trouble." I shoved my body into my sleeping bag and turned away from everyone. Mom would never have lied to me about having a twin sister.

The other girls settled down, but not before casting their vote for how they felt about the situation. Then someone turned off the light.

As I drifted off to sleep, a final question floated through my mind. Could Mom have lied to me all these years?

CHAPTER NINE

My obsession with Ali over the last week had switched to obsessing about the theory that we actually *were* twins. The girl's voices from the previous night bounced around my brain making me toss and turn all night. I ended up pushing my mattress further into the hallway the second time Brie kicked me and told me to stop moving around.

I was exhausted the next morning and for once I was happy that Ali was more popular than me. During breakfast, the girls wanted to hear more about her past, and their attention was on her instead of me. I wondered if my sleepy expression told them I wasn't willing to talk about it again.

The one detail that lined up with Ali's adoption was the fact that her real mother had given birth to her when she was very young. If anyone cared to do the math, they would know that my mom had given birth to me at a young age too. But I couldn't even fathom that Ali and I were twins. That would mean Mom had lied to me for years, and I had a sister I didn't even know about!

I shook away the thoughts and decided to prove this theory was wrong. I just wasn't sure how to go about it.

On the way home from Ronnie's, Grandma Ann asked me how the sleepover went.

"It was all right," I said. "We played games and watched a movie."

"That sounds fun!" she said.

"Or booooring," Lucas said from the backseat.

I whipped around and glared at him. He stuck his tongue out at me in his usual annoying manner.

I turned back around in a huff choosing to ignore him. I was already tired, I didn't need him bugging me right then.

While I stared out the window, Grandma Ann asked for more details about the night. I didn't want to be rude, but I wasn't in the mood to talk. I was concentrating on the conversation I would have with my mother when she arrived home.

"Casey?" Grandma Ann asked.

"What?" I asked.

"You seem to be in the clouds today. Are you okay?"

"Yes, I'm fine."

She clicked her tongue a few times. "You don't sound fine.'

I really didn't want to get into the specifics of Ali with her, but I knew her well enough that she wouldn't stop asking until she was satisfied with an answer.

"There's this new girl at school, Ali…" I told her the whole story from the beginning. She was always more attentive than Mom, and I found it easy to tell her everything I'd been feeling about the new girl. I kept Ali's secret about her mother's illness though, as I didn't think Grandma Ann needed to know about that.

I was finishing up my story when we pulled into the driveway. Lucas, who had been engrossed in his electronic game in the back seat, jumped out of the car, impatient to get inside and continue his game. Grandma Ann passed him the keys and we watched him walk up the steps towards the front door.

Without him there to overhear, I decided to continue. "All last night the girls were saying that Ali and I could be twins separated at birth. I don't think that's possible but what other explanation is there?"

Grandma Ann turned off the car and her hands dropped to her lap. She stared ahead as if she were in a trance.

"It's not possible, right?" I asked.

She pressed her lips together still not meeting my eye.

58

Oh, my —

I gasped. "Is it true?"

She snapped out of her trance and turned to me. Her face gave away everything. "Casey…"

My eyes welled with tears, but I wasn't sad, I felt utterly betrayed. I pushed on the door handle and shoved the car door open, throwing it closed behind me with a loud bang. Racing to the house, I disappeared through the open front door and sprinted for Mom's room.

I could clearly hear Grandma Ann's voice calling for me from the driveway. But there was no way I wanted to speak to her any further. Quickly slamming Mom's bedroom door closed, I turned the latch and locked it.

My breathing rasped in my ears, and my eyes darted around the room looking for something…anything that could prove what I already knew.

My gaze fell on Mom's cupboard. She had photo albums in there. I pulled out my baby album and whipped through each plastic page, the quick *thwapping* sound matched the pace of my racing heart.

"Casey!" Grandma Ann's voice came from the other side of the door. The knob jiggled, but she wasn't able to get it open.

"Leave me alone!" I shouted.

I expected her to fight. I expected her to yell for me to get out of my Mom's room, but instead, there was silence on the other side.

I didn't care what she said or what she did, I needed to find proof. I needed to see the proof with my own eyes.

I heard her feet shuffling down the hall away from the door. Then Lucas started talking animatedly about something, and Grandma Ann responded. I wondered how long it would take before she demanded that I open the door. I had to find something quickly before she returned.

I took a breath and continued through the album. Mom hadn't kept up with it over the past few years, she was too busy with work, I guessed. The photos were of me as a baby during birthdays and vacations. There were pictures of me with Grandma Ann and Lucas when he was a baby. But there were no other babies. No twin babies at all. There was nothing to suggest another baby had even existed! I went through the photos again, slower this time. I squinted at each one, trying to find something, anything, to prove I had a twin. After the third time going through the album, I closed it and shoved it away. It slid under Mom's desk, and I didn't care if it was ever found. It was a book of lies anyhow.

I left the room and decided to go right to the source. I confronted Grandma Ann in the living room, watching a show on TV with Lucas.

"Can I talk to you?" I asked her, my eyes blazing furiously.

Lucas looked over and shushed me. "You know this is my favorite part!"

Grandma Ann stood, her face pale and her mouth slightly open. I'd never seen her so nervous.

I walked down the hallway, organizing my thoughts and went into my bedroom. I sat on the edge of my bed but quickly jumped up and began to pace. It felt as though I had jumping beans under my skin. Was I ready to be told the truth?

Grandma Ann closed the door most of the way. "Casey—"

"So it's true? I have a twin?" I interrupted. Each of the questions I had, burst from my mouth at once. "Is my mom even my real Mom? Am I adopted too? Were we separated at birth for some reason? How come no one ever told me?" With each question, my voice began to crack a little more, until my vision blurred with tears.

"Please," I begged, "I just want the truth!"

Grandma Ann took a breath. "Okay. I will tell you everything. You deserve to know it all."

CHAPTER TEN

"You have to understand, Casey," she said. "Your mother was very young when she fell pregnant. Her boyfriend at the time, your birth father that is, decided to leave as soon as he found out. He said he wasn't ready to be a father, and he just left.

It was obviously not an ideal situation. And when we found out your mom was having twins the situation became even more complicated. Your grandfather and I wanted to see your mother graduate high school and go off to do promising things. We refused to let her get a job. She needed to focus on her studies, and she could not do both. And with your sick grandfather to care for, I was unable to add two babies to the household. The cost of his medical bills plus expenses for two babies was just not a possibility.

We found two separate families to adopt her unborn twins as there were no families willing to take two babies at the same time. But your mother would not have it. She refused to give up both of her children, and in the end, she chose to take you home. It was so hard for her to make the decision but she could not see both of you go."

I choked on a sob, unable to hold back my tears any longer. Poor Ali! If my mom had chosen differently, I would have been the one who was adopted, not her.

"Your mother was so stubborn," Grandma Ann continued. "She was little more than a child herself, but I couldn't change her mind. I'm so sorry, Casey."

"She made me promise not to tell you. She wanted to

wait until you were older to tell you the truth, hoping by that stage, you'd be able to cope."

She stared at me, her voice faltering as she spoke. This was clearly not an easy conversation for her to have. "Your mother had plans to find your sister long ago. But then she met your stepfather and then Lucas came along. It was only a year into their marriage before your grandfather passed and your stepfather skipped town."

Grandma Ann's voice was sad and furious at the same time, but she was forced to go on. "Everything fell apart for her, and she needed to focus on work to provide for you two. That's why I moved closer, so I could be around to help. And even though I knew you could handle the truth, to her it was never the right time. But you have to believe she didn't want to keep this from you forever. Neither of us ever expected you would find out on your own."

I rubbed my eyes, taking in everything she'd said. Knowing the truth had only made me feel worse. "So if I didn't find Ali, I might never have been told about my twin? Perhaps not until years from now, if ever at all?"

Grandma Ann avoided my eyes, answering the question without any words.

"Please leave," I murmured. I needed to be alone. I couldn't stand to have her near me.

Grandma Ann sighed, stepping toward me. "I think we should…"

"Go!" I shouted, backing away from her.

She jumped, surprised at my outburst. But she nodded and turned to leave.

Mom didn't allow locks on our doors so when

Grandma Ann left the room, I grabbed the chair from my desk and shoved the top of it under the knob. I wasn't sure if it would hold if she actually tried to get in, but it made me feel secure. Flinging myself onto the bed, I tried to process everything my grandmother had just told me. I couldn't believe they'd kept this from me. This huge part of me had been hidden under secrets and lies.

I didn't even know what to think anymore. I already knew my mom was self-absorbed, but I never thought Grandma Ann would betray me. As much as we didn't get along sometimes, she was supposed to be my support person, the one who I went to when Mom was busy. Lies were the last thing I'd expected from my grandmother.

"Sherry!" I heard Grandma Ann's voice through the door.

Was Mom home?

I got up from the bed. Mom was going to hear it from me. I opened the door and peered down the hallway but instead of my mother's face, I spotted Grandma Ann on the phone in the kitchen, her back turned toward me.

"I don't care about your meetings, Sherry. This is much more important and you need to listen! Casey knows!" There was a pause. Grandma Ann had her hand on her hip, and her head dipped forwards. "What do you mean, 'knows about what?'" she lowered her voice. "Casey found out about her twin." Another pause. "The girl showed up at her school. Anyhow, that's not the point. She knows and you need to come home now. She's not taking it very well." A longer pause.

I sneaked back into my room just as I heard Grandma Ann speak into the phone. "I'm worried about her."

I closed the door as quietly as I could, putting the chair back into place in front of the door. I didn't like hearing the worry in my grandmother's voice and even though I wanted answers from my mom, I wasn't sure if I could face her just yet.

Grandma Ann was understanding enough not to push me to come out of my room. She left a tray of food at my door, and after knocking gently and telling me that my dinner was there if I wanted it, she left me alone. But I had no appetite. Instead of eating, I finished packing for camp the following day and went to bed.

The next morning, I didn't remember any of my dreams but by the chaotic state of my sheets and comforter, I knew they weren't good ones.

I woke up before my alarm and lay in bed, trying to go back to sleep. But that was useless, as I couldn't stop thinking about everything that had happened. I was unable to comprehend the fact that Ali was my sister, my twin sister! The idea had been suggested by my friends but I honestly never thought it possible. I'd never considered that my mother would keep a secret like that from her only daughter.

When my alarm finally went off, I got out of bed, grabbed my clothes for the day and headed to the bathroom to shower. Afterward, I ran into Grandma Ann in the hallway. Her short gray-streaked hair was flat on one side from sleeping. There were thick bags of skin under her eyes. She hadn't slept well either.

"Good morning, Casey," she said.

"Morning," I said and flicked my gaze to my bedroom. She was blocking my way.

"Will you be joining me for breakfast? I'm making chocolate chip pancakes."

My stomach growled, betraying me. I shrugged. "I guess."

She moved in front of my bedroom door as if she thought I would run for cover as soon as her back was turned. The idea crossed my mind, but I was very hungry. Skipping dinner the night before was taking its toll and the thought of chocolate chip pancakes was making my mouth water.

I sat at the table while Grandma Ann went to the stove, pouring the thick pancake batter into the hot pan.

"Do you want to put the chocolate chips in?" she asked.

"No, you can do it," I said.

After a few seconds, the scent of chocolate filled my nose, and a feeling of warmth flooded my body. Even though I was hungry and I loved her pancakes, I wasn't going to give in as easily as she thought.

Grandma Ann flipped the pancake over and said, "I called your mother last night. She's coming home tomorrow evening. It was the first available flight that she could get."

"That's dumb," I said.

Grandma Ann lifted the pancake up from the pan with a spatula and moved it to a plate. "How so?"

"You should call her back and tell her not to bother. I'll be away at camp."

She placed the plate with the pancake in front of me. "I don't think camp is such a good idea."

I looked up at her. "I'm not missing camp because Mom is a liar. Besides, I don't want to speak with her anyway. I've been looking forward to this trip, and Mom's not going to ruin something else for me."

"Casey, that's not fair—"

I choked out a laugh. "Not fair? Mom lying to me for years is not fair. Let's see how she likes it."

I shoved the plate away from me and got up from the table. I wasn't going to give her the satisfaction of thinking she'd won me over with food.

"Casey," Grandma Ann pleaded.

"I'm not hungry. I'm sure Lucas will eat it."

And with that, I left the room. I shut my door and double checked that I had everything I needed. I thought of the things I'd say if Grandma Ann tried to stop me from going, but when she came to my room a while later, she only asked if she could help me carry my bags to the car.

On the way to school, I looked out the window, my head still spinning with everything that had happened. Having a look-alike was one thing. Now I had a twin, and she was in my class at school. The chances of that occurring were too bizarre for me to fully understand, but I guessed I had to now. It was the truth. I felt for Ali who had questioned her parents many times over the years. Now she would have her answers, and we were going to get through this together.

I wondered if she would be happy knowing that we were twins, or upset that her—and my—mother had given her up instead of me. Would she react the same way I had; angry and confused? Or would she be relieved? My stomach twisted. It shouldn't have been up to me to give her this news, but I had no choice. She deserved to know and it seemed that her adopted parents were not planning on sharing the secret. I took a deep breath, preparing myself for seeing Ali and revealing the truth.

CHAPTER ELEVEN

When we arrived at school, there were already a few students and teachers congregated by two yellow buses on the far end of the parking lot. Grandma Ann drove slowly toward them and I sensed her reluctance to leave me.

What I really needed was space and to escape her and the thought of her lies and betrayal. Going to camp would also be the perfect opportunity to get my head straight before I confronted my mother. I wondered if Ali would want to be there when I spoke with Mom but decided that I'd rather confront her on my own. After all, I was the one she'd been lying to for the past twelve years.

Pulling to a stop, Grandma Ann allowed the car to idle. I removed my seatbelt and put my hand on the door handle just as she spoke.

"Are you sure you want to do this, Casey? Your mother is coming home early, regardless. She wants to be here when you get home."

"Mom's coming home early?" Lucas asked excitedly from the back seat. "Cool!"

I ignored him. "I don't care if she'll be back early. I want to go on the school camp."

I wasn't usually so rude to my grandmother, but under the circumstances, I felt that I had every right and besides that, I couldn't help myself.

She nodded solemnly.

Getting out of the car, I opened the rear door and grabbed my bags, then closed the door a little harder than I intended. I could see Grandma Ann through the window, her expression sad. I felt bad, but she was as much to blame for this as Mom. Even though Mom asked Grandma Ann to lie, she could have said no. She was the responsible one, and she let me down too. I offered a little wave to her before she started out of the parking lot. Then watched the car pull away before lugging my bags to the bus.

When I got to the first bus, I was directed to stow my gear in the luggage compartment. Mrs. Halliday marked my name off her list and I climbed aboard. Brie waved to me from her spot in the middle and I slumped down into the seat next to her.

"How exciting is this!" Brie said, bouncing in her seat. "I'm so excited. I can't believe camp is finally here. I've been waiting so long for this day to come."

"Yeah," I said, staring at the seat in front of me.

"You okay?" Brie asked.

"I'm all right."

"Casey," Brie touched my arm, and I avoided her eyes. "What's wrong?"

When I didn't answer, she asked again, "We're best friends! We tell each other everything. So what is it?"

I glanced towards her and sighed. There was no way I could keep my news from her. "You have to promise not to tell anyone," I whispered. "I mean it. Like not even write it in your diary."

"Wow! This sounds good. I promise I won't tell a soul."

Looking tentatively around, she moved closer towards me, to make sure she could hear every word I said.

"Remember when Ali said that she was adopted?"

"Yes."

"Well it got me thinking, and when I said something to Grandma Ann about it, she got really quiet like she knew something. I paused for a moment, and Ali sat waiting impatiently for me to continue. "Then she told me that my mom actually did have twins when she was young. And Ali and I are those twins!"

"No way!" Brie exclaimed, bouncing up and down in her seat again. "I knew it!"

Her beaming smile showed the delight she felt in guessing our secret. She had known it all along.

"Shh!" I said, grabbing her arms and forcing her to sit still. I looked around the school bus, there were only a few classmates around us, but none of them had turned to see what the fuss was about.

Brie pressed her lips together as her eyes widened. "Sorry," she peeped quietly. "Go on."

"So Grandma Ann phoned Mom to tell her that I knew, and she was going to come home early—"

"Are you going to tell Ali?" Brie interrupted.

I shrugged. "I have to. It stinks being lied to, and I don't want to ever lie to her. We're sisters."

"I can't believe it!" Brie squeaked. "This is the most incredible thing I've ever heard."

I started to feel frustrated. "Keep it down." I wanted to be the one to tell Ali, and I wanted to keep this a secret until I spoke with Mom about everything.

Brie ignored me. "My very best friend in the whole world has a twin sister and didn't even know it."

I pinched her arm. "Brie, I'm beginning to regret telling you."

She laughed and covered her mouth. Then she mimed zipping her mouth and throwing away the key.

I looked out the window, wanting to get to Ali as soon as possible before Brie spilled the beans. I knew how bad it felt to have someone other than my Mom tell me the truth.

The bus filled up quickly and only when it was full, did the teachers start to direct students to the other bus. Ali was one of the last to arrive and was forced to join them. I sat back in my seat, upset about missing the opportunity to talk to her on the way to camp, but decided that I'd make a point of getting her attention when we arrived.

That plan went astray when we got to camp. The second we got off the bus, we were separated into cabin groups and instructed to grab our gear and go there with our assigned teachers. I spotted Ali in front of the other bus collecting her bags, but by the time I managed to get my own gear together, she'd already headed off with another group. I couldn't understand how we'd been thrown together every single day at school and then when I really needed to talk to her we had to be separated!

Luckily, Brie and I were in the same cabin. We spent the next hour or so unpacking and organizing our things. I had to keep an eye on Brie to make sure she didn't keep talking about the twins scenario. I'd be mortified if someone else overheard and got to Ali quicker than I could.

A little later, we were all instructed to assemble outside for some ice-breaker activities. The minutes stretched on. There were other groups in the distance and I spotted Ali a few times, but we were confined to our cabin groups so I didn't get any chance to talk to her. Even during lunch, Ali was surrounded by other kids and I felt as though the opportunity I needed would never arrive.

After more activities in the afternoon, we were finally given some free time until dinner and I could have jumped for joy. Leaving Brie with the other girls in our cabin, I rushed out the door in search of Ali but there were so many kids around, I never thought I'd find her.

I'd just about given up when I suddenly spotted her sitting on the top step of a nearby cabin. Racing in her direction, I saw a couple of girls filter out of the cabin holding bags and towels. They said something to Ali, and she smiled at them but shook her head. Watching for a second longer, I made sure no one else was around before approaching her. At last, it was the perfect opportunity, and I strode up to the cabin, stopping at the bottom of the steps.

"Hey," I said.

"Hey!" she said in return, her gaze flicking to mine.

"What are you up to?" I asked, suddenly feeling very shy. Filled with a nervous anxiety, I wasn't sure exactly what I would say or even if I was doing the right thing. But she needed to know. After all, she was my twin.

"Nothing much," she smiled in her friendly manner. Do you want to sit here for a bit?"

"Sure," I replied, taking a deep breath.

"How was your day?" I continued, making small talk. After thinking about this opportunity for the whole day, I was at a complete loss for what to say.

"It was fun. The girls in my cabin are really nice."

I pointed at a beaded bracelet that she had tied around her ankle. "Did you make that?"

She smiled. "Yeah, in the craft activity. Didn't you make one?" she asked, glancing at my bare wrists and ankles.

"Yeah, I did," I explained, "But I made it too tight and when I tried to loosen it, it broke," I continued. "All the beads fell off and it's in pieces in my bag."

"I could help you fix it?" she suggested.

I waved my hand and shook my head as if to say, "no big deal". We were quiet for a second, and I decided I couldn't hold it in any longer.

"I know this is random, but I need to tell you something."

"Okay."

I hesitated for a second, but then the words came tumbling out and once I started, there was no stopping. "After the sleepover, I asked my grandma if it was possible that my mom had given birth to twins."

I gauged her reaction before continuing. Ali sat stock still, waiting for me to go on.

Taking another deep breath, I answered her unspoken question. "Grandma said yes."

Ali took a deep breath of her own but said nothing.

I stared directly at her, and she stared straight back, listening intently as the words poured from my mouth. "I didn't think it was possible, but I guess she was very young when she got pregnant. She couldn't afford one baby, never mind two, so she was supposed to give us up to two different families since no one wanted twins. But she couldn't go through with it and decided to give up one… that was you…and she kept me. I haven't had a chance to talk to her yet, but I was so mad when I found out. I'm so sorry Ali. I wanted to tell you right away, but this is the first chance I've had!"

Stopping to take a breath, I watched Ali's expression change. Rather than a look of shock or dismay, her eyes were sparkling with excitement.

It was certainly not the reaction I'd expected.

CHAPTER TWELVE

Ali

I shook my head, trying to calm the racing thoughts. "I knew it," I said, firmly.

Casey's eyebrows furrowed together. "You knew what?"

A fluttering sensation settled in my stomach. "From the moment that I met you I had a feeling, deep down, we were connected. I can't really explain it but ever since the party, after seeing the two of us side by side in the mirror and then finding out we have the same birthdays, it's all I've thought about. To be honest, I was kind of avoiding you today." I wrung my hands in my lap. "I didn't want to freak you out."

"No way!" Casey exclaimed. "OMG! That is such a relief, I've felt just the same."

Nodding in agreement, I explained my own story. "I tried talking to my parents about you, but I didn't want to upset them. I've been going with them to the hospital every day for Mom's treatment. That's why I was late this morning. My dad and I took Mom to the hospital and then he dropped me off at school before going back." I took a breath.

"She hasn't been reacting well to the treatment. She seems to be worse rather than better. And I didn't want to bring up the issue of meeting you. Even though I was sure that you must be my twin sister."

"Ali," Casey said, placing a hand on my shoulder. "I'm so sorry. It could have been either one of us who was adopted, it was just the way it happened, I guess."

"It's okay," I said, trying to reassure her. "And besides, I love my parents...I mean, my adopted parents, they mean the world to me. The best news is that we've found each other!"

Casey nodded quietly, as she listened to me speak. "After Ronnie's party, I did some online research about twins being separated at birth. And do you know that there are heaps of cases worldwide? It's crazy!"

"Wow!" Casey replied, raising her eyebrows and her expression becoming more curious. "I didn't know that!"

I explained further, "Well from what I found, if separated twins are lucky enough to reunite, it's usually later in life after the parents finally tell them the truth."

Casey's mouth dropped open a little, as she realized that our situation was not so unique after all.

"And that's what would have happened to us if we hadn't just found each other," I added. "Even if it was by accident, I'm sure it was meant to be. You and I were destined to meet."

Tears welled in Casey's eyes as she wrapped her arms around my neck and pulled me to her. I clasped my hands around her back and squeezed. Her breathing was ragged in my ear, and I felt a tear slip down my own cheek.

"I can't believe this!" Casey whispered. "I have a sister."

"I know!" I said, pulling gently away and wiping my face. "And not just any kind of sister, a twin sister!"

We both began to cry, it was something neither of us could prevent.

"I've always wanted a sister," Casey said. "Maybe somehow, I knew you were out there, and that's why I kept hoping you'd appear in my life."

"Anything is possible," I replied, as I considered the impossible situation before me.

Noticing the girls from my cabin coming back from the showers, I glanced briefly towards them. Casey followed my gaze and moved a few inches away from me. This wasn't a conversation I wanted to share with the rest of my classmates, at least not yet.

That was something I'd have to discuss with Casey first. I just hoped they didn't notice our red eyes and the obvious fact that we'd both been crying.

The girls walked up the steps, immersed in their own conversation and barely taking note of us. We waited until they were inside the cabin before we faced each other again.

"We should meet after dinner and lights out," I suggested. "So we can talk more."

"Good idea," Casey agreed eagerly. "But I don't think we should share this with anyone yet. Do you mind keeping it secret? But I'm sorry, I have to admit I've already told Brie."

"That's fine," I said. "She's your best friend. And I really like her."

Casey bit her lip. "She only knows part of it. I think we should keep some of it to ourselves."

I nodded. "Whatever you think is best."

Casey let out a sharp breath. "Okay." She stood up, and we hugged again, quicker this time. "I'll see you after dinner and lights out."

"See you soon," I said.

Watching as Casey walked away, I couldn't help the excitement from bubbling inside me.

CHAPTER THIRTEEN

Casey

I made my way back to my cabin to get ready for dinner. Brie was there, laying on her bed reading a book when I arrived.

I sat on the edge of her mattress. "Hey."

She looked over at me and sat up right away. "I was wondering where you went off to. Did you talk to Ali?"

"Yeah."

"Spill!"

She beamed with excitement, desperate to hear my news.

I quickly pressed a finger to my lips, turning around to see if anyone else was listening. The other girls glanced over at us but soon returned to their own conversations.

Lowering my voice, I explained the details. "I told her about what Grandma Ann said. And do you know, she wasn't even that surprised? She said she knew it all along. But her mother did tell her she was adopted so I guess it made sense that we could be sisters and separated at birth."

I didn't tell Brie about the weird psychic connection between Ali and me. The entire situation was already strange. Brie knew enough, I wanted something to remain a secret. At least for now. Discovering that I had a real twin sister was freaky enough, I certainly wasn't sure that Brie would believe the psychic thing. I wasn't sure that I believed it myself.

"This is major," Brie said. "What are you going to do next?"

I shrugged. "I guess I'll wait until we get back home so I can talk to my mom about it all. I was so angry with her but now I'm not sure how I feel. I'm hoping Ali comes along too so we can confront her together. Can you imagine her reaction? That'll be payback for keeping it from us for so long. And besides, I'm sure Ali has a lot of questions. I know that I certainly do!"

Right then, I could barely wait for dinner to be over so Ali and I would have a chance to talk some more. As it turned out though, that never happened. There were several teachers patrolling the area and keeping an eye on everyone. Although I tried several times to escape from my cabin unseen, I didn't find a chance.

I just hoped that Ali wasn't waiting in the dark for me to arrive. Somehow though, I felt sure she'd know I wasn't coming.

When I finally climbed into my sleeping bag that night, I pushed the curtain aside and stared out the window in the direction of her cabin. Only a short distance away I had a real-life twin; a girl who looked just like me. As I closed my eyes, I pictured her face, my face, and I knew that right then, she was thinking the exact same thoughts as my own.

To our huge delight, the following day my cabin group happened to be paired up with Ali's for the activities for the entire day. I wondered whether it was luck or fate that had intervened. Whichever it was, I didn't really care, I was just grateful that it had worked out the way it had.

Immediately, I rushed to Ali's side, at the same time giving Brie an apologetic smile. But I knew I could rely on my best friend, who had already urged me to pair up with my sister. Brie was more than happy to pair up with Holly so it all worked out well.

Since confiding in each other the day before, my connection with Ali seemed stronger than ever, and my previous dislike was a thing of the past. In its place was the feeling that I was right where I was meant to be.

The first activity was archery. I'd had no idea that Mr. Pavoni was practically an expert at archery. He showed us how to properly hold the bow and where to place the arrow. This time, I was not upset when he paired me with Ali. It allowed us to spend even more time with each other, and out in the open, rather than in secret.

Mr. Pavoni did a double-take this time after making the pairing. Though he didn't say anything, he'd finally caught on that we looked alike!

Ali and I glanced at each other and smiled.

As it was her turn to try first, she held the bow the way Mr. Pavoni instructed, with one eye closed and focused on the target. She bit her lip in concentration, and let go. The arrow bounced on the ground a few feet in front of us.

She sighed and looked at me. We laughed.

Handing me the bow and still laughing, she asked. "Do you think you can do better?"

I took the bow from her and lifted an arrow from the bunch. "Probably not."

Moving my body into the correct stance, I placed the arrow on my finger. I took a deep breath and noticed I was biting my own lip in concentration. Smiling to myself, I recognized yet another trait that Ali and I shared. I let go of the arrow, and it flew straight towards the target. The arrow dropped a few feet from the target but it was still further than Ali's attempt.

"Alright," she said. "Gimme that. I want to try again."

I handed her the bow. Our fingers touched, and I could have sworn I felt an electric zing between our fingers. If Ali felt it, she didn't let on. Maybe my connection to her was stronger? Though when our eyes met, a certain spark lit her eyes. She did feel our connection. I knew it. I felt it deep down inside of me. She didn't have to say anything at all. I wondered what else would come up the more time we spent together.

On the way to the next activity, Ali and I laughed over the hilarious misses we'd made in archery. Mr. Pavoni said we'd have another session before camp ended, and I decided that I would try harder next time. There was a friendly rivalry between the two of us, and I was excited to give it another go.

"The way your arrow flew right over the top of the target!" Ali said, shaking her head.

"Hey," I said. "At least it reached the target!"

We both burst into a fit of laughter.

"What's so funny?" Brie asked.

I didn't realize she was beside me. "Brie, you had to be there," I scoffed grinning widely.

"Oh," she said, a little hurt.

Noticing her reaction, I felt bad and made sure to include her. "It's just that we missed the target every time. We were both pretty hopeless."

"Yeah, I saw that," Brie laughed, feeling proud of her own attempts, which I'd noticed were much more successful than my own.

"You're good at archery, Brie!" I grinned back, giving her a quick hug. She was my best friend and I reminded myself not to forget that. I'd hate to hurt her feelings, that was something she did not deserve.

With the three of us laughing over our archery attempts, we headed up the steps to the recreational building where tables were set up with a multitude of objects.

Breathing a sigh of relief, I realized we weren't making more beaded bracelets. I didn't want to embarrass myself again with my poor typing skills.

"Key chains," Ali said, recognizing the activity. "Cool."

Once everyone settled down, the teacher, whose name was Miss Tucker confirmed Ali's guess. "Once you have assembled your key chain, raise your hand, and I will come over and help you with securing it."

When she was finished, we went to work. Immediately, Ali and I reached for the same pink keyring. The table was filled with a huge variety and we could have chosen any of them, but instead, we targeted the same one. Glancing instinctively at each other, we laughed.

"This might sound strange," Ali said in a small voice. "But do you feel, like, odd around me sometimes? Not in a bad way, but—I don't know what I'm trying to say."

"Yes," I responded.

Her eyes widened. "I thought I was the only one?"

"No," I replied, smiling. "You're not." It was a relief to hear her say that. It was the one part of our friendship that neither of us had really discussed.

"What are you two whispering about?" Brie asked, leaning across the table to grab a piece of leather.

"Nothing," Ali and I stated at the same time.

"Are you two still doing that?" Lacey chuckled. "You're like clones."

"Close," I said under my breath.

Ali grinned, and I met Brie's eyes winking at her.

She smiled.

It was our secret and I knew it was safe with Brie.

CHAPTER FOURTEEN

Lunch break was next and then everyone was to take part in a ropes course. We had about ten minutes before having to be at our designated places when Ali abruptly turned to me with a proposition.

"You know what would be really fun?" she whispered quietly so no one would hear her.

"What?" I asked, finishing my glass of chocolate flavored milk. Wiping the excess from my lip with a napkin, I waited curiously for her to continue.

"When I was looking for information on identical twins, I found a heap of stories where some switched places and in many cases, their friends and family didn't even realize."

I looked around to make sure no one had been listening, but everyone was talking loudly and focused on their own conversations.

"You want to trade places?" I asked, raising my eyebrows curiously.

She shrugged and her smile widened. "Just until dinner. Don't you think it'd be fun?"

I chewed my lip. "I'm not sure." My cheeks flushed at the idea of playing a trick on my friends and teachers. What if it didn't work? And what if we were caught out? I'd hate for us to be sent home from camp.

"Come on," Ali pleaded. "If it doesn't work then it

doesn't work. We should try, though. This is the perfect opportunity. And it'll be fun!"

I took a breath, deciding to accept the challenge. "Alright. But only until dinner."

"Yes!" Ali said, pumping her fist in the air. "Okay, let's clear our plates, then head to the bathroom."

Following quickly behind her, we made our way into a cubicle each and passed our clothes under the wall to each other. When we emerged, we both stared into the mirror, laughing.

"Whoa," I said, unable to take my eyes off myself. Ali's clothes fit perfectly, and I imagined myself being her. I smoothed my hands over her soft shirt. Ali's clothes were a lot nicer than mine. Maybe this swap-thing wouldn't be so bad.

Ali reached for my hair.

"What're you doing?" I asked.

She looked at me in the mirror. "My braid is the only thing that sets us apart. Here, let me do it for you before we leave."

I watched the transformation take place as Ali expertly braided my hair.

Her fingers moved quickly down the strands until the braid was complete. She loosened her own braid and let the waves fall over her shoulders the way mine always did.

We checked ourselves over one more time before we heard the teachers telling our classmates to file outside.

"Ready?" Ali asked.

"Ready!" I said, high fiving her, before making my way to the door. My hands shook with anticipation of what we were about to do but at the same time, I felt a thrill work its way down my spine.

"Oh! And don't tell Brie," Ali said. "I want to see how long we can trick everyone for. If we can fool her, we can fool anyone!"

I hated lying to my best friend, but it was only a little prank. We played tricks on each other all the time, this was no different. Right?

"Deal," I replied with a smile, before stepping a little hesitantly out the bathroom door.

Convinced that we'd be caught right away, I felt my cheeks flush red, but no seemed to be taking much notice of us at all. Mrs. Halliday beckoned for us to keep moving and we made our way towards the throng that was already lining up outside.

"Let's go, ladies," Mrs. Halliday said.

"She has no idea," Ali said, confirming my thoughts.

I giggled into my hand. "This might actually work."

"I told you!" Ali exclaimed and beamed widely.

We were one of the last to arrive at the ropes course and headed towards Brie and the other girls.

"Here we go," Ali said.

I nodded and was about to take my place by Brie's side when Ali moved in front of me. Duh. That made sense. She was pretending to be me. I had to act like Ali now. I wasn't sure what that entailed. I wished we'd had a little time to prepare ourselves.

"I'm so not ready for this," Brie said to Ali.

"I'm sure you'll be okay. This looks fun," Ali said to her confidently.

Brie snorted. "Easy for you to say, you actually like all of this athletic stuff. You always have."

Ali glanced over her shoulder and shot me a grin. Even Brie was falling for this! I had to contain myself.

After safety instructions had been given, we were split into groups. Ali—as me—went off to the lower course while I was grouped with Brie and a few others for the higher course.

"Have you ever done something like this before?" Brie asked.

I almost remarked that I'd tried it at camp the year before, but held my tongue just in time. Tugging on the end of the braid that draped across my shoulder, I reminded myself that I was playing Ali, not Casey.

"No, I'm a little nervous," I replied instead, hoping that was something Ali would say.

A breath whooshed out of Brie. "Me too! I'm glad I'm not the only one."

Stumbling a little at first over how to respond, once I concentrated and channeled what I knew of Ali's personality, I fell into a rhythm that was both exciting and a little scary. I couldn't believe not one person guessed that we'd swapped. Not even my best friend had any idea it was me who was right beside her.

I wondered how Ali was doing and caught a glimpse of her a few times on the other side of the course. It really was striking to see me from across the way. But it appeared that she had taken to the transformation as well as I had.

From the high ropes course, we were directed straight to the dining hall and Ali and I decided to continue the charade during dinner. Sitting next to each other, it was easier to keep up the ruse as we fed off each other's comments. And being so close to her I could channel her inner thoughts much more easily. I didn't question the psychic connection we appeared to have. It had come out of nowhere and was unnerving at first, but already it seemed like second nature.

Excusing ourselves to the bathroom midway through the meal, we rushed to swap clothes, and we also wanted some privacy so we could talk.

"I can't believe it worked!" I said, laughing and in awe, the moment we were alone.

"I know!" Ali said from the next stall as she handed my shirt and shorts under the divider, and I did the same.

"Even Brie had no idea," I said. "She spoke to me as though I were you – she had no idea that we'd actually been friends for years!"

"I told you we'd get away with it," Ali replied cheerily and I could hear the smile in her voice.

After changing back into our own clothes, Ali braided her hair again, and I smoothed my own hair into long strands over my shoulders and moved my pink head band back into place.

Locking eyes in the mirror, Ali spoke, "I think we could do this again!"

I could not mistake the mischievous grin on her face.

"Yes, let's do it!" I agreed eagerly. If no one noticed today, then I doubt they would any other time."

An idea suddenly formed in my head, but I wondered if I should say it aloud. Glancing at Ali who was concentrating on braiding her hair, I decided that after everything we'd discovered, it would be silly to keep something from her.

Blurting out the words, I could feel my cheeks flush a little with embarrassment. "Do you like Jake?" I asked.

Ali shrugged. "I guess. He's been nice to me."

She continued braiding and then a moment later, she picked up on my meaning. "Do *you* like Jake?"

I cleared my throat. "Kind of."

Ali jumped up and down. "We have to do this again! Then you can talk to Jake, and pretend to be me. Maybe that'll help your shyness around him."

"I'm not shy—"

"You are around him!" Ali laughed "I've seen the way you behave. I don't know why I didn't put it together before."

I chewed on my lip, wanting to be certain before continuing with the idea. "Are you sure you don't like Jake that way? I mean it's obvious he likes you!"

I'd just discovered I had a twin and did not want to jeopardize our relationship, especially over a boy.

Ali sighed. "There's too much going on to think about boys. With my mom's illness and all. Besides, you liked him first. What kind of sister would I be if I got in the way?"

I smiled. "Okay, if you're sure about Jake, let's swap again tomorrow."

The excitement was working its way through me and already I could hardly wait for the following day to arrive.

"After breakfast," Ali agreed. "Let's meet in here and swap clothes again."

I nodded happily, following Ali to the door. As I watched her walk away, I wondered how I would ever get any sleep that night. My stomach fluttered with anticipation over Jake. I knew I had to pretend to be Ali, but it meant I got to spend time with him and it was certainly a start.

I could hardly wait for the next day to arrive.

CHAPTER FIFTEEN

As the weather forecast predicted clear blue skies with a blazing sun, water activities had been scheduled for the day. I was a little nervous about the canoeing activity. We weren't going on any wild rapids, but it still made my stomach turn to think about it. Sometimes I became queasy in boats, even on still water, and I would be mortified if I embarrassed myself in front of my classmates. And since I'd promised Ali we would swap places for the day, I didn't want to embarrass her either.

I didn't mention my nervousness when we swapped clothes and hairstyles in the bathroom that morning. She might change her mind and I really wanted Jake to notice me for a change, rather than being the onlooker, as was usually the case.

"Are you okay?" Ali asked.

"Yeah," I said a little breathless. I was glad for the divider between us so she couldn't see my face. "I didn't sleep much last night." I feigned a yawn.

"Me neither," she replied. "The girls in my cabin do not stop talking."

"Have you ever been canoeing?" I continued.

She snorted. "Casey, if I haven't been to a sleepover or a camp before, do you think I've been canoeing?"

"Maybe your Dad is outdoorsy?" I said with a smile. I

fed off Ali's excitement for the swap.

Ali's stall door opened. "No way. He's more of an indoorsy-type.

I adjusted the fit of Ali's two-piece bathing suit on my body, taking in the beautiful shimmering shade of blue and how lovely it looked against my skin, before lifting her shirt over the top. It was the latest style and I could hardly wait to show it off.

The hair swap had become a part of the routine too. Mom used to braid my hair when I was little, and I'd never had my hair braided since. Thinking of my mother reminded me of the shock she would feel when she eventually saw the two of us together. I could only imagine her reaction.

"Ready?" Ali asked as she finished the braid. I broke away from thoughts of my mom when I noticed the birthmark on her shoulder. I'd completely forgotten about it when I chose a sleeveless tank top to wear that day, but it was too late to go back to my cabin for a different one. "Remember to hide the birthmark. Keep your hair over it so it's covered. It's the only way anyone can tell us apart."

She glanced down nodding, too caught up in the excitement of what we were doing to allow her birthmark to be an issue. "Let's do this."

After breakfast was over, we made our way down to the river. Several of our teachers were already waiting by the canoes. Mr. Pavoni stepped forward and held his hands in the air, signaling for us to stop talking.

"There will be two people per boat," he said. "We're

splitting the classes into boy-girl pairs so find yourself a partner."

I turned to see Jake heading right for me. I flushed when his eyes locked with mine.

"Hey Ali," he said.

My insides deflated. Of course, he thought I was Ali, but for a split second, I almost wished he would have partnered up with the actual Ali since she was playing me. I only hesitated for a second before smiling at him. At least it would give me some time with him and maybe after he got to know me a little more, he'd eventually want to hang out with the real me. It was all very confusing, but I wasn't about to pass up the chance to be his partner, especially in our own little boat.

"Hi," I said.

"Want to be partners?" he asked.

"Sure!" I said a little too quickly and enthusiastically.

If my reaction was weird, Jake didn't show it. Instead, he grinned at me. "Cool."

I turned to find Ali who was partnered with Jordan Lockwood. He was in another class and I wondered how that had happened because it was likely that he didn't really know her. I wondered if she'd chosen him or it was he who had picked her.

With no time to worry about the Ali – Jordan issue, I followed Jake towards the pile of life jackets where he immediately offered to find me one. Passing it to me, he grabbed one for himself and then indicated a nearby canoe.

"I think we should take that one," he said, pointing to

one that had a red stripe across it. "Red is my lucky color."

I smiled. "Sounds good to me."

Standing by our boat, I realized that Jake was close enough that I could smell his minty toothpaste. He was concentrating on the instructions being given and I risked a glance towards him, taking in the fall of his long dark hair across his forehead. I then found myself wanting to brush it out of his eyes, at the same time wondering what it felt like to touch. When he suddenly turned towards me, I felt my cheeks flush and looked quickly away, hoping that he hadn't noticed me staring. That would have been so embarrassing.

With my stomach churning nervously at the thought of Jake as my rowing partner, my anxiety abruptly worsened when he maneuvered the canoe to the middle of the river. But before long, we'd fallen into a steady rhythm of rowing together and I began to relax a little.

He sat in the back behind me and I pictured his handsome face in my mind.

But all the while I tried to think of something to say.

Usually, I was chatty and outgoing, but around Jake, I was a different person. To my relief though, his constant chatter soon put me more at ease. "You're a pretty good rower," he commented from behind me.

Taking a quick glance around, I grinned, "I'm just doing my best not to capsize us." I wasn't sure if it was the calm water of the river or Jake's easy-going personality but I felt myself relax even further.

He laughed in response and I felt my insides flutter. My smile turned to a wide grin at the sound of his voice behind me. "Don't worry, I'll make sure we don't capsize."

"How do you know so much about this?" I asked.

"My parents love to go camping. We have a couple of canoes and we often take them out. It's such a fun sport. My dad and I usually use the canoes to go fishing."

"I always wanted to learn how to fish."

"Your Dad never taught you?" he asked.

I almost admitted that I didn't know anything about my dad, but caught myself just in time. I had to remember that I was Ali, and her father was present in her life. But with Jake so close, it was hard to concentrate.

"No, not yet," I replied, turning slightly towards him.

"I can teach you sometime," he said. "It's casting that's the trickiest. Apart from that, there's nothing to it."

Glancing over my shoulder, I smiled. "That'd be great."

"Cool."

"Cool," I repeated quietly to myself, finding it difficult to believe that I was really in a little boat on a river with Jake .... as my partner.

But then I remembered that he thought I was Ali and some of the thrill disappeared. I wanted him to like me, Casey, not the girl who was my twin. I wondered how he'd react to know that I'd tricked him.

But then I considered the idea of not telling him what we'd done. If I built up enough confidence, perhaps I could approach him on my own. Ali had made it clear she wasn't interested, so maybe his interest in her would switch to me when he realized how well we got along.

It was all so complicated! But I decided to shake off the worry and enjoy my time with Jake. I'd just have to figure out the rest later.

We canoed for the next hour and I became more comfortable as the time went by. Even when Jake pretended to capsize the boat, swaying it from side to side, my squeals turned to fits of laughter. Then when he really did tip the boat over and we were both tossed into the cold water, I gasped when I came up for air. Splashing him, I pretended I was annoyed but then he splashed me back and the game was on. When he turned the boat back over and climbed back in, he reached down to help me up. I was sure that the day could not get any better!

During lunch, I filled Ali in on my morning.

"I was watching you guys," she said. "You and Jake were having so much fun! I knew this swap was a good idea."

"How did you do with Jordan?"

Ali smiled. "Not so well, but it was fun trying."

I happened to look up at the same time Jake was staring at me from the next table. He gave me a little wave and my whole body flushed.

"Wow, he really likes you," Ali said, noticing him too. "He can't stop looking this way."

"I know, right? It's so strange."

Ali and I giggled together which caused a few looks from the girls at the table. Brie's eyebrows were raised. Her eyes darted between us.

I didn't want to ruin the game, so I stopped laughing and continued eating my grilled cheese.

On the way to free swim time, I confided in Ali about Jake. "You know, at first I was really jealous of you getting along so well with him."

Ali's eyes widened. "Oh no! I told you I don't like him like that."

"I know," I said. "But I didn't know that at the time. It was pretty annoying that he never gave me any attention and then you arrived, my absolute look-alike, and he could not take his eyes off you."

Ali shook her head, denying that it was true. But I knew it had been the case and I wasn't the only one who'd noticed.

Clearly, there was something about Ali that attracted people to her. Even Jordan Lockwood, from a completely different class, had rushed to be her partner for canoeing.

But rather than feeling jealous, as I would previously have done, I felt grateful that she was so willing to help me. I smiled appreciatively at her as I thanked her again for swapping identities.

Draping an arm around my shoulders, she replied, "Anything for my sister."

The temperature had spiked that afternoon and all of my classmates, except for a select few who sat under the shade of the trees, were in the water. The teachers had set up a floating volleyball net, and there was a roped off lane for races. Ali, Brie and I found a spot away from the activities, happy enough to enjoy swimming on our own.

"Let's see how long we can float on our backs!" Brie suggested.

We flung our bodies back and allowed the slow current to move us over the surface of the river. My mind drifted to the morning and how much fun I'd had with Jake. I didn't realize how long I'd been floating until Mrs. Halliday's frantic voice called out.

"Ali!" Mrs. Halliday called. "You're drifting away, swim back to shore please."

I looked over my shoulder at Ali who was closer to the shore than I was. She had a confused look on her face. I followed her gaze and realized Mrs. Halliday was looking at me!

I dipped my legs into the water, and waved to my teacher, signaling that I'd heard her. I swam closer to Ali, noticing her bare shoulders.

"Casey," I whispered pointedly.

Ali turned to me with a smile.

"Your birthmark," I said in a voice just above a whisper.

She lowered herself under the surface until only her neck and head were visible. "Thanks," she said.

Thankfully Brie hadn't noticed our exchange.

"Hey Ali," Jake said as he swam past us, a friendly smile on his tanned face.

Ali poked me in the side under the surface of the water.

"Hi, Jake," I said, smiling.

He made a point of splashing water at me, before swimming away again,

I looked at the girls. Brie was staring at Ali. I knew that she was waiting for "Casey" to react. And I could see the surprise register on her face when she saw Ali's wide grin and nod of encouragement. Clearly, she was quite confused as to why "Casey" would be acting that way when Jake was showing such obvious interest in "Ali."

With an effort to distract her, I splashed Brie with a handful of water and suggested we race each other to the shore. Then, without waiting for a response, I began to swim, fully aware that she would not be able to resist a challenge. Sure enough, she fell into pace beside me and raced me to the shore.

Quickly I grabbed our towels and threw mine to Ali who immediately wrapped it around her shoulders. It had taken no effort whatsoever for her to pick up on my meaning and once again, I was grateful for our psychic connection.

Unfortunately, it began to rain during dinner, so the campfire planned that evening was postponed until the following night. Instead, we were given permission to hang out in the recreational building where there was a ping pong table, a pool table and several comfy couches.

There was also a variety of board games. Ali, Brie, Lacey and I played checkers.

"I'm so thirsty!" Lacey said, getting up. "Anyone want water?"

When we all nodded in response, Brie offered to help. "I'm going to grab more cookies too. I'll go with you."

The girls left and Ali and I sat quietly alongside each other, Ali yawning widely.

"I'm not looking forward to going to the cabin tonight," she moaned.

"Why not?" I asked curiously. It was the first time I'd heard her complain about anything.

"The girls in my cabin talk all night about boys and makeup. It was okay for the first night, but I can't sleep when there's so much noise."

Out of nowhere, I was struck with a brilliant idea. "Why don't you sleep in my cabin tonight? The girls in my cabin all want to sleep, so no one stays awake very late. As soon as it's time for lights out, that's pretty much it for us. And no one will notice you're not me."

"Oh, that's okay," Ali said chuckling. "We've probably done enough swapping for one day."

"Ali, I'm serious," I insisted. "Why not? If you're tired, then take advantage. It won't bother me, I can sleep through anything."

"Really?" Ali sat upright in her seat, the idea obviously catching her interest.

I nodded. "My mom used to tell me how surprised she was that I could sleep through Lucas's crying when he was a baby. Trust me. I'll be fine. You look exhausted."

She hesitated, staring quietly towards me and I could almost hear her brain ticking over with the idea.

"Besides, your decision to swap places gave me a chance to hang out with Jake. It's the least I can do."

"Alright, if you're sure it's ok?" she asked once more.

"Yes, absolutely," I smiled at her reassuringly.

A breath whooshed out of her. "That will be amazing! Thanks so much, Casey."

"What are sisters for?" I asked with a smile.

CHAPTER SIXTEEN

Ali

The last hour of downtime went by quickly. Although I hadn't admitted it, I was a little nervous about sleeping in Casey's cabin, but as Casey reminded me, if no one noticed throughout the entire day that we'd swapped places, then it was highly unlikely that anyone would notice when we were sleeping.

When I followed Brie inside, I stayed close by her. Casey had said her bed was next to Brie's. She also explained where she'd put her clothes and toiletries. As the cabin layouts were all the same, it was easy for me to figure out where everything was. I didn't intend to use her toothbrush, but a little toothpaste on my finger was better than nothing and I did like to brush my hair before bed. I was sure she wouldn't mind if I borrowed her hairbrush.

One of the girls, Amanda, who for some strange reason had decided to dye her hair green for camp, seemed to be in charge when it came to the sleep schedule.

"Five minutes, girls," she said, clapping her hands. She sounded like a teacher, but I was looking forward to getting into bed so I didn't mind her bossy attitude.

The weight of sleep began to press on my eyelids. I changed into a set of pajamas from Casey's designated drawer and sat on her bed. But my usual habit of brushing my hair to one side had been a terrible mistake.

Brie let out a little gasp, and I glanced up at her.

She bolted over to my bed and sat next to me, pointing at my exposed shoulder and my birthmark.

I quickly covered it with my hair.

Brie's eyes darted around the room before they settled on mine. "Ali?" she asked in a low voice.

"Shh," I said.

"Where's Casey?" she asked.

"In my cabin. She said I could sleep here tonight since the girls in my cabin are so loud. They just don't sleep!"

Brie shook her head vigorously. "But—but—how long have you been pretending to be Casey?"

I swallowed. Casey trusted Brie but I'd been caught out. I just wasn't sure how Brie would feel about Casey keeping this from her. I'd hate for Brie to alert the other girls to our game. If the teachers found out what we'd been up to there was no way of knowing how they'd react.

"Most of yesterday and all of today." I stared guiltily at Brie, holding my breath anxiously.

Brie clapped her hands over her mouth.

"Don't say anything," I begged.

Brie looked a little hurt. "How come neither of you told me?"

"We wanted to see how long it would take anyone to notice. And then Casey started talking to Jake and—"

Brie snapped her fingers. "They were hanging out all day! I wondered why Casey—or you—didn't mention it. She told you about her crush right?"

I nodded.

Brie shook her head, dumbfounded. "And they were hanging out all day! She must be so excited!"

I smiled. "She is."

"Whoa," Brie said. "I should be upset that you two kept this from me, but I'm so happy for Casey."

"Me too. But, Brie, you must keep our secret. I'm not sure if we're going to swap again tomorrow, but if we do, you can't tell anybody at all."

Casey had already mentioned that Brie could keep a secret, but sometimes in her excitement, she let details slip. I was careful not to say anything about my mom around her. I didn't need anyone to feel bad for me.

"I cross my heart," Brie said, making an imaginary 'X' over her chest.

Amanda clapped her hands again and then she flipped the light switch by the door. The room was abruptly shrouded in darkness. I blinked a few times, letting my eyes adjust to the sudden change.

Brie squeezed my arm. "Good night. Hope you sleep well, *Casey*."

Her over-accentuation of Casey's name was a little obvious, but I let it go. My body craved sleep, so I snuggled under the covers of Casey's bed and closed my eyes, falling quickly into a deep coma.

CHAPTER SEVENTEEN

Casey

The next morning, I was the first one to wake and at first, I was disoriented. But after clearing the sleep from my head, I remembered I was in Ali's cabin. Ali had been right about her cabin-mates. I'd managed to drift in and out of sleep but I was sure they'd been chatting and giggling for most of the night. I ignored most of it, except for their gossip over the boys in our grade which did catch my interest, especially when Jake's name was mentioned. A girl called Ashleigh went on and on about how cute he was. It sounded to me that she had a crush on him herself.

"He's so cute!" I heard her gush. "Don't you think he's the best-looking boy in our grade?"

They all took turns at guessing who he liked. That was until one of the girls, I couldn't tell who, shushed the others and mentioned Ali by name. They assumed she— meaning me—was asleep but didn't want "her" to wake up and hear them talking about Jake.

I smiled against my pillow. It had been obvious to everyone that Jake preferred Ali and possibly liked her, well me. It was all so confusing. Maybe it would be best if I told him outright that he'd been hanging out with me instead of Ali. At least we could start our friendship off properly, and he'd see that he really preferred me over her. I was sure Ali wouldn't mind, she didn't like him that way anyway.

I was already showered and dressed before any of the girls woke up and I left the cabin ahead of them, making my way towards the dining hall for breakfast.

On my way, I caught sight of Ali and Brie who'd obviously got up early as well and I hurried to catch up.

"Hey, Ali!" Brie said. "Decided not to braid your hair today?" She looked at me with a grin and I caught the cheeky expression on her face.

Shoot! I didn't realize that I got ready this morning as Casey, leaving my hair down. "Oh, uh. Yeah, I decided not to."

"I told her," Ali said, in a matter of fact voice. "She found out, so I had no choice!"

I looked innocently from one girl to the other, pretending I didn't know what they were talking about.

"Oh come on!" Brie said laughing. "Admit I had you there for a second."

112

I grinned back at her as she explained how she'd found out. I'd always known that Brie would be the hardest one to fool but if it hadn't been for Ali's birthmark, I was sure there was no way she could have known.

Then I realized that Brie had a point, "Should I braid my hair?" I asked Ali.

She shook her head. "No. I'm beginning to like it down too. I bet no one will be able to tell us apart."

I played with the hem of Ali's shirt. I was sure people would be able to tell right away who was pretending to be whom. Ali's clothes were much nicer than mine. But I didn't say anything.

Ali had been right, though. As the kids came into the cafeteria and passed our table, most did a double-take.

My heart thudded in my chest when Jake put his tray down at our table and slid into the seat next to mine.

"Is anyone sitting here?" he asked.

"N-no," I stammered.

"Cool," he said.

"Morning, Jake," Ali said.

My eyes widened, and I looked at her. There was something in her expression that told me to keep my mouth shut.

"Hi, Casey," he said.

Brie kicked me under the table, and I gave her a tiny shrug.

"Did you like canoeing yesterday?" Ali asked him.

"I love canoeing." He picked up a piece of toast from his plate and started eating.

"Me too!" Ali said excitedly.

"Really?" Jake said.

"Yes, I love outdoorsy things."

My breathing quickened, and I started to understand what she was doing. Ali's natural outgoing attitude was helping me get an "in" with Jake. She was pretending to be me, starting the conversation with Jake and then when we switched back I wouldn't have to be so nervous. At least that's what I thought she was doing. It was hard to tell sometimes with Ali. At times, I felt we shared one brain, which was ridiculous but entirely possible considering we were twins.

"Me too," he said.

His gaze darted between Ali and me. "You know, I always thought you two looked alike, but today you look like twins."

"Everyone says that," Ali said.

"I'd say it was a compliment," I added.

Ali smiled at me, and we all continued eating. Ali chatted some more with Jake and each time he replied, I felt butterflies fluttering crazily in my stomach. This whole camp had been a dream come true and I'd almost forgotten what I would be going home to in a few days. Deciding to push that thought from my head, for the time being, I focused on enjoying the time I had left.

We had a few minutes left before breakfast ended when Ali and I excused ourselves from the table. I had an idea, and I wasn't sure if Ali would go for it, but there was no harm in asking.

After we'd swapped back into our own clothes, I outlined the plan.

"You want to swap houses too?" Ali asked as we stood in front of the mirrors. Whether it was a pure habit or because of the hot steamy air outside, I wasn't sure, but she began to braid her hair.

"Don't you want to meet your real mom?" I asked.

Ali considered this.

As much as I wanted to know more from Mom about giving up one of her kids, I was still angry with her. And it would be perfect payback for her to face the child she had given up for adoption. I didn't say this to Ali. Once Ali was at my house, I'd make a point of visiting and then Mom would have to face the two of us. I wasn't sure Ali would agree to the second part of the plan, so I had to have her in the house already when I arrived. Then Mom would feel awful for what she had done. As much as I loved the idea of having a twin sister, I wasn't ready to forgive my mother just yet, for the years of lies.

I smiled, imagining the shocked expression on my mother's face.

"I don't know," Ali said.

The bathroom door burst open, and a few girls entered. Ali and I moved just outside the door so we could keep talking in secret.

"Why not?" I asked.

Ali finished her braid, wrapping a hair tie around the end a few times. "I don't want to upset my mom if she finds out we did this. Her condition is getting worse, and I think this would hurt her."

"She won't find out," I said. "I promise. How about we only do it for one night? And I can keep you updated on her as much as you want."

Ali sighed. "I really do want to meet my birth mom..."

I let her think about the plan for a few seconds while my insides twisted with anticipation.

"Alright, I'll do it," she answered, suddenly coming to a decision. "One night couldn't hurt."

Jumping up and down with excitement, I threw my arms around her in a quick hug. "That's so awesome!"

Ali grinned. "I finally get to meet my real mom. Wow! I can't believe it!"

"It will be great," I said, pumping her up. Everything was falling into place. And both of us would get what we wanted.

"And let's keep this to ourselves," I added. "Except for Brie. She likes to be included, and I trust her to keep this secret."

"Deal," she said.

"Oh! Thanks for talking to Jake as me," I said.

Ali smiled and draped her arm over my shoulder. "Anything for my sister."

I smiled back. I loved having a twin.

As the camp grounds were soaked from the drenching of overnight rain, we did indoor activities all day. I crossed my fingers that we'd still be able to have a campfire that night. All day I formulated a plan with Ali that would put Jake and me together. My hopes were high as a few times he approached me to talk about whichever activity we were doing.

I imagined Jake and me sitting together, making smores by the fire…it was going to be a perfect night.

Usually, my imagination took me away to experiences I knew deep down would never happen. But miraculously, the campfire plan worked! I almost jumped for joy when Mrs. Halliday announced that the campfire was still on.

Ali, Brie and I arrived early, looking for the perfect seats. The bonfire was lit and the fire was raging.

"Is this too close?" I asked, checking out the other kids arriving and searching for Jake in the crowd.

"It's fine," Brie said. "Look, there he is."

I swatted her hand, hoping he didn't see her pointing towards him. Her enthusiasm was going to mess everything up.

Jake was with his cabin-mates. He looked so good in his black skinny jeans and light blue t-shirt. Without even thinking about it, I caught his attention and waved him over.

Surprised at myself, I felt nervous butterflies fluttering crazily inside me. Calling him over was something I would never have even considered before, but it was my chance to talk with him as myself instead of Ali doing all the work for me.

"I saved you guys a seat," I said, indicating the spaces

beside me.

He and Jordan sat down, and the other guys in his group scattered, sitting in other unoccupied seats.

"Thanks!" Jake grinned, and I noticed the pleased expression on his face. "This is a good spot.

My cheeks flushed as I smiled back, and the butterflies in my stomach continued their crazy dance.

Feeling a little awkward at first, I was soon grateful for Brie's excited chatter, it helped so much to have a chatty person in the group and before long all of us were talking non-stop about our day. A couple of times I caught Jake smiling at Ali, and I had to control the small twinge of jealousy that I felt inside. Ali however, made a point of taking little notice and before long most of his attention was directed towards me.

By that time, I was so much more at ease with him and able to relax and just be myself. The two of us even had a smore eating contest, which he won by two whole s'mores. Laughing at his efforts to fit in his fourth s'more, I clutched my own stomach which was already so full. The heat from the fire had become quite hot and a few of the others had moved away, but I didn't dare budge from my spot beside him. We were getting on so well and there was no way I wanted to leave his side. I also noticed that when his friends moved away, he continued to stay alongside me.

When we were eventually sent back to our cabins to prepare for bed, Ali grabbed hold of my arm and whispered in my ear, asking if we could swap for one more night. She wanted to make the most of the opportunity to practice switching identities, especially if we were planning to swap houses.

I agreed that it was probably a good idea and as I was so happy about the Jake situation, I would have agreed to anything right then. I watched as Ali raced ahead so she could reach the cabin before the other girls and change into my pajamas.

But even though I had to pretend I was Ali again, inside I was soaring! Jake wanted to be near me all night. Me! Not Ali. And I felt as though all my dreams had come true.

I made my own way back to Ali's cabin, grabbed the bathroom before anyone else and then climbed into bed, not bothered at all by the light still shining brightly and the non-stop chatter of the other girls. When Molly, the girl who slept in the bunk above Ali's bed, asked me what I thought about Jake, I smiled awkwardly and tried to brush the question away. But I could not help the red flush that crept onto my cheeks and I knew it was a dead giveaway.

Molly laughed, commenting on how cute she thought Jake was and each of the others agreed. They assumed it had been Ali sitting with Jake at the campfire all night and found it hard to believe that the new girl already had the hottest boy in the grade interested in her. Shaking my head with embarrassment, I could not help my wide grin. Then, to escape any more questions, I yawned and rolled over pretending to go to sleep. I just wanted to be alone with my thoughts and the image of Jake's beautiful smile in my head.

The girl's voices were a distant sound that I pushed away as I focused on visions of the campfire with Jake alongside me.

CHAPTER EIGHTEEN

The next morning, I woke up to the sound of the other girls frantically rushing around the room, complaining that they'd overslept again and were going to be late for breakfast. I blinked open my eyes, the edges of my sight blurry. My head ached, and when I got up from the bed, I realized I was in a lather of sweat and my pajamas were sticking to my body.

I told the girls not to wait for me. I wasn't at all hungry and asked them to tell Casey and Brie that I'd meet them at the stables after breakfast. Our groups were scheduled to do horseback riding that morning and it was going to be the highlight of the whole camp.

I made my way to the bathroom to get showered and dressed. But I could feel my legs giving way beneath me and fumbled my way back to the bed. Suddenly everything went black.

The next thing I knew, Mrs. Halliday was sitting on the bed alongside me. I glanced at her worried expression as she placed her hand gently on my forehead,

"Ali, you're burning up!" Her brow was wrinkled in concern. She offered me a glass of water, but I could only manage a small sip.

"It looks like you have a nasty fever," she said, as she placed a cool cloth on top of my forehead. "I'm not sure that you're well enough to stay."

Sitting up abruptly, the cloth fell onto the bed as I shook my head weakly. "No, I'll be fine, honest. Maybe I can just skip this morning's activity and get a little more sleep. I'm sure I'll feel much better in a little while."

The last thing I wanted to do was go home and miss out on the rest of camp, especially when I'd finally become friends with Jake. I could not let them send me home.

Then another thought struck me. Right then, she thought I was Ali, so there was no way I could have her sending me anywhere. My head was throbbing and I could feel the flush of my skin. I felt hot all over and just wanted to sleep.

Trying my hardest to convince Mrs. Halliday, I gave her a small smile and tried to reassure her that after a short rest, I would be fine.

Shaking her head reluctantly, she stood to leave.

"Okay, Ali. I'll just be down on the grass with the archery groups. You'll be able to see us from your cabin door. If you need anything, just call out. I'll keep coming back to check on you, but if you don't improve, I'll have to call your parents."

And with that, she was gone. But by then, my head was in such a thick fog that I could do nothing but close my eyes. All I wanted was sleep and within seconds, I drifted off.

CHAPTER NINETEEN

Ali

After breakfast, our group was instructed to line up at the stables for horseback riding. I looked around for Casey, who had still not appeared and I wondered what was taking her so long. I was so excited. It was another first-time experience for me, and I simply couldn't wait! When I glanced towards the horses lined up waiting, I hoped to be given the beautiful white one that stood quietly at the end of the row. Once again, Casey's group and mine had been placed together for this activity, which was a perfect opportunity to talk more about our house swap.

When the instructors arrived and asked us to gather closer, I looked around for Casey once more.

"Casey still hasn't shown up," I whispered in Brie's ear and she glanced around worriedly.

"I don't know where she could be!" Brie exclaimed. "She was really looking forward to this activity, I can't believe she'd miss it!"

Making my way to Mr. Pavoni who was our supervising teacher that morning, I pointed out to him the fact that Casey still hadn't arrived.

"Mrs. Halliday just called me," he said quietly in my ear, not wanting to interrupt the instructor's spiel as she explained what we would all be doing.

"Apparently, Ali is unwell and she's resting in her

cabin," he continued. "Hopefully she'll feel better later and can join in with a different group tomorrow."

Frowning with disappointment, I looked up the hill towards the cabins and thought of Ali in bed on her own. It was so unfair that she had to get sick. I just hoped that she'd be okay. Then when we were asked to line up for a riding helmet, I was forced to shake thoughts of Casey away as I concentrated on all the instructions being given.

The pony I ended up being paired with was a chocolate brown horse named Trina. And as soon as I was asked to lead her around the enclosed arena, I found that she was very quiet and very obedient, perfect for a beginner rider such as me.

When I later realized that the beautiful white horse was much friskier and less obedient, I felt relieved that I'd been given Trina to ride. She did exactly as I asked, even if it was the wrong command. But try as I might, my mind was not fully focused on riding. My thoughts kept wandering to Casey hoping that she was okay.

For some reason, I felt a constant niggling inside that something was not right and I could not help but worry.

After almost an hour into the ride, I began to lose interest, my focus still on Casey. We had another half-hour to go, but all my thoughts were directed towards my twin. The minutes dragged on, and when we finally got back to the stables, I jumped off Trina, tied her to some timber fencing as instructed, and headed in the direction of the cabins.

"Al—Casey!" Brie called.

I turned to her and gave her a look. She'd nearly given us away by calling me the wrong name.

Brie jogged over to me. "We have to help put the gear away and clean the stables."

"Really?" I asked, my frustration worsening. All I wanted to do was check on Casey.

Brie shrugged. "It's more than just a horse ride. We have to learn responsibility or whatever. We do it every year. I know you're worried about Casey, but we have to do this. Casey's probably still asleep. I'll go with you afterward and we can check on her."

I sighed heavily, glancing back towards the cabins, but with no other option, I was forced to follow Brie and try to get the work done as quickly as possible. My anxiety over Casey was getting worse, and I could not control it. Eventually, my hands were practically shaking with the anticipation of seeing her again.

Finally, we were finished and Mr. Pavoni told us we had fifteen minutes before lunch to go and change if we wanted to.

I was desperate to get to the cabins. More specifically, my cabin.

With Brie at my side, I could feel the throb of my pulse quicken as I raced up the hill. Something was wrong. I had no idea what, but I felt my concern worsen with each step. The top of the hill was so close yet so far. The muscles in my legs burned. If I stopped, I would probably fall over and not reach the top. I pushed through the uncomfortable cramps in my legs and abruptly stopped at the top of the steep incline. I leaned over, catching my breath. Then, as I glanced up, my worst fears were realized and all I could do was stand and stare.

The familiar car pulled out of the lot. The girl in the backseat turned her head. She had the exact same profile as me. Where was she going? Why was she leaving? And now what was I supposed to do without her?

"Ali?" Brie asked. "What's wrong?"

I shook my head, unable to believe what I was witnessing. "Everything!" I exclaimed. "That was my parent's car, I'm sure of it."

Brie stared at me with a confused expression. "It could be one that looks like your parents' car. Why would they be here?"

My stomach dropped.

Mrs. Halliday's voice floated up from the other side of the hill. I rushed over to her. She was informing the others that we had a short amount of time before lunch.

"Mrs. Halliday!" I said, rushing over to her.

"Yes, Casey?"

I cringed at my sister's name. Why did we ever play this silly game?

"There was a large yellow car here. It was driving past the cabins and I could see a girl in the back."

Mrs. Halliday pressed her lips together in a thin line. "I'm sorry Casey. I know you and Ali were getting close. She was too ill to stay at camp. I had to call her parents to come and pick her up."

Brie grabbed my arm and squeezed.

Mrs. Halliday turned to speak with another teacher.

I turned to Brie, speechless and in shock.

Brie's face abruptly filled with comprehension. "Did she—?"

I nodded. "Casey was in that car!"

***

Book 2

Caught Out!

CHAPTER ONE

Ali

Brie and I stared at each other as realization flooded us both. Casey had been taken home by my parents. *My* parents! And they had no idea that she was my twin and not me!

How could Mrs. Halliday do this to us? Casey would have been fine with a little sleep. Now my parents had taken home someone who wasn't me! What was going to happen now? My parents would surely know the difference between their own kid and her twin. And I dreaded how upset they would be if they found out the truth.

I pushed my hair back away from my suddenly hot face.

"What do we do?" Brie asked. Her eyes were teary with fright.

I looked over my shoulder at Mrs. Halliday who was a few feet away talking with another teacher. What could we do? I knew Casey and I were supposed to switch places eventually, but this wasn't part of the plan. We needed more time to prepare for the swap.

There was nothing we could do right then. I wasn't going to tell Mrs. Halliday what had happened. Maybe it would somehow turn out okay.

"We can't do anything," I said in a low whisper. "If I tell anyone that Casey and I switched places then we will both be in trouble."

I also knew that if my mother found out I was aware of my biological family, she'd be very hurt. If she wanted me to know, surely she would have already told me about them herself. There was also the fact that I wanted to meet my real mother. And if I spilled the beans then that might not ever happen. My head was fuzzy thinking about all the things that could go wrong for us in the situation we'd suddenly found ourselves in.

"But Casey is in a car with strangers!" Brie exclaimed, throwing her hands out to her sides.

I grabbed her hands and pulled them down. I didn't want Mrs. Halliday to come over and ask what we were talking about. "They're not strangers," I said. "They're my parents. She will be fine. They will take good care of her."

I knew that for a fact. Dad had been taking care of Mom for a long time. And Mom loved any opportunity to treat me like a little kid again.

"This is not a good idea," Brie said, her hands were shaking. "Maybe we should tell someone. They can call your parents, turn the car around and bring Casey back. You can just say that it was all a big mistake."

I was trying to play it cool but Brie was making it very hard. My own anxiety about the situation was making my stomach hurt. "Casey wouldn't want that," I said, knowing it was the truth. "We spent most of the camp pretending to be each other. She will be fine. We wanted to swap homes anyway."

"Casey wanted to do that?" Brie asked. She seemed a little surprised that Casey and I had a secret she wasn't in on.

"Yes. She did. We both did."

The sound of a whistle in the distance made us both jump.

"Come on ladies!" Mrs. Halliday said, waving us over. "It's lunchtime."

Brie was chewing on her bottom lip.

I wrapped my arm around her shoulder. "Keep pretending I'm Casey and everything is going to be fine."

She nodded.

I hoped that Casey was well enough to be able to trick my parents or else we were going to be in so much trouble.

During lunch, I was barely able to eat anything. Brie sat next to me and hardly said a word. The other girls didn't notice but I wanted her to act normal as if nothing was wrong. I hoped she wouldn't change her mind and tell the teachers about Casey and me. Casey did mention that it was very hard for Brie to keep a secret. I decided to stick by her the rest of the day to make sure she didn't say anything.

Since it was the last day of camp, our craft project was to make a picture frame out of different materials. We were given longer than normal in that session so we could really personalize it. I couldn't concentrate on making the frame because I was so worried about Casey. But I had to take my own advice and pretend nothing was wrong.

There were a few Polaroid cameras floating around and we were supposed to take a picture with our friends and put it in the frame. Ashleigh and a couple of girls from my cabin lined up with some other friends to take a group photo. They were all having so much fun.

It would have been a really cool project to do with Casey but she wasn't there to enjoy it with us. Instead, just Brie and I took a picture together. When it developed, I realized it was a bad photo of me. I wasn't really smiling as I was so upset on the inside. So I made Ronnie take another one. That one turned out better and after seeing the other kids having such a great time, I started to relax a little and enjoy myself as well. I painted the frame pink and pasted little gems on it.

Then I thought of Mom and how she'd love the frame. She kept all my projects even though I wasn't very artistic.

Thoughts of Mom made me think of Casey again. Swapping places was part of the plan, but we needed more time to prepare. I had no idea how to act like Casey around the people who knew her best. It was easy at camp since we were both there and could play off each other. At her house, I would be on my own and wasn't confident at all.

I swiped at a tear that tried to escape my eye. I imagined Mom finding out that Casey and I had lied to her. Would this secret that Casey and I had between us, affect her health even more? Would she be disappointed in me? Our little family was a team and would lying to her break that apart? I didn't want to make her condition worse than it already was. I hoped that Casey would manage to convince them she was me, or else we'd have more to worry about than getting into trouble.

CHAPTER TWO

Ali

Before dinner, we were instructed to go to our cabins and get into our pajamas. There was going to be a pajama party after we ate. Everyone seemed really excited about it. I was happy for the few minutes of downtime. It gave Brie and me some time to discuss what was going to happen in the morning. We'd barely had a chance to talk all day since we were rarely alone. We needed privacy to talk about the swap and now I was running out of time.

"I feel so unprepared," I said to Brie. We were sitting on her bed since it was the farthest from the others. We had a little while before we had to leave. And the other girls had started an impromptu dance party so the music and their shouting was loud enough to mask our conversation. "Casey and I were supposed to spend this last day and night preparing so our families wouldn't find out about us."

It was nice to be able to share my feelings with Brie. For years, I'd never had anyone to confide in about my wanting to know my biological family. Now I could talk to Brie and Casey, though I wished Casey was there too.

"Don't worry about it," Brie said. "Casey and I are best friends and know practically everything about each other. I can help you and it will all turn out okay."

It surprised me that she had changed her mind about the swap. I didn't ask her about it, though, we didn't have much time. "Okay," I said warily. "Where do we start?"

Brie's eyes wandered to my shoulder. I'd already changed into Casey's last clean pair of pajamas. I was wearing a light purple tank top and a pair of matching shorts. I didn't realize by wearing a sleeveless top, I could give away the only thing that made Casey and me different.

She pulled my hair loose and moved it over the birthmark. "Make sure that stays covered. Even if Lucas doesn't notice, Grandma Ann and Casey's — er — your mom will."

"And Lucas is Casey's brother, right?" I asked.

Brie nodded. "And Casey and Lucas don't get along. He *can* be really annoying sometimes. Her mom makes Casey babysit him all the time which she hates doing. She usually watches Harry Potter when she's with him. She's seen the movies like a million times and Lucas likes them too. I'd say that's the only thing they have in common. At least it keeps him quiet for two or three hours."

I remembered Casey's love for Harry Potter. I imagined sitting on the couch with both Casey and Lucas watching movies. I wondered if that would ever happen. Having a sister was a surprise enough, now I had a brother too. Well, half-brother, but he was still mine.

"I've always wondered what it was like to have a brother," I admitted. "Growing up an only child gets lonely. I can't wait to meet him."

Brie held up her hand. "This is really important. Casey and Lucas do not get along. At all! If you go home to their house after being at camp and you're suddenly nice to Lucas, then you will definitely be caught out."

I couldn't imagine being annoyed with someone I'd never met but at least while I was playing Casey, I had to look and act the part. "Got it, what else?"

"While we're on the subject of family," Brie started, "Grandma Ann is your *real* mom's mom. Your mom often goes away on business trips and Grandma Ann stays with Casey and Lucas. She helps out anytime your mom is too busy with work. Which is a lot. I think I see Grandma Ann more than I see your mom."

"My mother works a lot?" I asked. I hoped when I was there, she wouldn't be on a business trip. That would make this preparation all for nothing. Though I was sure that when we agreed to the plan, Casey would have known if our mom would be at home.

"Yes, she works all the time," Brie said. "It sort of takes over her life at times. It's one thing Casey is very sensitive about, but she never complains to her mother since it's the only way they have money."

I picked at a small hole in the hem of Casey's nightshirt. Looking down, I realized I'd made it bigger. I tried to push the sides of the hole together to make it smaller again but it wasn't working.

Brie hesitated for a moment. "Speaking of money, they don't really have a lot. At least not as much as your family does."

I swallowed. I never tried to make it show that we had money. It wasn't something I bragged about but I guessed that Brie could tell by my clothes. When my mother was well enough she loved to take me shopping. I never needed designer clothes but it was bonding time with my mom and she wanted to spoil me. I didn't know how much time we had left with her so they were special moments that I treasured. But I wouldn't hesitate to trade all the clothes in if only she could get well.

"Casey is given a small allowance from Grandma Ann," Brie continued. "She usually saves up for a while until she finds something she really wants. Often it's clothing that looks like a top brand but is much cheaper."

I nodded.

"Oh!" Brie said. "She doesn't wear much jewelry but she loves bracelets. She has one that Grandma Ann gave her for her birthday. She only wears it on special occasions."

I didn't wear much jewelry either. I preferred buying clothes instead. That was another strange coincidence between my twin and me.

A few of the girls in the cabin started giggling uncontrollably and Brie and I turned to see what was so funny. They were huddled together and stared back at us, laughing and making silly peace signs. At first, I thought that for some reason they were laughing at us.

Then I realized they were laughing over a bag of chocolate covered pretzels that they had almost devoured. Home brought food was banned from the cabins and I wondered how long they'd had the bag hidden. The chocolate wafting through the air made my mouth water. It smelled so good.

I turned back to Brie. "What type of food does Casey like?" I'd hate to mention a food Casey disliked at the dinner table. I would be found out for sure.

Brie went over a long list of things Casey liked. I had to stop her from rattling on and changed my question. "Name one thing she doesn't like."

Brie closed one eye in concentration. "Casey hates pumpkin and pumpkin flavored anything. She thinks it's disgusting and will tell everyone how much she hates it. I think for the short amount of time you are with her family, just avoid any mention of it."

I smiled. "Okay."

"And I think you need to act a little more casual. You're very proper," Brie said.

I thought I acted normal. At least no one told me otherwise. "What do you mean?"

Brie rolled her eyes. "You stand so straight. You just

need to relax more. It's hard to explain but I've noticed that difference between you and Casey, since finding out your secret."

I shrugged. "What should I do?"

Brie pursed her lips together. "Casey's very expressive when she talks. She moves her hands a lot. And she uses certain words when she speaks. I think if you use those more it would help."

"Okay, what words?" I wondered if I should be using a notebook for all the little things I needed to know about Casey, but I didn't want any evidence of our secret.

"For instance, she tends to use the word 'dorky' a lot," Brie continued, "mostly when she's talking about Lucas. She also says 'duh' and 'flawless' a lot as well."

"Got it," I said. "What else does she say?"

"What else does *who* say?" a voice said, from directly behind me.

CHAPTER THREE

Ali

Brie's eyes went wide and I quickly turned around to see who had eavesdropped on our conversation. It was Holly. She had her hands on her hip and her eyes were narrowed. Her pajamas were mismatched with a blue shirt and pink and red checked flannel pants.

How much of the conversation had she heard? Casey didn't seem to hang out with her much so I wondered if she'd be able to tell I wasn't her!

"Holly!" Brie said in surprise. "What's up?"

Holly's dark brown eyes moved back and forth between Brie and me. "What're you talking about?" She leaned closer to us and lowered her voice to a whisper. "*Who* are you talking about?"

Brie and I were silent for a few seconds. My stomach felt like I had just swallowed a ton of rocks. I needed to be quicker on my feet if I was going to pretend to be Casey. What would Casey do?

Thankfully Brie spoke first. "Casey was quizzing me on some Harry Potter lines. I'm trying to win a trivia contest."

It wasn't the best fib but Holly seemed to believe her.

"Oh, well that's a little weird," Holly said and then came right up to my side. "I don't know much about Harry Potter. It's not really something I'm into. No offense."

"No problem," I said. She was a little too close to me so I moved further onto the bed. I knocked my knee into Brie's leg.

Holly looked over at me and I wondered what her problem was, until I felt the sliding movement of my hair over my shoulder.

Brie gasped lightly, only loud enough for me to hear.

"Have you always had that birthmark?" Holly asked, pointing to my shoulder.

I knew Holly and Casey weren't that close. And I just hoped that Holly didn't know too much about Casey. But it seemed like a good time to test out my lying skills in preparation for the following day.

"I usually don't wear sleeveless shirts. I get really hot when I sleep, though, so I don't like wearing sleeves to bed. I've had it since birth but it's normally hidden under my clothes."

"Oh." Holly appeared to believe what I said and carried on speaking. "Well, anyway, that's not why I came over here." She sat on the bed. It wasn't big enough for three people and I had to balance myself by holding the edge of the bed to stay upright.

"I had to tell someone!" Holly continued, a secretive grin forming on her face.

"What is it?" Brie asked, eager to find out the gossip.

Admittedly, I was curious too. Holly's excitement was infectious. And I'm sure Casey would have wanted to know as well. I was already doing a good job pretending to be her!

"Jake Hanley is, like, obsessed with Ali Jackson. The new girl! Can you believe it?" Holly opened her mouth in surprise as if she didn't already know.

That wasn't the news I was expecting. My cheeks started to feel very hot and I glanced at Brie whose eyes were darting from me back to Holly.

Holly didn't have a clue about our silent conversation and continued speaking, "Ronnie overheard Jake talking about Ali to his friends and apparently, she was all he could talk about. How crazy is that? She's been at our school for less than a week and already the coolest boy in our grade is like, in love with her! I don't know her that well but there must be something special about her."

Holly looked to us to say something but after a

moment her face fell. "Oh no," she said, chewing on her bottom lip. "Casey. I'm so sorry. I completely forgot that Jake is your crush and here I am going on about him and Ali. O-M-G you're like the last person I should have told. I was so excited to tell someone that I didn't even think about it."

Brie and I looked at each other. At first, I wasn't sure what to say. I was stunned to hear that Jake liked me. We'd worked so hard over the past few days to get him to like Casey. Ronnie must have misheard. I knew how stories could get misunderstood when too many people were telling them. Surely she had it wrong.

Brie snorted and then covered her mouth, embarrassed at the sound she'd made.

My mouth dropped open. Brie's eyes widened as if silently telling me to laugh too.

So I did. I laughed and then we fell over each other onto the bed in a fit of giggles.

Holly laughed uncomfortably and looked at both of us. I wasn't sure if Brie's idea to fool her was working. "So, Casey, you don't care? You're not worried about Jake liking Ali?" Holly asked, slightly confused.

Brie spoke between giggles. "*Casey*. Do you care Jake likes *Ali*?"

I bent over in fits of laughter when Brie called me Casey. I wasn't even sure what we were laughing at anymore but it certainly eased the tension that I had bundled up all day, ever since I saw Casey leaving in my parent's car. "Holly, don't worry about it. Jake can like whoever he wants."

Holly stood up from the bed. She tugged at the hem of her sleeve. She was frowning with confusion, unsure what was going on. "I'm heading to the dining hall. You two should come too. You don't want to be late and get into trouble."

"We'll be right there," I said, wiping the tears from my eyes. Brie was still laughing uncontrollably.

Holly and the rest of the girls left the cabin. We got a few looks from the group but no one said anything.

It took a few minutes for us to get control of ourselves and then we headed off as well. We were the only ones outside walking so we knew we were going to be late.

"We should hurry up," Brie said.

We both took off and it turned into a race. Brie had said Casey was athletic and I intended to help keep up her reputation.

We reached the hall at the same time and were out of breath when we walked in. Once we were inside I looked at the big clock in the middle of the room. We had made it with only seconds to spare.

Jake was the first person I saw. My stomach did a little flip-flop. He wore gray sweatpants with a red and gray t-shirt and I had to admit that he looked really good. He flicked his hair from his eyes as he walked toward his table holding a tray of food. He definitely noticed us, although he didn't smile or say hi or anything like he normally did. But he didn't know I was Ali. Instead, just like everyone else at camp, he thought I was Casey.

Maybe what Ronnie had overheard was true. It was a weird feeling to know that he liked me and not Casey. After my mom's diagnosis, boys were the last thing on my mind. I was too worried about my mother's illness to be thinking about boys. But if Jake was talking about me to his friends then he must be serious. Casey wasn't going to like that one bit. I couldn't betray my sister like that, even for a really cute boy.

"You see," Brie whispered, breaking me away from my thoughts. "You have nothing to worry about. No one has any idea that you're not Casey. This is all working out. The only thing is Jake. I'm not too sure how Casey will feel about him liking you and not her," she warned as she moved towards the food line.

I frowned and followed her. I just hoped the Jake

scenario wasn't going to be a problem. I had enough to worry about as it was. We were last in line and by the time we reached the serving table, there wasn't much food left, but I wasn't that hungry anyway. I wasn't concerned about fooling the kids and teachers at camp and school. Casey and I had already spent a few days doing that. The hardest test for me would come when I went to Casey's home. I'd have to take all the advice from Brie and hope that everyone was tricked into thinking I was Casey and not some impostor. This was not going to be simple.

At the same time, I pictured a sick Casey, lying in my comfy queen-sized bed, in my bedroom, at my house. I imagined Dad making his homemade chicken noodle soup for her. I wondered if she was good at fooling my parents. At least she could say she was unwell if she said or did anything out of the ordinary. I wouldn't have that excuse to help me!

Then I remembered that it had been hours since Casey had left with my parents. If they suspected anything, wouldn't there have been a phone call if they'd figured out our secret?

Brie and I sat down at the table with the other girls from our cabin. They were talking excitedly about the pajama party that the teachers were setting up in the other room.

But all I could think about was my twin and I pictured her smiling face in my mind. Poor Casey. I hoped she was okay!

CHAPTER FOUR

Casey

I wasn't sure how long I was asleep, but my chattering teeth woke me from whatever dream I was having. I pulled the covers tighter over my freezing cold body.

Somewhere in the distance, I heard a door open then close. Whispering voices filled my head. My eyelids were heavy and the blankets around me were scratchy. I felt disorientated and confused. Blinking my eyes, I squinted at my surroundings. I could see bunk beds and an array of belongings scattered around the cabin. I realized suddenly that I was still at school camp. I tried to move my legs but they felt heavy and stiff. All my muscles were achy and my head throbbed.

"Hello?" I mumbled, not wanting to open my eyes. The room seemed too bright for my pounding head.

"Ali," Mrs. Halliday's voice came from somewhere in the room. "I called your parents. They are here to take you home."

"I'm not...." My eyes snapped open and I instantly became more alert, clamming my mouth shut just in time. I was still pretending to be Ali. So, of course, Mrs. Halliday would think "Ali" was sick and not Casey. And she'd called Ali's parents!

With a sudden panic filling my senses, I turned and focused my gaze on the two strangers standing next to my teacher. They were both tall. Ali's mother had brown hair cut into a short cropped style. I wondered if that was a wig. Her blue eyes were concerned. She was almost too thin. And I could imagine how scared she was for "her daughter" to be sick at camp. She rushed to my side and knelt down on the floor next to my bed. Her cool hand moved over my face and I sighed. Ignoring the fact that a stranger was touching me, her hand felt really nice against my hot skin.

"Ali, where are your things?" Ali's dad asked. He had short dark hair and a serious expression. I watched him as his eyes darted around the cabin.

I wasn't sure I could do this. I tried to swallow but my throat felt as though it were closing up.

"Over here, Mr. Jackson," Mrs. Halliday said and led Ali's dad to her pink suitcase which lay under a shelf at the foot of her bed. He opened the bag and started to pack away Ali's things from the shelf above.

"Can you sit up?" Ali's mom asked, pulling my attention away from her dad.

I really didn't want to sit up. If I sat up then I would have to go with these people. I didn't want to go with them but I also didn't want to get into trouble. Ali had said her mom was sick and she didn't want Ali to know her biological parents. If I told them that they had the wrong twin, I had no idea how she'd be affected. My mind flooded with images of her collapsing on the spot, overcome with shock, and my anxiety instantly worsened.

I had no choice but to play along.

Unease worked its way through to every part of me as I allowed Ali's mom to help change me out of the sweat-soaked clothes I was in and into something dry and clean. She picked out a comfortable pair of the softest yellow pajamas I'd ever felt. The fabric was like silk against my skin. The matching set was probably expensive like everything else Ali owned.

Once I was changed, Ali's dad gave me a pair of flip-flops and I stuck them on my feet.

"Do you think you can manage to walk?" he asked.

"I think so," I said and tried to stand up again. The room swam around me as a wave of dizziness hit, and I almost fell back onto the bed.

He wrapped his arm around my shoulders and held me tightly against him while his other hand held the suitcase.

I leaned heavily on him as we walked out of the cabin. Ali's mom and Mrs. Halliday followed us.

Outside, a gentle breeze moved over my face and I sighed. As we moved closer to the car, I thought of a million things I should have said to them.

I'm not your daughter. Mrs. Halliday, please call my real mom.

Sorry for the confusion Mr. And Mrs. Jackson, but you're taking the wrong twin home.

None of those excuses left my mouth. There was nothing I could do but go with them.

Their black SUV could probably fit ten people inside. It was huge!

Ali's mom thanked Mrs. Halliday for taking care of me and then sat in the front seat of the car. I noticed she moved very slowly and carefully. Ali had gone with her to her latest treatment a few days earlier. I wondered briefly if it had helped or perhaps that was how she moved normally.

Ali's dad helped me into the backseat. He buckled my seatbelt and wrapped a blanket around me, tucking it around my body to keep me warm. I wanted to protest, but then I began to shiver and was grateful for the soft warmth around me.

Mrs. Halliday poked her head into the car, a very worried expression on her face.

"Get better soon, Ali. I hope you make a speedy recovery."

"Th-th-thanks," I said through chattering teeth.

The door closed and I leaned my head against the window, my eyelids were heavy again and all I wanted to do was sleep.

I took a quick glance towards the campground that we were leaving behind, and in the distance, I saw myself and Brie running toward the car. My breathing quickened and I sat up straighter. That wasn't me in the distance, it was Ali. I was suddenly alert and awake. What must Ali be thinking? Did she recognize the car or was she playing some game with Brie? I tried to send her a mental message that our swap had officially begun.

Ali's mom turned around in her seat and rubbed the top of my leg. "You can relax now, hon, we're going to get you home and call the doctor to come check on you." Her voice was soft and soothing.

I nodded and took one last look at my best friend and my sister and closed my eyes. There was no turning back now. This was our plan. It was happening sooner than expected and with no real preparation. I wondered about Ali's eagerness to swap places, thinking that it had not been a good idea at all. We were messing with our parent's lives and lying to them. My stomach twisted with fear. I didn't want to hurt Ali's parents and I wasn't sure if Ali would be able to fool my mom and Grandma Ann. We were in way over our heads.

The movement of the car rocked me to sleep. It felt as though only a few minutes had passed when the car rolled to a stop in front of Ali's house. I looked at the clock and realized I'd been asleep for a while.

The driveway was long, I couldn't even see the street from where the car was. The house was much bigger than mine and much fancier as well. There were four big white columns in the front and the whole house was made of light gray colored stone. I felt as though I was at a celebrity's house and not my twin's.

Ali's dad helped me out of the car and towards the front door. I wasn't sure where Ali's mom had gone. My head started to hurt again and I was shivering uncontrollably as he led me through the house. The floors were made of some sort of stone and appeared to be spotless. Lucas would ruin these floors in two seconds if he ever came here. I guessed with a sick mom and a working dad, they had someone to keep the house clean.

Ali's dad was patient with me as we climbed the

stairs to the second floor. There were two hallways off the stairs and we went down the right one. The second door on the left was Ali's room.

When he opened the door, all I could focus on was the huge bed in the middle and the four fluffy pillows on top of it. They looked softer than clouds.

Ali's dad moved the thick white quilt, which seemed lighter than air, aside and helped me to climb into bed. It was much taller and larger than the bed I slept on every night at home. And I had been right about the softness. I sank my head gratefully onto the pillows while Ali's dad tucked me in once again.

"Dr. Spencer will be here soon," he said and placed a kiss on my forehead.

The doorbell rang and Ali's dad chuckled to himself. "Or he's here now."

Ali's mom came into the room with a large glass of water and placed it on the side table.

Behind her was a man with thick dark hair, dressed in navy blue pants and a light blue collared shirt. He certainly didn't look at all like a doctor. He was dressed like he had been at church that morning. Maybe he had been. What day was it? I couldn't keep track. My head was spinning and all I wanted was sleep.

"Hello, Ali," Dr. Spencer said, with a friendly smile.

"Hi," I croaked.

"Alright, I'm going to examine you now. I will be quick so you can get some rest."

Ali's mom stood behind Dr. Spencer as he examined me. He took my temperature and checked to see if I was in pain anywhere. He also put his freezing cold stethoscope on me which didn't help my comfort level.

When he was finished he turned to Ali's parents and assured them that I had some sort of virus and that I should stay in bed and drink lots of fluids. I could have told him that.

"Thank you, doctor," Ali's mom said, shaking Dr. Spencer's hand.

"It's my pleasure. Little Ali here rarely gets sick, so I'm happy to help when I can." He winked at me and smiled.

"Call me if her temperature doesn't come down after twenty-four hours or if she is suffering from any worse symptoms."

"We will," Ali's dad said. "We'll give her some quiet time now, so she can sleep."

Ali's mom blew me a kiss and wrung her hands together as she left the room. This illness seemed to be affecting her as much as it was me. I hoped it wasn't contagious. Ali would never forgive me if I made her mom even sicker than she already was.

CHAPTER FIVE

Casey

The room was so quiet without Ali's parents and Dr. Spencer in it. At my house, Lucas would be doing something annoying or I'd hear Mom's fingers clicking over the computer keyboard. But Ali's house was so big that those things could be happening and I'd have no idea. There was so much space here.

I closed my eyes and leaned against Ali's fluffy pillows. I tried to drift off to sleep but after a few minutes, I was still wide awake. I opened my eyes and looked around the room. It was twice the size of my own room, probably more. The walls were painted a cream color and all the furniture was a pristine white. Across the room stood a large computer desk and a laptop computer. I couldn't believe she had her own computer! I always had to share with my mom. And she was rarely away from it so the only computer access I had was maybe once a week at home or when Mom was away. A tall dresser stood to the right of the bed. I wondered how many other designer outfits were neatly folded or hanging inside.

I closed my eyes and tried to sleep again but after another few seconds, I knew sleep wasn't going to come.

Smoothing my hands over the quilt, I shivered. I was so sleepy before Dr. Spencer had come in. Now that I was firmly placed in Ali's life, my brain had caught up with the entire situation and gone into overdrive. My stomach sunk thinking that we had done it. We'd made the swap. It was far from what we'd imagined and whether we liked it or not, we had done it. But now what?

I listened for movement from Ali's parents but I didn't hear anything. They were giving "Ali" time to rest. I pushed the quilt off my body and immediately regretted it. I started to shiver again. Jumping off the bed, I shuffled over to Ali's closet, my teeth chattering uncontrollably. I found a pair of slippers and a robe and shoved those on. I tied the robe around me and clinched it as tight as I could. The inner lining of the slippers was incredibly soft and I wiggled my toes inside of them. Once I was comfortable and warm, I began to wander around the room; my intense curiosity making me forget about how unwell I'd been feeling only moments earlier.

At first, it all seemed very strange. I was intruding on Ali's life by going through her closet and putting her clothes on, but we were sisters. Weren't sisters supposed to borrow clothes from one another? I wasn't sure if borrowing houses was a thing but ours was a very unusual situation.

I thought of Ali and her distraught expression as she watched her parents' car pull away from the campground. What must she be thinking right now? Would she and Brie be able to convince everyone that she was me? And what was going to happen when Ali went to my house tomorrow? She didn't have an illness as an excuse for forgetting things. Ali was going to be faced with my mom, Grandma Ann, and Lucas. And without my help! We went into this with no preparation.

My temperature suddenly spiked and I found it hard to breathe. I knew it wasn't part of the virus. I was going into full-blown panic mode. Our intention to reveal ourselves to our parents had been a good idea at the time, but not like this. If they were to find out that we lied there would be serious consequences. I was especially concerned about Ali's mom and her poor health. This was supposed to be a fun idea. And I wasn't having fun at all.

I pressed my palms against my eyes and took a deep breath then let it out slowly.

There was no backing out of the situation now. We had to move forward. Ali was very smart and she also had Brie to help her. I hoped they had enough time. I, on the other hand, had no help. It was one thing to pretend to be Ali at camp. We were together most of the time so if I messed up, Ali could cover for me and vice versa. Now I was on my own.

I moved my hands away from my face and looked around the room again.

Ali's mom had closed the curtains, darkening the room. I was curious to see more about the house so I peeked through the curtains and my mouth dropped open. Ali had a view of the most beautiful garden I'd ever seen. It looked like it had been plucked right out of a magazine. Not a leaf was out of place. And the mixture of colors was gorgeous. What a lucky girl to wake up to that view every morning.

I turned around, closing the curtains behind me. The bright light from outside hurt my sensitive eyes and it took them a second to adjust to the dimness of the room. If I was going to play Ali, I had everything I needed in this room to help me. A girl's room was her sanctuary, now I had to find Ali's secrets.

I went over to her computer. Maybe she had something on there that could help. I opened it up and my finger hovered over the power button but I didn't press it. What if there was a sound when the computer was powering up?

I couldn't alert Ali's parents seeing me out of bed and asking questions. I needed as much uninterrupted time as possible. I started to look through her drawers, opening them slowly. It would be great if Ali had a diary that outlined everything I needed to know. But after looking through all the drawers I had no such luck. Besides, I was invading Ali's private life enough already. A diary might be stepping over the line. I would be mortified if someone read my personal thoughts.

I took another breath and looked around. Next to the desk was a bookcase that was built into the wall. I spotted all seven Harry Potter books on one shelf and smiled. I took the first one off the shelf and realized it was a first edition. My jaw dropped. First editions were very expensive. I carefully placed it back on the shelf and clasped my hands together. I didn't want to ruin it with my fingerprints. Having those books in my room would be my most prized possession. I wondered how many other rare editions she had.

And that's when I saw it.

A thin pink phone rested on one of the shelves. Ali had followed the 'no phones at camp' rule just as I had. I knew some of the kids had sneaked their phones into camp but if they were caught then they had the risk of the phone being confiscated. The culprits would also be on cleaning duty for the entire camp session. Brie and I had both left ours at home and obviously, Ali had done the same thing. If that rule didn't exist, we'd be able to contact each other right now.

I grabbed the phone and turned it over. The case had a picture of Ali and her parents at some theme park. She was younger in the photo. Her mom had long curly blonde hair and looked like the picture of health. I felt bad that she was so sick now.

I pressed the button to turn the phone on. The seconds waiting for the screen to light up were the longest of my life! I kept listening for someone in the hallway but I didn't hear a thing. Being an only child was great, no dorky brothers to interrupt your time alone.

The screen flickered. I was giddy with relief until the request for a 4-number password appeared on the screen.

"No way," I said to myself, grumbling.

I pressed 1-2-3-4 into the phone and the numbers on the screen shook and the phone vibrated, telling me I didn't have the right combination.

I heard something in the hallway and gasped lightly. I pressed the phone against my body and rushed to the bed. Kicking off the slippers, I jumped into the bed and covered myself with the quilt. I laid there, heart hammering in my chest and waited for one of Ali's parents to come into the room.

I didn't hear the sound again and no one came in. Releasing the breath I'd been holding, I pulled the phone out, holding it in front of me.

I sat up against the pillows and pulled the quilt up to my neck.

"What would your password be?" I said to the phone, hoping an idea would strike me. There were so many combinations. It could take hours to try and figure it out.

I chewed on the inside of my cheek and stared at the phone, trying and failing over and over again. I tried numbers that I would have used, but I forgot I was playing Ali. What numbers would she use? I wracked my brain, hoping the right ones would come to mind.

I then decided to try and channel her thoughts. I wondered if the strange psychic connection we had could work over long distances.

Suddenly, in a flash of recognition, it came to me! I typed in the numbers that popped into my head and then the main screen opened before me.

CHAPTER SIX

Casey

I couldn't believe it! Ali's passcode was the exact same one as mine! 1010, the tenth of October, our birthday. When I first got my phone I used the year of my birth for the passcode and Mom said that was too easy to crack. That's when I came up with using the date and month. I couldn't believe Ali had the same thoughts!

I wondered when she came up with the idea to use that code. I made a mental note to ask her the next time I saw her. Which really couldn't be soon enough.

The background on her phone was a bouquet of flowers which looked very similar to the ones in her backyard. I flipped through the apps on the screen, wondering where to start. This was the vault to finding out more about Ali and her life. I hoped I could find some information to at least get me through the weekend and then to school on Monday without alerting anyone to our secret.

I felt a little guilty for snooping but it was necessary for this situation. And it wasn't like Ali kept a diary on her phone. I would only find the information I needed and was sure she would understand.

Opening her Instagram account, I scrolled through her photos. She liked to post photos of a very cute orange and white cat.

I clicked on the caption on a more recent photo and discovered that her cat's name was Sox. Several of the pictures showed Ali kissing or hugging the cat against her. In my short time away from her, I almost forgot how alike we were. It almost looked as though I was hugging the cat. If it weren't for Ali's braided hairstyle, I doubted even my brother would be able to tell the difference.

The funny thing was that just like Ali, I also adored

158

cats. I'd always wanted one. So I didn't need to fake any affection when I finally met Sox.

A few of her older posts showed her packing her old room. Then there were a some of her standing outside her old house. That one was even nicer than this one if that was even possible.

And she liked to take selfies with her new clothes. Apparently, she went shopping a lot. I already knew she had great style and more money than I did, but it was different seeing it up close. Ali had a good heart so I knew she wasn't trying to show off but it still made me a little jealous.

I started to get distracted so I had to refocus on the task at hand. Scrolling higher I looked at the more recent posts and stopped at one that I hadn't noticed before. The picture was of Ali in the cafeteria during lunch. She was taking a selfie with her food, and Jake was in the background sticking out his tongue and making a funny face. One of the hashtags on the post was #photobomb. She had even tagged Jake in the photo!

My insides tingled at seeing him. I wondered if he was thinking about me at all. We had such a great time canoeing and swimming together. I thought we'd really hit it off. Even though I was "playing" Ali at the time, I still had the feeling we now had a deeper connection. And at the bonfire, he didn't move from my side the entire time.

I hoped Ali was continuing what we'd started with Jake, especially while she pretended to be me. It would be so awesome if I went to school the following week as myself and Jake talked to me like he had at camp. I couldn't help but smile as I looked into his eyes through the Instagram photo. We were meant to be, I could feel it.

My finger hovered over his name. I wanted to click it to see if he'd posted anything lately, but I didn't. I knew he wouldn't have during the time we were at camp since no phones were allowed. And thinking of Jake would only distract me.

After looking through most of Ali's pictures and getting as much information about her life as I could, I moved on to her text messages.

There were a few from her parents and one really long thread with someone named Meg. They seemed very close but they also texted in mostly emoji's so I didn't understand what they were talking about. If they were close friends, they probably had inside jokes that I didn't understand.

I flipped back to Instagram to find Meg. After checking Ali's friends, I only found one Megan. I clicked on the account and it opened. I feared it would be locked and private but then I remembered I was on Ali's phone so technically I wasn't a stranger to this girl.

I looked at Meg's pictures and saw a recent one that she'd posted of herself.

There were also a lot of her and Ali before Ali moved to town. The hashtag #BFF ended each one of them.

I went back to Ali's texts and saw that Meg and Ali

texted almost every single day. One of the more recent ones had Ali telling Meg she was going to be away from her phone while she was at camp. I hoped Meg didn't know exactly when Ali was coming back. I didn't want to have to reply to someone who most likely knew Ali better than her parents did.

Ali didn't have many other texts from people. One was from Ronnie, texting Ali the address to her house the day before the sleepover. Even though Ali was well-liked at school, she had only been there for about a week. Not enough time to fill her texts with fun plans and inside jokes yet.

I opened her music streaming app to see what she liked to listen to. I almost squealed when I saw she had a whole playlist of Hailee Steinfeld songs. I loved her! Ali's other playlists were similar to the ones on my phone. Yet another thing we had in common.

I looked through the music stored on her phone and it was filled with hundreds of songs. I scrolled through them and was awestruck at the collection she had for herself. What it must be like to be able to get whatever you wanted, whenever you wanted. While we looked alike, our families were totally different. She had two loving parents who came to her rescue at a moment's notice and offered to buy her the best of everything. I had an annoying brother and a liar and workaholic for a mom.

My brain started to get fuzzy the more I stared at the screen trying to learn more about Ali. I decided to take a break and nap for a little while. I wasn't going to be able to use all this information if I didn't get better.

I placed the phone on the side table and turned it on silent before rolling over and lifting the quilt over myself.

I snuggled into the pillow and shoved my hand underneath to prop it up. As comfortable as I was, the pillows were very soft. I was used to being propped up a little more. I adjusted my arm and felt something hard move behind the pillow. I wrinkled my nose and moved my arm again. Something was definitely back there.

I grabbed the object and pulled it out. It was a book.

It had a soft brown leather cover. Maybe Ali liked to read old books before bed? I flipped through it and a pen fell out, bumping me in the chest before falling between two pillows at my side. Inside the book was handwriting. It wasn't a book. It was Ali's diary.

I sat up and immediately regretted it. The room spun for a minute and I closed my eyes to get my bearings.

When the spinning stopped, I looked down at the book again. This was a step I wasn't sure I was prepared to take just yet. Although I had just been snooping around in her phone, I wasn't sure this was the same thing. A diary was much more private.

But the more I thought about it, the more I realized that a phone only offered surface details. If I was really going to play the part of Ali, I needed deeper information. Perhaps I could quickly scan through the pages and pick up what I needed. And I could start at the most recent entry and go backward so I wouldn't be getting too far into her personal life.

I weighed my options for a few seconds before deciding to open the diary. Flipping through to the recent entries, I found the one that was written the night before we left for camp.

Ali had just finished dinner, and it was her mom's home-cooked chicken casserole. She made a note that it was "DELISH" and her favorite meal of all time. My mouth started to water. Maybe her mom would make it for me so I could see how good it really was. Then Ali wrote about her excitement for camp and making new friends.

I flipped to the previous entry and it was dated the day before. The writing was scrawled which probably meant she was in a hurry. She wrote that she had spilled her mother's green tea all over one of her favorite shirts that morning and was super bummed about it. She wrote about the morning ritual and how she made the tea for her mom each morning before school. Then Ali went on about how upset she'd been lately because of her mother's illness, she was so afraid of her mom dying. She knew it would happen eventually, but she didn't want to lose her best friend.

My eyes teared up thinking about how Ali must be feeling. She might have seemed okay on the outside but she really wasn't. I was the first of her new friends that she had confided in about her mother. She obviously needed to talk to someone outside of her diary and I intended to be there for her once we were together again.

We had so many things in common, but this was one big difference. Ali was incredibly close to her mom and I wasn't close with mine at all. It broke my heart to know that she was hurting over this. I hoped that we could switch back soon so that Ali could be with her mom for all the time she had left.

I was about to continue onto the next entry when a sound at the door made my entire body freeze.

CHAPTER SEVEN

Casey

I quickly laid down and turned away from the door. My heartbeat was so loud in my ears I wasn't sure if I had imagined the sound or not. I held my breath for as long as I could while my heart continued to do a fast-paced dance around my chest.

The door clicked and I squeezed my eyes closed. I waited for another sound but nothing happened for a few minutes.

When I was sure I was alone, I slowly opened my eyes to look around the room. I turned, glancing over my shoulder. There was no one else in the room with me. I spotted a mug on the side table with a string from a tea bag laying over the side. Steam rose from the liquid.

I let out a huge breath and sat up again. That was close.

I had a feeling Ali's mom had brought the tea since she was also a tea drinker. I'd have to make sure I was as quiet as a mouse while I continued to learn all I could about the girl and the life I'd stepped into.

I had never tried tea before. Mom didn't keep it in the house. And anytime Grandma Ann offered some to me I always refused, thinking it was an old lady's drink. But if Ali's mom had brought it to me, Ali had to be a tea drinker too. So I decided to try it.

I grabbed the handle of the mug, careful not to touch the piping hot sides. I blew on the tea until most of the steam was gone and took a sip.

I winced when the tea burned my lips and tongue, but the actual taste of the tea was really good! It had a sweetness that soothed my throat. Taking another sip, I placed the mug on the table and returned my attention to

Ali's phone, getting back to learning as much about my twin as possible.

I switched between reading the diary and scrolling through her phone. Things we had in common kept cropping up and soon I felt more comfortable playing Ali. Eventually, though, my eyes became heavy with the need for sleep and I was forced to push the phone and diary under the covers and close my eyes.

It was a while later that I was woken by the sound of the bedroom door opening again. I kept my eyes closed as someone shuffled into the room. The next thing I heard was the sound of something sliding across the surface of the bedside table, a few feet away from me. I tried to keep my breathing even to keep up the pretense that I was still asleep.

"I love you," Ali's mom whispered and then shuffled out of the room again.

I waited until the latch clicked before I opened my eyes. The room was dimmer than before and the clock on the bedside table read six-thirty-five. I'd been asleep for almost two hours.

On the bedside table was a tray. On the tray was a plate covered with plastic wrap and a glass of water. I sat up to get a better look. My stomach growled and I pulled the tray in front of me.

I lifted the plastic from the plate and the scent of the delicious lasagna floated up into my nostrils. It smelled so good! The food was very hot so I took a sip of water and then took a bite of the bread that was also on the tray. The inside of the bread was warm too and it tasted better than any store-bought bread I'd ever had. It must have been homemade. Ali loved her mom's cooking and I now knew from everything I'd learned about Ali, that all their food was made by one of her parents from scratch.

I could barely wait to dig into the lasagna. I was careful not to burn my tongue but I had to eat it! If possible, it tasted better than it smelled. I couldn't slow down. The last time I ate was at camp and that food didn't even compare. And the frozen food my mom served us almost every night tasted like cardboard compared to this. I wondered if Ali had the recipe. If she did I'd want to make this every night when I returned home; maybe teach my mother a lesson on how to really cook for her kids.

By the last bite, my stomach was very content and full. I licked all the morsels off the fork and placed it quietly on the tray. After finishing the water, I scooped up any remaining sauce with the rest of the bread then placed the tray back on the table and sat back against the pillows, finally content.

I stared up at the ceiling. It was getting dark outside and with the fading light, I could see an outline of stars on the ceiling. They looked like they were painted with glow-in-the-dark paint. They were so pretty! Ali must have felt like the luckiest girl every night.

My mind wandered while I gazed at the indoor stars. I wondered how Brie and Ali were doing at camp. I hoped Brie was helping Ali prepare for the next day. Both of us had our work cut out for us. I hadn't had much time with Ali's parents up to that point, so convincing them was going to be tough. And I knew it would also be tough for Ali. I just hoped she was ready. Thanks to her diary and phone, I felt much more prepared than I'd felt earlier, but that would be tested in a matter of time.

My stomach began to twist and I forced away all thoughts of what was ahead. There was nothing I could do but wait and hope that everything would work out fine. I would continue thinking of Ali like I did when we swapped at camp.

The stars reminded me of the night of the bonfire. There had been so many in the sky that night. I couldn't help going back to that scene over and over in my head. Jake could have moved at any point but instead, he chose to stay next to me. It had been a dream come true! I couldn't wait to see him again. I hoped that Ali had been able to hang out with him during the last day and night of camp. That way when Monday came around I could switch back to being me and everything would return to normal; except maybe I would have a boyfriend!

My eyes started to grow heavy again and I knew I needed more rest if I was going to get better. I turned onto my side and snuggled deeper into the soft bed. As I closed my eyes, an image of Jake's smiling face appeared in my mind. His beautiful brown eyes stared back and his hair looked soft enough to touch.

Sighing contently, I grinned to myself as I fell into a deep sleep.

CHAPTER EIGHT

Ali

The final morning of the camp was a flurry of activity, especially after our late night at the pajama party the night before. I did manage to talk to Jake a few times. Obviously, he thought I was Casey but he seemed distracted. I hoped I hadn't done anything to ruin her chances with him. Though a small part of me wondered if he was upset because "Ali" had gone home. I tried to shake away the thought. I shouldn't care about the rumor that he liked me. I was going to be a good sister and ignore it so Casey could have her crush to herself.

The girls in Casey's cabin rushed around to pack their bags at the very last minute. Brie and I had packed the night before so we could sleep in. But because of the amount of noise in the cabin, sleeping in wasn't an option. Instead, we headed for the showers and were among the first to use them. By the time we left a huge flock of girls was headed our way.

When we got back to the cabin, we had it all to ourselves.

I stood by the mirror and started to split my hair into three even strands.

"Ahem!" Brie faked a cough.

I turned around and looked at her, confused. "What?"

"Casey," she put a lot of emphasis on the name, "combs her hair after a shower and leaves it loose."

I dropped the strands and reached for the brush. "Oh no. I forgot."

"Well it's good you forgot here instead of when you're at her house."

The weight of our swap came crashing over me. Today was the day I had to prove that I was Casey to the people who knew her best.

"You're going to be fine," Brie said encouragingly. "You know enough to get through the weekend. The biggest thing to remember is your relationship with Lucas."

"I know," I said. I combed my hair and parted it down the middle like Casey always did. My hair was still wet, creating a watermark on my shirt.

I stood back from the mirror to inspect my look. I'd chosen a pair of worn jean shorts and a pretty pink top that had sequins on the sleeves. Casey's knock-off converse sneakers completed the look. I had to admit she was creative with her choices in fashion. With the right combination, no one would be able to tell that her clothes were off-brand.

I took a deep breath and let it out slowly. My hands began to shake with nervousness. I went over to Casey's bed and sat. My legs were like jelly as each minute closer to departure time ticked by.

Brie sat next to me and put her arm on my shoulder. "Everything is going to be fine," she repeated. "When you get home, find Casey's phone and text me if you have questions. I'll check my messages constantly, in case you need something, so you don't need to worry about a thing."

I smiled. "Thanks."

"No problem!"

On the bus ride home, Brie and I sat in the last row huddled together, going over the final details of Casey's life. The trip seemed much shorter on the ride home, probably because I was dreading what would happen when I got there.

What if Casey's family knew it wasn't her the second I got off the bus? Casey had managed an entire day pretending to be me without my parents storming back to camp and demanding their real child. Now it was up to me to have the same success. My nerves started up again and I had to take several deep breaths to calm myself down.

Before I knew it, the bus pulled into the school parking lot. I couldn't help looking at all the cars for my real mom. While I was cramming my brain with Casey's likes and dislikes, I totally forgot that I was about to meet my biological family! I'd been dreaming about this moment for years. It hadn't worked out as we planned but it was only seconds from happening.

I couldn't help the big smile on my face.

The bus parked at the far end of the lot and parents began to get out of their cars. Most of my other classmates were disappointed that they were going home but I couldn't get off the bus fast enough!

"Do you see Grandma Ann?" I asked Brie.

She leaned over to get a closer look out the window. "No, I don't see her. But I'll let you know when we get off the bus."

It was hard to let anyone cut in front of me, but I allowed Brie to head down the aisle first since she knew who Casey would be going home with.

The last step off the bus was my final moment as Ali, for a couple of days at least. I tried to push aside thoughts of my parents and all my personal preferences and channeled my sister's energy.

"Here we go," I said to myself.

I stuck close to Brie's side while she looked for my grandmother.

"That's surprising," Brie said.

"What?" I asked. "What's surprising?" I wasn't sure I could handle a surprise at that moment.

"Your mom actually came to pick you up," she said under her breath.

I looked at the crowd to try and find her. But I had no idea who I was looking for. "Where is she?"

Brie leaned close to my ear and whispered, "Over to the right. Next to the white car. There's a bald man in a checkered shirt. Next to him is your mom." She grinned and gave me a thumbs up.

I swallowed and looked for the bald man. And there he was, waving over his son, who was one of my classmates. Next to him was one of the prettiest women I'd ever seen.

Her long brown wavy hair was in a low ponytail. Even from this far away I could see her brown eyes. My brown eyes. She looked like an older version of Casey and me. I couldn't believe I was about to meet my real mom!

When my biological mom's eyes met mine, a fluttering sensation took over my insides. She appeared relieved and gave me a close-lipped smile with a hesitant

171

wave.

"Oh my gosh," I said to Brie. That beautiful young woman is my real mom! I started to tug at the hem of my shirt, wondering if I'd chosen the right outfit for our first meeting.

"I know you're excited, but whatever you do, remember not to be too friendly," Brie said. "*Casey* isn't very happy with her mom right now. Remember how she lied?"

"Yes," I replied. But I couldn't help the excitement from bubbling to the surface.

"Just keep your distance. Be angry. You left for camp really upset with her. Casey can be stubborn at times so just do that and remember all the stuff I told you."

I nodded a few times, understanding what she was saying even though my body buzzed with excitement. "I'll talk to you later okay?"

I grabbed Casey's sleeping bag, pillow, and overnight bag and started toward my real mom. My pace quickened, my legs had a mind of their own! I had to force myself to slow down.

Be upset, I thought to myself even though it was the exact opposite reaction that I felt!

When I finally reached her, my excitement turned to shyness. My hands held onto Casey's bag so tightly, that they started to sweat.

"Hi," my mom said first. She chewed on her lip while waiting for my response.

I wondered how upset Casey would be days after their argument. I glanced over my shoulder and found Brie with her mother.

She gave me a small thumbs up.

I took a breath and turned to my mom. "Hi," I said quickly. I hoped I sounded aloof enough.

My mom came closer to me and leaned down to give me a hug. My hands were full so I was unable to put my arms around her. I inhaled. She smelled like the sweetest perfume. I couldn't help the goofy smile on my face. But when she pulled away from me, I put a serious expression on. Casey wouldn't be grinning like an idiot after she was so upset with her mom.

"Let me take those for you," she offered.

I handed her everything at once and she awkwardly grabbed the items.

She turned to the car and I mentally chided myself for being so uncomfortable. Casey had lived with our mom her whole life. She wouldn't be this awkward.

I went to the passenger seat of the car and opened the door. *Be aloof. Angry. And most of all, be Casey!*

I got into the seat and buckled my seatbelt. The car shook as the trunk door closed. My mom got into the driver's seat next to me. She jiggled the key ring in her hands. I noticed a photo keychain on the ring. I strained my eyes to see what the picture was even though I was sure Casey would already know.

"Casey," she said, and turned hesitantly in her seat to face me.

"Yeah?"

She took a deep breath as if what she was about to say was hard for her. "Casey, we need to talk. I know you must be very tired from camp, but would it be okay if we don't go straight home? Grandma Ann and Lucas are there, and I think we really need some time to ourselves right now."

I nodded slowly in agreement. As Ali, it was everything I wanted! But would Casey want that? Would she want to be alone with the mother who had lied to her all these years? Casey and I were sort of in the same place. My mom had kept everything from me as well. Would I give her a chance to explain? If it had anything to do with my biological mom I would have agreed in seconds. I wasn't sure about Casey though.

"Listen," my mom said. "How about we go to your favorite cafe." She snapped her fingers a few times. "What's it called? I always forget the name."

I tried to remember if Casey or Brie had mentioned anything about a favorite cafe. My mind went completely blank. I couldn't even remember the name of one cafe in town even though I'd been to a few already. My mouth opened but nothing came out.

"Oh! I remember now," my mom said. "Aromas. On the Boardwalk. That's the one you love, isn't it? How about we go there. You can order your favorite hot chocolate. Or whatever you want…"

Her words trailed off, waiting for my response.

I smiled tentatively, suddenly afraid to speak! Everything I wanted to say to her since I found out I was adopted disappeared from my mind. My real mom was talking to me like a real mom did with her daughter. If it was up to me, we wouldn't need to go anywhere else. I was happy to be sitting in the car with her.

Her eyebrows rose as if asking me a silent question.

I nodded, agreeing to go with her.

She smiled, showing sparkling white straight teeth. "Okay then." She put the keys in the ignition and started the car.

I sat back in my seat and turned toward the window, trying to hide the silly grin from my own face.

CHAPTER NINE

Ali

During the drive to the cafe, we didn't talk much. My mom turned on the radio and I got excited when a Hailee Steinfeld song came on. I mouthed the words and bobbed my head to the music. She even turned up the song, knowing I obviously liked it. I knew Casey was a fan too so that part was easy to play along with.

When we arrived at the Boardwalk, she parked a few stores down from the cafe. We walked together in silence. I knew she was nervous, I could tell by the way she was playing with her keys. I was just happy to be there with her. Getting some answers was a bonus. But I had to be careful and not ask too many questions about things that Casey already knew. I didn't want her to suspect anything about our swap.

The inside of the cafe was as normal as they came. Small wooden tables that seated no more than four people took up the center space. There was a tiny bar with stools on the right side. There weren't many decorations on the walls but the large front window brought in a lot of light from outside, brightening up the space.

We sat down at a table in the back of the cafe. An older woman came over to take our order. My mom ordered a coffee and I ordered a hot chocolate. I really wanted a tea but my mom had suggested the hot chocolate. It was obviously what Casey preferred. I only drank hot chocolate when we ran out of tea at my house.

When the waitress left our table to make our order, my mom began to talk.

"Casey, I'm so sorry you found out this way. I had intentions to tell you everything at some point, but that opportunity never came around."

She looked at me despairingly and then took a breath before continuing. "All of this happened when I was very young. I thought I was in love but when I got pregnant my whole life turned upside down. The boy I was with at the time didn't want anything to do with the situation. And even though Grandma Ann and your grandfather were supportive, his failing health made things that much harder financially."

She was staring directly at me, her eyes not wavering from mine. All I could do was sit silently and take in her words. "Then I found out I was having twins and I knew I had to give up both of you to good families, ones who would be able to take care of you the way that I wasn't able to. Initially, I wanted someone to take the both of you but no families at the time wanted twins. Then when you two were born something inside of me changed. I knew I couldn't take both of you, but I also couldn't let go completely."

I leaned against the table, fascinated by our story and hearing it from my real mom!

She reached across the table and took my hand in hers. Her eyes were shiny with tears. "I had to keep you, Casey."

The sound of my twin's name made me flinch. What had been wrong with me that she decided to take Casey over me?

The waitress returned with our drinks. She placed a glass mug that contained the hot chocolate in front of me and I stared down at it. Hot chocolate was the last thing I felt like right then.

My mom took her hand back and thanked the waitress.

"If you need anything else let me know," the waitress smiled, and then left our table.

"That's the main gist of the story," Mom said. "That is exactly how it happened."

She glanced questioningly at me, waiting for my response. But I had no idea what to say. What questions would Casey ask? From what Casey told me, she'd only heard her grandmother's story, so I supposed any questions I had, Casey would probably have too.

"How did you choose who to take?" I asked, as it was the detail that bothered me most.

My mom took a sip of coffee and then sighed deeply. "I didn't. You chose me. There was something in your eyes that said you needed me more. I don't really know how to explain it, I just had a feeling and went with it."

That didn't help me feel any better but I guessed there wasn't any more she could say.

"Who is my father?"

"His name is Jonathan Cartwright."

"Where is he now? Did you ever contact him about me?"

She took another sip of coffee before responding. "Last I heard he was married and living in London. I contacted him when you were still young. And after he purposefully missed our meeting, I thought we were all better off."

I felt bad for Casey. At least I grew up with a father. Brie had told me Lucas's father, Casey's stepfather, had run out on our mom too. It seemed like everyone in both our families had let us down.

"I still can't believe you lied to me all these years. I missed out on twelve years with my sister. My twin." And suddenly I realized I wasn't just mad at my real mom. My own parents, even if they were my adopted family, had lied to me. I knew I was adopted, but hiding a twin from me? Did they know there was a twin involved? They had to. My mom said that the families didn't want two kids which was why they were going to split us up to begin with. Why did all the adults in my life think it was okay to lie about this?

Tears welled in my mom's eyes and she opened her mouth a few times to speak, but nothing came out. She took a deep breath and eventually said, "I'm so sorry."

I nodded. I knew she was sorry, but that didn't make up for everything that had happened. A tear fell from her eyes and she quickly swiped at it then took another sip of her coffee. She avoided my eyes.

My stomach twisted. As much as I wanted this to be about me and Casey, our mom was hurting too. I didn't think she'd meant to hurt us by keeping this secret. She meant to tell Casey, but how would anyone bring that up? For me, the adoption was something I knew about, so my parents had the opportunity to discuss it at any moment but had decided not to. I wasn't sure which parents were more at fault.

"What can I do to make it up to you?" my mom asked.

I knew what I wanted and it was something I knew Casey wanted too. "I want to spend some time with you. I want to get to know you. I feel like you never have time for me. I just want to know my mother."

After I said what was in my heart, I felt much better. Our swap plan had started off with me wanting to know my real mom. And now I was going to have that chance.

CHAPTER TEN

Casey

I rolled over in bed and opened my bleary eyes to see Ali's mom standing there holding a tray. I sat up quickly, adjusting the blankets around my body as if she'd be able to somehow tell that I wasn't her daughter.

"Good morning," she said.

"Morning." I didn't think I would be face to face with Ali's parents right away. At least it was only her mom instead of both of her parents at once. Anxiety filled my stomach and I had to swallow down the dread from seeing

Ali's mom. I hoped I was ready for this.

She placed the tray of food on the side table then sat on the edge of the bed. Yellow fluffy scrambled eggs covered most of the plate. Alongside were two slices of toast and a heaping pile of bacon. My mouth watered.

"Your dad left for work early this morning. He's coming back in a few hours, though. I thought I would treat you to a lovely big breakfast. I know it's more than you usually eat but it will help you get your strength back.

At this distance, I noticed her breathing was a little ragged. Was she winded from carrying that tray upstairs? Her skin was pale and her hands trembled in her lap. I wasn't sure how sick she really was but since Ali's dad was coming home early from work to help care for me, I knew she wasn't doing well.

"How are you feeling?" she asked.

I should have asked her the same thing. But Ali already knew how sick her mom was and I didn't want to say anything that might make her suspicious about who I was.

"I'm feeling much better," I replied with a small smile.

She clasped her hands in her lap, hard enough that her knuckles turned white. It looked as though she was trying to take hold of her shaking hands.

I reached for them, knowing it was something Ali would do. "How was your treatment this week?" I was grateful that Ali kept track of her mother's appointments in her phone calendar. She'd had an appointment on Thursday while Ali was at camp.

She squeezed my hand and then reached for the tray. "I'm fine. The doctors are waiting for more test results but they are very hopeful."

As she placed the tray on my lap, I noticed she was avoiding eye contact. She was trying to reassure her daughter but was doing a poor job of it. I didn't push for more information. I remembered Ali's diary entry about her fear of her mother dying. I just hoped that her mom was okay until we swapped back. Then Ali could spend as much time with her mother as possible, before something happened.

I picked up a piece of toast from the tray and took a small bite. The awkward silence between us stretched on. I finished the whole slice before Ali's mom said something.

"How was camp?" she asked.

I looked over at her. She was smiling, eager to hear about how Ali spent her days away. I remembered Ali thought of her mother and herself as best friends. Even though I felt bad about her being sick, Ali would have wanted to share everything about camp.

"It was fun," I said.

"What activities did you do?"

"Well, we did a craft every day."

"That sounds fun. What did you make?"

The more questions she asked, the more comfortable I felt talking about camp. Eventually, I outlined each day before she asked.

"The canoeing was really fun," I said remembering my time with Jake. Technically "Ali" had gone with Jake so I didn't have to lie about that part.

"Dad will be very surprised to hear you enjoyed the outdoors."

"I hope they have the trip again next year," I said.

Ali's mom's smile turned to a frown. I had a feeling her illness was bad but now I really knew. Did she not expect to be around next year? My eyes teared up. I felt so bad for Ali.

She sighed and forced a smile. She didn't ask another question but instead looked at me with an odd expression.

"What is it?" I asked. I smoothed my hair down over my shoulder. I was feeling a little uncomfortable and hoped that she hadn't picked up on anything.

She shook her head. "I've heard that school camp can be life-changing for some kids – but there's something very different about you, Ali. I just can't figure out what it is!"

I cleared my throat. I knew exactly what it was. I had been falling back into being Casey. But I needed to be Ali! I avoided her eyes and focused on the food in front of me, shoveling the eggs into my mouth. They were so good! Much better than the ones my own mother made.

"I really feel like I fit in at school," I said when I was finished clearing the plate. I munched on the last slice of bacon, hoping that was something Ali really felt. She actually really did fit in better than I did so it wasn't a lie.

"That's wonderful, Ali."

Just then, the bedroom door opened wider and I wondered if Ali's dad had come home sooner. Instead, an orange and white cat entered the room.

"Sox!" I said excitedly. "Come here Sox, it's so good to see you!" I'm sure Ali would be excited to see her favorite cat.

Sox meowed and then leaped onto the bed, as he walked, the tip of his thick tail curled over like a question mark.

I reached for him and pulled him closer to me. I patted his little head and stroked his back. He took a step away from me but I gently picked him up and placed him into my lap again. I had to do this a few times and then he jumped out of my arms onto the floor and sprinted out of the room.

Ali's mom's forehead creased. "That's odd. He normally never wants to leave your side!"

Sox probably sensed that I was an impostor and not Ali. I didn't want Ali's mom to question it again so I shoved the quilt off me and leaped from the bed. "I think it's time I got out of bed and had a shower. I probably smell like camp and he doesn't like it." It was a good excuse. At least I hoped it was. And at least I'd managed to change the subject before

Ali's mom mentioned anymore about Sox's escape from the room.

She placed my plate and cutlery on the tray and picked it up. Maybe she wouldn't have as much trouble now that the plate was empty.

"I think I'll take a shower now and get dressed." I went to Ali's closet and started to pick through her clothes. I wanted her mom to leave before I did something else that was different to Ali.

"It's a little cooler today," Ali's mom said. "Make sure you wear a cardigan or jacket."

"Thanks," I said, staring at Ali's clothes. Why wasn't she leaving?

"I want to ask you something," she said and I slowly turned around to face her.

CHAPTER ELEVEN

Casey

"Are you okay with me leaving for a little while to get some groceries?" she asked, raising her eyebrows questioningly.

"I won't be gone long but if you preferred that I stayed, just say so."

I tried not to act as relieved as I felt. I was sure I'd been caught, and the hammering of my heart was like a bass drum in my ears.

"I want to make the chicken casserole that you love," she continued.

Ali had written about the casserole in her diary and I was aware of how much she enjoyed it. I made a show of gasping sharply and smiling. "Really? That would be amazing and I'm sure it'd make me feel even better."

I knew it was the right reaction when she smiled too. "I know it's your favorite. And I love making it for you. So I'm going to run over to the store and pick up some ingredients while you shower and get cleaned up."

Was Ali's mom well enough for a grocery trip on her own? I thought about offering to go with her but with both Ali's parents gone, I'd have an opportunity to check out the house and become more comfortable in Ali's surroundings. It was too good an opportunity to pass up.

"Are you sure you're okay with that?" she asked. "I won't be gone that long."

"It's fine," I said. "Take your time." I meant every word of that, and smiled widely with relief.

She came over and hugged me. Without hesitation, I wrapped my arms around her and squeezed her too. Ali was so lucky to have a mom who cared so much for her. I didn't remember the last time that my mom had hugged me or Lucas. I didn't realize how much I needed it, especially after being sick.

Ali's mom stroked my hair while holding me against her. I closed my eyes and took in every second. I hoped that she could feel Ali's love for her through me.

She kissed the top of my head and went to the side table to pick up the tray. "I'll see you in a little bit, okay?"

"Okay," I said.

"Love you."

"L-love you too," I said, stumbling over my words.

She left the room and I stood there for a moment, taking everything in. It had been my first real interaction with Ali's mom, and everything seemed to have gone well. At least I thought it had. She seemed to be acting normal and wasn't questioning anything I did. Although I made a point to find Sox and get him used to me. That confrontation with the cat could have ruined everything.

The sound of a car engine made my ears perk up. I raced to the window and pushed the curtain aside. A small red car pulled out of the driveway. I moved the curtain over my face so Ali's mom wouldn't see me. She turned the car onto the road and then drove away. I waited by the window for a few minutes to make sure she hadn't forgotten anything and returned sooner.

I turned and headed out into the hallway. I decided to start with the first floor so I could at least be back upstairs when Ali's mom came home. I went down the huge staircase and stood in the massive entryway. I looked up at the tall ceiling and the expensive-looking chandelier hanging down from it. There were two rooms on either side of me. One was a dining room with a long table that had twelve chairs around it. The other was a living room with two large couches and a fireplace. On either side of the fireplace were bookshelves built into the walls. Each shelf was bursting with books. I wondered how many more first-editions Ali's family had. With a house like that, they seemed to have a lot of money to spend on such things.

Further into the house was a kitchen that was probably the size of my kitchen and living room combined. All the surfaces were white and with the sun coming in through the large window that overlooked the garden, the room was blindingly bright.

The refrigerator had glass doors so I could see everything inside. It was the cleanest refrigerator I'd ever seen! Mine was usually covered with spills from juice or whatever else we stored in there. I was fairly tidy and blamed Lucas for a majority of those messes.

While exploring the rest of the first floor, I found a study with a big wooden desk (probably for Ali's father), two bathrooms and another living room. The second living room was more casual since it had a huge widescreen television and the sofas looked much more comfortable than the ones in the other living room.

I couldn't believe how beautiful this house was. It was the most expensive home I'd ever been inside and it was the place where my twin lived! How exciting!

I went to the front door of the house and peeked outside. Ali's mom still hadn't returned but I knew I needed to hurry so I could finish exploring. She would probably expect me to be showered and dressed by the time she arrived back. Ali wouldn't need to be wandering around her house instead of getting cleaned up.

Upstairs, there were four bedrooms in addition to Ali's and each of them had their own bathroom. I didn't spend much time in those since I had a funny feeling that my time was running short. Inside Ali's bedroom, there was another door that led to her bathroom. The bathroom was bigger than my bedroom and it was very clean. I went through the drawers and saw that I had everything I needed to present myself as Ali.

After showering, I braided my hair into Ali's

signature style and went back into her bedroom to find some clothes.

I started to get excited when I made my way to her closet. Since meeting her, I'd admired the designer clothes she wore. Even though our styles were different, I still loved the way she was dressed every day. And since we looked alike, it was almost like looking in a mirror, except Ali had a lot of money to spend.

I tried on a few outfits, combining some white skinny jeans with a gorgeous pink crop top. I soon realized I was looking for items that were more Casey and not Ali. Putting those ones neatly back on the shelves, I decided to go preppy, like Ali would.

I then discovered a spotted blue dress with a dark blue trim on the sleeves and collar. I completed the style with a thin leather belt that I found hanging on a rack. Moving in front of the mirror, I adjusted the belt around my waist, then took notice of the soft and silky fabric and how nice it felt against my skin.

Since I normally bought discounted clothes, I wasn't used to the high quality but I knew Ali's things needed to be handled with care. I couldn't help but treat them like precious items.

My toes dug further into the carpet and I wondered which shoes to wear. On one side of Ali's closet were dozens of pairs of shoes. There were a lot of ballet flats, some heels, but I wanted to be comfortable, even in Ali's style. I decided on a pair of white sneakers. I pulled on some ankle socks and put the shoes on, once again going to the mirror.

Unable to stop my wide smile, I grinned happily at my reflection. When Ali and I had swapped at camp, we only had the mirror in the bathroom showing us from our waist up. With Ali's full-length mirror I could see how alike we really were and how easy this swap was to pull off.

I looked over my shoulder at the clock. It was still early. Ali would be arriving back from camp in a few hours. I sighed, wondering what to do next. I wanted to talk to Ali but I had to wait until she could get to my phone.

I went over to the side table and picked up Ali's phone. I stared at it for a few seconds, wondering if I should wait or send her something. My fingers entered the password and I opened a text message. I typed in my own phone number and thought about what to say. I needed to be careful with my wording in case nosey-Lucas found my phone and read it. He didn't know my password but "Ali's" text would pop up on the screen if he turned it on. Although Lucas might not be interested in my texts with classmates, I knew Grandma Ann might be. Especially since I'd told her about Ali already, she would probably ask about the text. She noticed everything.

I typed a few lines before deleting the words. It took a few minutes to work on my message before knowing I had it right.

Hey, it's me. I'm feeling much better now. Everything is okay so far. Call me as soon as u get a chance. Ali.

I pressed send and let out a big breath. Now all I had to do was wait.

CHAPTER TWELVE

Ali

After the cafe, my mom took me to Casey's house. The open conversation we'd had made me feel lighter inside. But when we pulled up to the driveway my stomach churned with worry. I'd received all the answers I wanted, but I had to remember I was still playing Casey. Grandma Ann and Lucas were the people she spent the most time with so I had to work hard to make them think I was Casey.

Casey's house was much smaller than mine, but it was so cute and I felt instantly at home.

My mom and I carried Casey's things up the driveway and with each step, I felt even more anxious than I had when I got off the bus.

My mother opened the front door and walked inside. I quickly followed her and entered Casey's home. Instead of the huge entryway that I was used to, we walked right into the living room. I kicked off my shoes, not wanting to get dirt from outside onto the carpet.

She raised one eyebrow after I placed Casey's sneakers by the door next to each other. "They were dirty from camp," I said, hoping it was an acceptable excuse.

She smiled at me. "They must have taught you some extra manners at camp."

I smiled back, wondering how much my twin didn't care about keeping the house clean. My parents were very neat but that was more for my mom's benefit. I guessed the cleanliness had been passed on without me knowing!

"Mom!" a younger boy called from the other room. He came bounding into the room and hugged my mother.

She gently patted his back. "I wasn't gone that long."

My insides were bursting when I saw Lucas. He had

short reddish hair and big blue eyes and was wearing a yellow cap that had been stuck on backward. Even though his coloring was different to mine, I could still see a resemblance between us. I wanted to scoop him up into a hug, but Brie's warning rang in my head.

Before I had a chance to speak, he burst out with a laugh. "Oh you're back, it's been so good without you!" He broke into a fit of giggles.

I couldn't help but laugh at that. He was too adorable! Even if he was insulting Casey.

Someone else came into the room and I felt even more overwhelmed to see Grandma Ann. She had short dark hair that was streaked with gray and wore a pair of burgundy rimmed glasses. She wore a white blouse with a light blue cardigan over it. I didn't know what I was expecting, but when her blue eyes met mine I couldn't help but run over to give her a hug. At least I'd get to hug someone in this room!

"Oh!" Grandma Ann said and laughed.

I couldn't help but smile too. This was my real grandmother! My adopted mom's parents had passed away years earlier and we rarely saw Dad's parents. But it was different to be around my biological family. My dreams were finally coming true.

"Hugs for me and you and Lucas laughing? We should send you to camp more often," Grandma Ann commented. Her tone was only half-joking.

I backed away from her and shrugged. "I'm happy to be home and to sleep in my own room. The girls at camp were loud at night."

They didn't need to know that the *real* Casey had slept fine while the girls in *my* room were the chatterboxes. It seemed to be a good excuse since Grandma Ann didn't push it further.

"Dinner will be ready in a little while," Grandma Ann said to me and my mom. Then she turned to me and said, "Why don't you bring everything to your room and start unpacking."

A break from Grandma Ann's questioning looks was just what I needed. I didn't have any trouble remembering where Casey's room was. The house was only one floor and Brie had drawn me a map the night before. I'd memorized it quickly and it was stashed at the bottom of Casey's bag.

Lucas spun quickly around and pointed his fingers at me. "Casey! I want you to see my school project. It's so awesome!"

He ran out of the room and I tried hard not to laugh. He had a lot of energy!

I followed him towards the bedrooms. As much as Brie had tried to explain Casey's home, seeing it in real life was something different. There were family and school portraits all around the room, on the walls and even on the television stand. Walking down the hallway, I saw more pictures and had to stop myself from really looking at them. Casey would have seen these pictures a million times already.

"Casey!" Lucas called from his room. His head popped out through the doorway and he waved me in. "Come on!"

I knew Casey's bedroom was on the way, based on the map, and when I reached Casey's door, I was surprised to see that it was open. The lights were off and I had the urge to go inside and explore. But I didn't want Lucas to come out again so I put Casey's bag down in the doorway and went into Lucas's room.

Lucas had just finished explaining his science project to me when our mother came to the door and announced it was dinner time. "Go wash your hands guys, dinner's ready."

Lucas groaned and I wanted to do the same, but for another reason. I really wanted a chance to explore Casey's bedroom since I knew she'd had a head-start exploring mine. I wanted to know more about my twin but with my mom's stern expression, dinner would have to come first.

I waited for Lucas to finish washing his hands in the bathroom across the hall. As I stood there watching him, I wondered how three people could share one bathroom. I supposed I was a little spoiled as I'd had my own bathroom for as long as I could remember.

Lucas ran down the hallway when he was finished and I quickly washed my hands. I wanted to sneak a minute or two in Casey's room but when I left the bathroom, Grandma Ann spotted me from the kitchen and waved me over.

"We're all waiting on you," she said.

Grandma Ann had baked a whole chicken and it was served with a platter of mixed vegetables and rice. The chicken reminded me of my favorite meal Mom always made me, chicken casserole. I hoped she was doing okay after her treatment. I wanted to call her but I knew I couldn't. Maybe I could find a way to get in touch with Casey and see how they both were doing.

"So, Casey, tell us about the camp," Grandma Ann asked, as she carved the chicken.

I told them about all the activities we'd participated in. Since she and Casey had an argument about me before camp, I expected her to ask about "Ali". But she never did. I was slightly suspicious but was more relieved that we didn't need to go into that topic again. I wanted to get to know my real family without the drama that Casey had experienced before camp.

There were a few instances where I was almost caught out but luckily, Lucas kept interrupting the conversation, clearly wanting the attention on himself. He always seemed to have something to say which probably really annoyed Casey. Right then, however, it was distracting everyone and working in my favor. It was hard to be quick to respond as "Casey" when I had both my mother and Grandma Ann asking me questions, one after the other. Although, I thought I was doing okay.

When the questions about camp stopped and everyone was enjoying the meal, I scooped a second helping of vegetables onto my plate. I went back in with the spoon and found a few pieces of pumpkin, adding them as well. Whatever spices Grandma Ann used were so good. It was much better than the camp food.

As I was eating, I noticed Grandma Ann watching me, a surprised expression on her face.

"So you've suddenly taken a liking to pumpkin?"

I shrugged. "It's my favorite vegetable." As the words came out of my mouth, my stomach lurched and I wished I could stuff them back in. I backpedaled. "Since camp. It's become my favorite since camp. Umm, I don't know what it was but the pumpkin there tasted so good. And now I love it…" I heard the forced tone in my voice and I couldn't believe I'd messed up so badly. Brie had gone on and on about Casey's dislike for pumpkin. And I had completely forgotten!

Now I was sure that I was caught. And I'd only just arrived. Not even one night had passed and I'd ruined everything.

My stomach clenched for about the hundredth time that day. Grandma Ann frowned again but she said nothing else. I waited for her to call me a liar and an impostor but she didn't.

Lucas took the opportunity to chatter on about his science project and I stared at my plate, suddenly not hungry at all.

The meal couldn't be over quick enough. Once Grandma Ann stood up and took her plate to the sink, I jumped up, willing to help her. It was something I thought Casey would have done.

"You can go and unpack if you like," Grandma Ann said. "I'm sure you're tired after being at camp all week. Your mother and I will clean up."

I took the opportunity and left the room, heading straight for Casey's.

Once inside her bedroom I closed the door and pressed my back against it, taking several deep breaths. I hoped the rest of my time as Casey wouldn't be so stressful. I wanted to talk to the only person who knew I was in this situation. Brie. I found Casey's phone next to her bed. It was connected to the charger. I unplugged it and turned the screen on.

There was only one text on the screen and it was from my phone number.

CHAPTER THIRTEEN

Casey

It was nearing dinner time and I'd developed a nervous habit of checking Ali's phone every few minutes. What if something had happened and she and Mom were on their way over here to take me back? I tried to stop those negative thoughts but with no texts or calls from Ali, I couldn't help thinking the worst.

When Ali's mom returned from the grocery store, I gave her the excuse that I was tired and locked myself in Ali's room for the rest of the day. Thankfully Ali had an iPad and I could sit in bed and watch movies on it, which distracted me for a little while. Ali's dad had come home earlier and checked to see how I was. He had work to do at home so he left me alone for the remainder of the day to rest. I knew what it was like to have a parent work from home, but the difference was that my mom rarely checked in on me or Lucas. She locked herself away in her bedroom and we wouldn't see her for hours at a time.

Thinking of my mom made me think of Ali again. I reread the text message I'd already sent and stared at it, wondering if I should text her again. But decided against it. If Lucas had been spying in my room—like he usually did—I didn't want to give him a reason to go through my phone. I was doing a good job at being Ali and I wasn't going to ruin that over a text message. She would call me when she could.

During dinner, the text tone I'd been waiting to hear went off.

Both Ali's parents looked at me oddly.

"Do you have your cell phone at the table?" Ali's dad asked.

I looked at him and nodded. "I made a new friend at

camp and she said she was going to text me when she got home."

"You know the rules," Ali's dad said.

"Oh, Chris, Ali's made a new friend," Ali's mom said, smiling at me. "I know how hard it's been for you with the move."

Had it been hard on Ali? Did her parents not know she was one of the most popular girls in our class since the second she'd stepped into the school? I wondered if she was just being nice to the other kids when they gave her so much attention. Maybe she didn't feel like she'd made actual friends. If that was the case, she was a very good actor.

"Can I call her back? I'm finished with my dinner." I pushed my empty plate away from me. The chicken casserole had been delicious, just like Ali said in her diary. I'd had two whole servings.

"Sure," Ali's mom said.

I jumped off the chair, took my plate to the kitchen then ran up the stairs to Ali's room, closing the door firmly behind me.

Taking the phone quickly from my pocket, I read the message. *Sorry! I just got your text. I'm alone now.*

I pressed the icon for voice call and went into the bathroom, locking the door behind me. I didn't want to risk Ali's parents overhearing our conversation.

Ali picked up on the first ring. "Casey!"

"Ali!"

"Oh my gosh. I can't believe it's you. How's my mom doing?"

I thought Ali would be asking about me. But her mom was very ill, it was only right that she was Ali's main concern.

I took a breath and responded. "She said they're running more tests but the doctor is hopeful."

I didn't tell her I had a feeling that was a lie. Ali didn't need to be swamped with worries about her mother right then. We had no chance of swapping back until Monday at school and then she'd be able to spend every day with her mom if she wanted.

"That's so great!" Ali said, and I could hear the relief in her voice. "How are you feeling?"

"Much better. I don't know what happened to me. Did anyone else at camp get sick?"

"Not that I know of. We were really worried about you. And when I saw you drive away from camp in my parents' car, I totally panicked. I couldn't believe what was happening!"

"I couldn't believe it either!" I admitted. "And I was panicking too. One minute I was sick in bed and felt like I was dying, and the next minute I was driving away with your parents. I still can't believe that it happened!"

"I know!" Ali agreed. "We were planning to swap and then it just happened without any warning at all. It's so crazy the way it's all come together!"

"I know!" I laughed. "It's the most amazing thing ever. And Ali, your house...it's enormous!! Plus it's so beautiful! Your parents are lovely as well. They care so much about you, Ali. And it's wonderful to have a dad around."

I knew I was prattling on but I had so much to say. This whole experience was like nothing I'd ever known. I'd never admitted to anyone that I wanted a dad in my life. I pictured Ali's father's smiling face and how handsome he had looked in his suit when he came home from work that day.

Being around both of Ali's parents made me realize what I'd missed all these years. I felt as though I could live with Ali's family forever.

Ali's voice broke in and interrupted my thoughts. I could hear the excitement in her words as they poured through the phone.

"Casey, meeting my real family is incredible. I had no idea our mom would be so young and so pretty! It's just amazing to finally meet her. And Lucas is so cute, Casey! I adore him. And Grandma Ann…oh my gosh, I have never had a grandma I could be close to."

Had Ali gone to another house? Sure our mom was young, but she was shut-off and cold while Lucas was a huge dork with too much energy. Grandma Ann was the only exception. I knew I was lucky to have her, she was the only one who I could relate to. Thankfully though, it seemed that so far Ali had managed to fool them all.

As if reading my thoughts, Ali burst out with a confession and told me that she was almost caught out by a piece of pumpkin. She said that Brie had warned her but she'd totally forgotten. I cringed thinking of that disgusting vegetable and wondered if I'd need to eat some when I got back home to prove that what she'd said about suddenly liking pumpkin was true. I didn't know when we were going to reveal our swap but I really hoped I wouldn't have to eat pumpkin any time soon.

I decided not to own up about finding her diary, but I did admit to snooping on her phone. She only laughed and said it was fine as she was snooping through my room right then, while talking to me on the phone. We laughed about sharing the same passcodes, another coincidence to add to the growing list.

I couldn't resist asking her about Jake. I was dying to know what happened after I left. She seemed to hesitate slightly, but to my disappointment, she said the last days were so busy they barely had time to chat. I figured I would just have to wait until school on Monday, and smiled at the thought of seeing him again.

When we were finally done catching up on everything, I suggested that Ali keep her phone on her so we could text throughout the following day.

She agreed. It would be helpful to have instant contact with each other in case we ran into any situations where we needed help.

"Oh! I forgot to tell you. Our mom is taking me out tomorrow," she said.

"Really?" I asked. That wasn't normal. Mom must be

feeling guilty about keeping her secret from me.

"Yes, I'm so excited to get to know her more. We're going shopping!"

I couldn't remember the last time my mom had taken me shopping. I decided that she must be feeling very guilty.

Reminded suddenly of something Ali's parents had mentioned during dinner, I pushed thoughts of my mom away. "Ali, your parents said they have something organized for tomorrow as well. Apparently, they have tickets to the musical, *Wicked*. They bought the tickets ages ago and your mom said she's feeling well enough to go."

"I totally forgot about that!" Ali's surprised voice cut through the phone.

"Are you upset?" I replied, concerned. "I'm so sorry about this. I don't think the tickets can be changed. If they're not used tomorrow, they'll be wasted. I don't know what we can do—"

"Don't worry about it, Casey," Ali assured me. "I'm spending the weekend with my birth family. I can see *Wicked* some other time. And I'm so happy that Mom is feeling good. She loves musicals and she's been really excited to see this one."

I let out a breath. "Oh, that's good! I'm actually excited too. You know me, I love anything with music and magic!" I was relieved that Ali was okay with it. I'd never seen a big production before and I'd heard that it was amazing. Everyone who saw *Wicked* seemed to love it. I knew I would love it too.

A knock on my bedroom door startled me. I lowered my voice. "Ali, I have to go. Let's talk tomorrow."

"Okay, I'll talk to you then, *Ali*."

"Bye, *Casey*." I giggled and hung up the phone, stuffing it back into my pocket. I felt so much better talking to her. The swap was going well and we were both having a good time. Tomorrow was going to be a great day!

CHAPTER FOURTEEN

Ali

The next day, my mom took me to the mall. I was still getting used to calling her "Mom". Each time I said it, I reveled in the word, knowing that she was my real mother, the one who had given birth to me, 12 years earlier.

I'd always loved shopping with my adopted mom but going shopping with my real mom made it that much more special. For about an hour, we wandered around, chatting about everything.

Then I spotted the store that I'd discovered the week before. "I love that store!" I pointed towards it and took her hand, pulling her closer. There were some new items on display and I wanted to try them on.

"Really?" my mom asked looking at the front window. "I've never been in here before."

"It's great," I said and headed straight for the new items in the designer section. While flipping through them, I noticed my mother frowning.

"These prices are very high," she glanced at me, her eyebrows raised questioningly. "I know I have a lot to make up for, but sorry, Casey. Buying expensive clothes isn't really in the budget right now."

My face flushed. I looked down at the price tags, and took note of the figures displayed there. I'd never really taken much notice of how expensive my clothes were. Mom always just bought whatever I liked. Brie had mentioned that Casey's family weren't as wealthy as my adopted parents were and I felt instantly ashamed.

"Oh, I don't want to buy anything from here," I said quickly. "I just like looking at their things. So then when I do buy clothes I can try to match the styles."

Spotting the saleswoman coming toward us, I moved away from the rack and took my mom by the arm, then led her to the exit. Across the way was a big SALE sign. I think I can find a bargain in this store."

My mom seemed a little happier now that we were out of the boutique shop.

I found a cute little sleeveless top from a rack that had sale items on it. My mom tagged along with me and we ended up finding a pretty blue skirt to match.

"I need to try on this outfit!" I exclaimed.

While my mother waited for me outside the changing room, I made sure to double check the price tags. Relieved to see that the prices were very reasonable, I tried the outfit on. Both the top and the skirt fitted perfectly and I twirled around in front of the mirror, the skirt twirling with me.

I could barely hold in my excitement when I opened the door to show off the outfit to my mom. "What do you think?"

She stood up from the seat she was sitting on and smiled. "It's very cute. I love it on you!"

I turned back to the mirror and checked myself up and down to make sure everything fit. Then, in the blink of an eye, my gaze fell on the one thing I needed to hide. Sucking in my breath, I stared at the heart-shaped birthmark on my shoulder and then quickly moved my hair over the top to cover it. My mom didn't appear to have noticed the mark even though she was right behind me, watching as I took in my reflection in the mirror.

"Okay," I said in a rush. "I'm going to change back now." I went into the change room and closed the door. That had been so close!

When I was done putting Casey's clothes back on, I came out of the dressing room holding both items in front of me. I didn't want to impose myself on my mom by purchasing two items. And what if Casey didn't like them? I noticed she didn't have any skirts in her cupboard but every girl needed a skirt!

"I think I'll just take the skirt. I don't need the top."

"No, honey," my mom said. "The whole outfit looked really great on you. This shade of blue is my favorite color and it looked so pretty against your beautiful skin. I want to buy it for you."

"Are you sure?"

"Yes," she said, taking the outfit from me. "I'm absolutely sure."

"Besides, with the school fair tonight, it would be nice for you to have something new to wear."

I let her convince me. It was a really cute outfit. And I got a little excited thinking about a school fair. The fair was something I hadn't even been aware of until Lucas mentioned it at breakfast that morning. As I was away at camp for the whole week, I guessed that I'd missed the reminders at school. But Lucas could barely wait and it was all he'd been able to talk about. I just hoped Casey wouldn't mind missing out. Although I suspected that she'd much rather see *Wicked* than go to a school fair.

206

Mom paid for the outfit and when we walked out of the store she put her arm around me. "This is so nice, Casey. I'm having such a lovely time."

I closed my eyes and hoped I could hang onto this memory forever. "Me too."

"I've missed spending time with you. I promise I will make more time in the future." She smiled at me, a warm genuine smile that lit up her beautiful face, and I could feel my heart melt.

I smiled back. "I'd really like that, Mom." I just wished Casey was with us and we could be a family together. I also hoped that when Casey returned home, she could forgive our mother for the secret she'd kept for so long. Having a close relationship with your mother was more special than anything.

"Are you hungry?" my mom asked, breaking through my thoughts.

I nodded. "Yes, I'm starving!" Shopping did have a way of making me hungry.

"There's this great little cafe nearby," she said. "I'm not sure if I've taken you there before."

"As long as there is food you can take me anywhere."

My mom laughed and I did too. Her smile was infectious and I couldn't stop staring at her, she was so beautiful. I just wished she'd smile more. Ever since my arrival home, she'd been very serious. I guessed the way that Casey left might have had her worried, but everything was going to be fine now, I was sure of it.

At the cafe, we were seated right in front, so we had a clear view of the street.

"They have a really good lunch menu here," she said, placing her napkin on her lap.

I did the same and looked at the menu. We both ordered the turkey club sandwich without even discussing it! Like my mental connection with Casey, it appeared my mom and I had the same taste in food.

When we were left alone again, my mom leaned closer to me, her arms were folded on the table. "Casey, I don't want to push you but I've noticed you've been avoiding the topic of your twin since we spoke yesterday. Like I said, if you have any questions for me, I'm here to answer them. I would understand if you're upset with me but I'm willing to be open with you. I think we really should talk about this. And if by some bizarre coincidence, she is now in your class at school, we must work out what we're going to do. She has her own family. It's all so complicated."

"I know," I replied, an awkward sensation working its way into my stomach and causing me to lose my appetite. What my mom had said was true. The fact that I'd ended up in Casey's class was an extremely bizarre coincidence and I did have my own family. But they were my adopted family and I'd only just met my real one. The one I'd been born into. Only a week earlier, I had no idea where they were and I certainly was not aware that I had a twin sister.

But right then, I didn't want to spend all my time with my biological mother, the one who I had only just met, talking about my twin. We had a lifetime to do that. I wanted to get to know my real mom without any messy drama.

"Ali?" a familiar voice suddenly called from behind me. Caught unaware and deep in thought over the conversation with my mom, I quickly turned around, but then instantly realized my mistake. I wasn't supposed to be Ali right then, I was Casey!

I searched in the direction of the voice, wondering who it had come from and when I spotted him walking towards me, my whole body froze.

There I was, face to face with Jake Hanley.

CHAPTER FIFTEEN

Ali

The sight of Jake's beaming smile took me by complete surprise.

"Hi, Jake!" I replied, my stomach churning anxiously. From the corner of my eye, I could see my mother's curious expression as she stared at the boy in our midst.

Quickly trying to right the situation, I explained, "I'm actually Casey!"

He smiled at me. "Oh wow! Sorry! It's so hard to tell you two apart. But I could have sworn you were Ali."

I laughed. The sound was forced but I was doing my best to convince him. "It's not the first time that's happened."

My mom continued to frown and my insides were a flurry of panic. I didn't want her to become suspicious. "Mom!" I said a little too loudly. She jumped a little and looked at me. "This is Jake. He's in my class at school."

"It's nice to meet you," she said. Her frown had eased a little and she gave him a small smile.

"You too," Jake smiled back.

"Did you go on the school camp as well?" Mom asked.

"Yeah, I did," he replied. "It was awesome, wasn't it Casey?"

"Yes, it was," I grinned. "I loved it all. Especially the campfire."

On the night of the campfire, Casey had been herself and Jake had chosen to hang out with her for the whole time. After that night, I was certain that he liked her, but after being told he had a crush on me, I wasn't sure what was going on.

I didn't want a boy to come between me and my twin,

and I hoped that when Casey returned to school as herself, everything would work itself out.

A small part of me was jealous though. I couldn't deny that deep down, I kind of had my own crush. This whole thing was very confusing.

After chatting a little more about the camp, Jake blurted out, "Have you heard from Ali? Is she okay?"

As much as I loved spending time with Jake, this situation was becoming more and more awkward. My eyes darted between Jake and my mom. The silence stretched on much longer than it needed to.

I shook my head. "I'm not sure how she is." It wasn't a complete lie. I didn't know how "Ali" was doing at that exact moment. I pictured Casey in my room, pretending to be me around my parents. In the house where I should have been right then.

"Are you going to the fair tonight?" Jake asked, his voice made all thoughts of Casey disappear.

I turned to my mom, her eyebrows were raised as she took in the conversation between Jake and me.

"Umm, yeah, I think so," I replied hesitatingly. I knew we'd made plans earlier but now I wasn't so sure what was going to happen. If I was going to be around Casey's family, then I'd have to be better at acting like her. Right now, I wasn't doing so well. I blamed Jake and his handsome face, he made my brain turn to mush.

Mom slowly nodded her head. "Yes, we've planned to go tonight. We like to support all the school fundraiser efforts. We will probably see you there, Jake, if you're going."

Jake grinned again. "Yeah, I plan to go too." He looked at me for a moment too long and heat moved across my cheeks.

The waitress returned with two plates of food and Jake moved to the side. "Well, I have to go. I guess I'll see you tonight."

I nodded and sat down again. "Yeah, see you there." Thinking of seeing Jake again created butterflies in my stomach.

"It was nice to meet you, Mrs. Wrigley," Jake said and waved to the both of us.

I turned around and sighed, picking up a french fry from my plate.

"What's wrong, Casey?" Mom asked. "Don't you want to go to the fair? It's a perfect opportunity for us all to have a family night out. I know that Lucas will love it. And Jake seems such a nice boy. I'm sure it'll be fun. I think they advertised fireworks and all."

"Yeah, it sounds fun. I just wasn't sure if you wanted to go," I said, trying to make up some excuse for my change in attitude.

Mom grinned and pointed to the bag at my feet. "And you even have a new outfit to wear."

I knew Casey would be convinced at that point, so I nodded my approval and lifted my sandwich, taking a bite. It was so good!

"Jake certainly seems to have taken an interest in you, though, Casey," my mom added with a slight grin.

Yes, that's what I'm worried about, I thought to myself, ignoring my mom's comment. I took a sip of my soda to wash down the food and the uncomfortable lump in my throat.

I was halfway through my meal when Mom brought up "Ali" again. "I still can't believe the chances that your twin has turned up at your school. The likelihood seems so crazy, I'm finding it hard to comprehend." She shook her head in disbelief. "Somehow I feel it was meant to happen. And you two were destined to meet. What are the chances?" She said the last part more to herself than to me.

The chances that out of all the schools in the world, me going to Casey's, had been very small.

"Do you want to see her?" I asked, wondering if my

mom even cared for me—Ali—at all.

"Of course I want to meet my daughter, your sister, but it's all so complicated," she said. "How am I going to do this? Casey, how am I going to explain everything to her?"

"You explained it to me," I said. "Ali will understand, I'm sure of it."

"You've met her. What's she like? Has she told you anything about her family?"

A vision of Ali's face flashed through my mind.

I took a deep breath, and answered her, "She's just like me!"

CHAPTER SIXTEEN

Casey

Sitting in the plush chairs of the theater, I found myself smiling like a crazy person. The day had been the most magical of my life! Both of Ali's parents were so attentive, definitely something I wasn't used to. A few times throughout the day, I forgot I was playing Ali. I wanted to be a part of this little group and I finally found a place where I fit in. Ali's dad was so nice and so funny! He made me laugh many times with his silly jokes. Having a dad was something I'd only dreamed about and even though we weren't blood-related, I could see him in my life. And Ali's mom was the sweetest person in the world, I'd quickly become attached to her.

I played with the hem of Ali's skirt, smoothing my hands over the silky fabric thinking back to earlier. While going through Ali's closet, I felt like someone in a modeling competition. Ali had so many gorgeous clothes that it took me a while to find the perfect outfit for the play. There were a lot of things that were varying shades of blue. I couldn't believe we had the same favorite color too!

It wasn't until I found the pretty sequined top and fitted skirt in my favorite shade of sky blue, that I knew I'd found the outfit I had to wear. If only Jake could see me now… I smiled thinking about him. Pretending to be Ali had built up my confidence and I decided to be more open with Jake when I saw him again. The worst that he could do was turn me down, right? Ali wouldn't have let that stop her. Her parents had raised her well and I decided to learn from her example.

Ali's parents returned from the bathrooms just as the lights started to turn down, signaling the start of the show.

I couldn't believe how wonderful it all was. The

costumes, the scenes, the singing and the dancing was all incredible. Every part of the show was so amazing. It was no wonder so many people had raved about it.

During intermission, we talked about our favorite parts. Mine was the song, "Popular". The girl playing Glinda was so perfect for the role. And she was very funny. I didn't expect to have so many emotions while watching a musical. Maybe when I went back into my own life, I could convince Grandma Ann to take me to see another show for my birthday. I knew Mom would have another work excuse so I wouldn't bother asking her. She probably wouldn't enjoy it anyhow.

During the big showdown scene between Elphaba and Glinda, Ali's mom squeezed my arm. I turned to her and saw Ali's dad crouched over.

"What's going on?" I asked.

Ali's dad mouthed the words, "Let's go."

I stood up and followed him and Ali's mom out of the theater.

Once we reached the lobby, I could see why we were leaving. Ali's mother's face was very pale and she looked a little sweaty.

"I'm so sorry," she said, breathing heavily. "I'm not feeling well."

I glanced at the door wistfully. We were so close to the end, I wanted to see how the play turned out. But Ali's mom was more important. I took her hand as we walked to the car together.

Ali's mom was hot with a fever, so we couldn't have the heat on in the car. I tucked Ali's coat around me, thankful it was thick and warm, unlike most of my worn coats that were too thin for cooler weather. I wiped a tear from my cheek, feeling just awful for the poor woman in the front seat. Ali needed to be with her mother. What if something terrible happened and Ali wasn't here?

I didn't know what to do. Did I tell Ali and make her worry or not tell her and then have the chance she might be mad at me because I didn't let her know?

At the house, I helped her mom up the stairs and then her dad took over.

Ali's mom kissed my forehead. "I'm sorry, again sweetheart—"

"Don't be sorry," I interrupted.

"I'll be fine in the morning," she said. "I promise."

I nodded and watched them head down the other end of the hallway toward their bedroom. I hoped she was right. But I had a feeling she was holding back the truth from her daughter.

Thinking of Ali, I wondered how her day had gone with our Mom. I went into Ali's room and grabbed her phone. I'd left it behind when we went to the theater, determined not to be distracted by anything during the performance. I was surprised to see that I had no messages from Ali, even though she said she'd be in touch with me too.

There were several messages from Meg but I didn't respond to them. I hoped she'd assume Ali was still at camp.

I thought it best to let Ali reply to Meg herself, when she got back home on Monday.

I began a text of my own to Ali. *What's going on?* I typed into the message box. I didn't mention anything about her mom until she asked. Besides, if Ali's mom was fine in the morning, I didn't want to worry Ali unnecessarily.

Sitting on the edge of the bed, I stared at the phone. Ali, where are you?

CHAPTER SEVENTEEN

Ali

Lucas ran down the hallway at top speed when he was finished getting ready.

"Come on, Casey!" My mom called from the other room. "We're heading out now."

I looked down at the new outfit we got from the mall, knowing that my mom would question me if I didn't wear it. I tried to adjust my hair over the heart-shaped birthmark on my shoulder but it kept sliding off. Even if Casey's friends didn't notice, her family certainly would. Why hadn't I chosen a top with sleeves? My obsession for fashion got in the way of hiding the only thing that could ruin the entire swap.

I searched in Casey's closet and found a light jacket to throw over the top. Looking in the mirror above Casey's dresser, I felt happy with the result. The jacket gave a little bit of Casey's casual fashion sense to the preppy outfit. It was the perfect combination of our styles.

Lucas burst into Casey's room and grabbed my hand. "Let's go! Let's go!"

I laughed and allowed him to drag me into the living room. He started jumping up and down with excitement.

"It's amazing how a few days away can make such a huge difference," Grandma Ann commented while she put on her coat.

I was reminded of the conversation I'd overheard earlier between Grandma Ann and my mom. I didn't mean to eavesdrop but I walked by my mom's bedroom and heard Casey's name, I stood outside and listened.

"You two seem to be getting on so well. It's as though this news of a twin sister was the best thing that could have happened," Grandma Ann had said. "But what are you going to do about contacting her family? You need to get this all out in the open as soon as possible. I mean, what if your other daughter is at the fair tonight? Have you thought about that?"

My mom gasped as if she had burned herself. "That's something I didn't think of! I wish I'd never agreed to the fair. How could I have been so stupid?"

"Well, it's too late now," Grandma Ann said. "You're going to have to face her and her family sooner or later, so you need to be prepared."

That was actually one thing they wouldn't have to worry about, since her second daughter was standing only feet away from her and was happy to be in her real mother's presence. I didn't think my adopted parents would mind meeting my real mother either. At least I hoped not. They were aware that I wanted to know about my past so having everyone in the same town would make it easier for us all.

I just didn't want them to know that I'd tricked them. That was something I was sure would really upset my adopted mom and she was sick enough as it was. I did not want to risk making her condition worse.

But I pushed that thought aside and focused on the idea of Casey and I keeping our swap, secret. No one would ever find out. Instead, everyone would finally meet each other properly, without any more secrets or swapping of twins or lies. The thought made me giddy. And Lucas's excitement rubbed off on me as well. I started to really look forward to the fair. But I knew the main reason for my excitement was Jake. I couldn't wait to see him again, even if he did think I was Casey.

On the ride to the fair, Lucas chatted on about which rides he was going on and how much junk food he wanted to eat, and I became caught up in his enthusiasm. I decided in that moment, to push away all thoughts of Jake. I only had a limited amount of time with Casey's family before I had to get back to my real life and I didn't want to waste it.

When we reached the fair, we headed straight for the food stalls. Lucas was hungry and wouldn't stop complaining until Grandma Ann offered to buy him a slice of pizza and fried dough with powdered sugar for dessert. I went with chicken fingers and fries, knowing Casey would have picked those. And I knew I chose correctly when Grandma Ann didn't offer another comment about how much "Casey" had changed at camp.

We walked toward the games next, waiting until our stomachs settled before going on the rides. That part of the fair was across the way, but I could hear people screaming and laughing even from that distance.

I had to ask my mom several times which game she wanted to play. She finally answered that she didn't like games and that they were a waste of money. I frowned. She continued to be distracted, her eyes darting around the crowd. And then it came to me. Was she worried that "Ali" was going to show up there? It made sense from the conversation I'd overheard earlier.

I knew Casey was with my parents at the play. I questioned if I should say something to my mom or not. This was one of the few times we'd all be together and I didn't want it to be like this. But would bringing "Ali" into the conversation ruin the mood as well? I was so confused! In the end, I said nothing.

There were a few kids from school I recognized and we exchanged waves. I hadn't thought of it but what if Brie was there? I hadn't contacted her since arriving at Casey's but I was suddenly so keen to see her.

It was my turn to search the crowd for Casey's best friend. And then I felt a hand on my arm. I turned around to see Brie, dragging me away from Casey's family.

"Can you get away for a bit?" she asked.

"Let me ask."

I went back to my mom, Grandma Ann and Lucas.

"Do you mind if I hang out with Brie for just a little while?"

Lucas's face fell with disappointment and my heart broke for him. We'd been getting along so well and now I felt as though I were abandoning him.

But in what appeared to be typical Lucas style, he spotted one of his friends and was immediately distracted. "Hey Kyle!" he called to a kid in the nearby crowd. "Mom, can I hang out with Kyle?"

"Maybe just for a short time," my mom said, "if its okay with Kyle's mom, that is."

"Awesome!" he said, and took off to ask permission. Mom waited for Lucas to check with Kyle's mother and when she waved in acknowledgment, Mom turned back towards me.

"That's fine, Casey. How about we meet back here in

an hour?" I nodded in agreement, instantly relieved at the thought of being myself for a while.

I headed back to Brie and she waved at my mom and Grandma Ann. She then waited until they were completely out of earshot before speaking. "I need details! Have you heard from Casey? How is she?"

"Yes, I heard from her. She's better."

"Oh good! How are you and how's everything going?"

"So far so good," I said. "I really love spending time with Casey's family."

She leaned closer to me. "Have they figured it out yet?"

"I don't think so. Although Grandma Ann keeps insisting that 'Casey' has been acting differently since camp."

"That's not good," Brie said, her eyes filled with worry.

"It's fine," I said. "They don't suspect I'm actually myself, only that Casey is a little different."

I felt a tapping on my left shoulder and turned around but no one was there. Hearing a chuckling sound, I whipped around to face the other direction, and saw Jake with his fist pressed against his mouth, trying to stifle a laugh. "Gotcha!"

I smiled.

"Hey, Casey!" he grinned.

"Hey," I said, nervously brushing my hair out of the way.

Brie's eyebrows were raised questioningly, and her eyes darted between Jake and me.

"I saw Jake earlier at the mall today," I said as an explanation to Casey's best friend, even though it didn't stop her questioning expression.

"Do you girls want to hang out with me and my friend, Wyatt? He's visiting town, our parents have been friends for years."

"Sure!" I said. It was something Casey would want to do and even though I had a feeling Brie was desperate to ask me more questions, I didn't want to miss the opportunity to hang out with Jake.

"Oh cool, you got the unlimited ride pass too!" Jake asked, pointing to the neon green bracelets on our wrists.

"Yeah, *Casey* and I love rides," Brie said.

I lightly bumped her shoulder and she glanced at me with a questioning look. But I ignored it and grabbed her by the arm. "Come on, Brie," I coaxed, "this'll be fun!"

And leading her along beside me, we headed off with Jake who was waiting with his friend nearby.

Jake dared Brie and me to go on the scariest roller coaster at the fair. It didn't have any loops but it was very fast and had sharp corners. Brie and I rode together and we screamed the entire time. I even heard Jake and Wyatt screaming a few times too. We were laughing so hard when we got off the ride, I was gasping for breath.

"Oh my gosh!" Brie exclaimed. "That one is my favorite!"

She pointed to one ride that looked like a giant spider. The arms of the "spider" moved up and down while the attached buckets spun on their own.

All four of us ran to the ride and were the last bucket to be filled. The bucket didn't have a seatbelt, only a bar to keep us in place. The ride started slowly. Brie took hold of the round saucer in the middle of the bucket.

"What's that for?" I asked.

"For this!" she twisted the saucer and my body jerked to the side and slammed into Jake.

"I'm so sorry," I said through fits of laughter. I realized the movement of the saucer made the bucket move.

Each of us had a turn and no matter where we moved the saucer we all ended up piled on each other. When Wyatt had his turn, he spun the saucer so quickly that we were all plastered to our seats and pressed against each other. I found myself glued to Jake, laughing the hardest that I had in a long time.

We decided to go on one more ride before the fireworks. We chose the ghost train. A tiny roller coaster took us up and down small hills while being completely in the dark. Jake and Wyatt kept jumping up out of their seats and trying to scare us.

By the time we found my mom and Grandma Ann, I realized I'd put Casey completely out of my mind. I was reminded of my twin as I watched my mom chat with a few other parents who were grouped alongside them. I'd had such a good time as myself that I'd forgotten I was part of someone else's life. I felt a little guilty about leaving them for so long but they didn't seem bothered in the least.

"Hey, Mom," I said when we approached the group.

Jake and Wyatt were talking to the other parents. How funny that they'd all ended up together as we had!

"Hi, Casey. Did you have fun?" my mom asked.

"Yeah, we went on a bunch of rides."

Jake came to my side. "Hi, Mrs. Wrigley. Is it okay for Casey to watch the fireworks with us?"

"Absolutely," my mom said, giving me a small wink.

My cheeks burned, I hoped Jake didn't see that wink!

"I'll be here when they're done. Come find me," she said.

"Okay!" I answered with a wave.

Everyone from the fair gathered on the large open space of grass right outside the entrance. The four of us found a spot near the fence so we were able to sit down and lean back on it while we watched.

Brie sat next to me and Jake sat on the other side. Our arms brushed together when we sat and my stomach fluttered with butterflies.

"I love fireworks," Wyatt said to Brie, he'd chosen to

sit on her other side. I thought they were hitting it off quite well.

"These ones are okay," she said with a shrug. "But the Fourth of July ones are really big."

The lights around us dimmed and everyone started cheering and clapping. I joined in with them, my body buzzing with excitement.

Jake and I talked during the downtime in between each set of fireworks.

"I like the ones I can feel in my chest, like BOOM," he said, placing a hand on his heart and mimicking the sound.

I laughed. "Me too!"

During the finale, the fireworks were going off all at once. And then I definitely felt them in my chest like Jake had described. I couldn't help but smile and cheer as the memories from the entire night made me giddy with delight. The night had been absolutely magical...and for once I really believed nothing could possibly go wrong.

Brie leaned closer to me and said into my ear, "What's going on with you and Jake?"

CHAPTER EIGHTEEN

Casey

The sound of a text message filled my ear, waking me from a dead sleep. I fumbled in the darkness to check the text. The bright screen made my eyes water and I closed them, slowly opening them again until they adjusted. The top of the screen read ten-thirty-seven. When had I fallen asleep? I still had all my clothes on. I sat up and switched on the lamp that was on the bedside table. I rubbed my face as I read the text from Ali.

Everything's going well here. How about u? How was the musical and how's mom?

I switched her phone to vibrate so any more incoming texts wouldn't wake her parents. I wasn't sure if Ali's dad was asleep but I didn't want him barging in on me either.

The musical was great! Your parents are wonderful!

I tried to keep the message upbeat, hoping Ali wouldn't think anything was wrong. I didn't want her to worry. Her mom had convinced me before going to bed that she'd be better in the morning. But then Ali asked about her mother again.

How's mom?

I sighed. Now that she'd asked me twice, I needed to say something. I wasn't going to lie, though, I didn't want her to think I'd hidden things from her if she found out her mom wasn't well at all. So I typed a message back.

She wasn't too well tonight but said she just needs to rest.

I watched the three dots blink on the bottom of the screen and waited for Ali's response.

I'm so worried about her! I don't want to do anything to upset her or make her worse. But our mom wants to meet her other daughter. She's been asking me all about "Ali" and she thinks it's time we all met.

225

I watched and waited as Ali continued to type. Then her next message appeared on the screen.

But I'm scared it will be too upsetting for my mother. If she finds out the truth right now it might make her condition worse. I don't know what to do!

I took a deep breath and sighed heavily. This was getting really complicated. If only Ali's mom wasn't so sick. I paused to think for a moment before typing a message back.

Just try to avoid the subject for another day…at least until Monday when we can switch back. Hopefully by tomorrow your mom will feel much better and we can work out a plan.

I waited for Ali to reply.

Okay…I'll text u tomorrow. Make sure u let me know if she gets worse!"

I will. Talk to u tomorrow.

OK!

I changed out of my clothes and into one of Ali's matching pajama sets. Climbing back into bed, I flipped off the light and stared up at the glowing stars that were scattered across the ceiling. With all the talk of Ali's mom, I'd completely forgotten to ask about the shopping trip with my mother. I wondered how it all went and what else they'd been up to. I could barely wait until Monday so I'd be able to see her again. There were so many questions and so much to talk about. I just hoped that she wasn't too bored while staying at my house and that Lucas wasn't annoying her too much.

I guessed I would just have to wait and see. As much as I was enjoying being with Ali's family in her beautiful home and could stay there forever, I could not wait to see my twin again.

CHAPTER NINETEEN

Ali

The next morning, I woke early for once. I was still so excited about the night before and could feel the smile on my face the moment I opened my eyes. For a short while, I stayed in bed and relived every minute of the fair in my mind. It had been such a relief to hang out with Brie and be myself for a while, rather than pretending to be Casey. But the best part was definitely when Jake came along. I could still feel the fluttering of butterflies in my stomach, and sighed at how wonderful it had all been.

Then I thought of my twin and her crush on Jake. And reality came crashing over me. A knot of guilt began to take its place firmly in my stomach and the smile vanished from my lips. Why did it all have to be so complicated?

But when my mom's face abruptly appeared in my mind, all thoughts of Jake disappeared completely. My mom was my biggest concern and she was the only one I really needed to be worrying about right then. Glancing at Casey's phone on the table beside the bed, I could see there had been no texts of any sort. That was a good sign and I breathed a small sigh of relief. Realizing it was still too early to be texting Casey, I decided to get out of bed and take a shower instead.

After quietly rummaging through her cupboard for some clothes to wear, I found a pair of black cut off shorts and a pink t-shirt, and pulled them from the small pile that was stacked neatly on the shelf. Being careful to make as little noise as possible so I didn't wake anyone, I reached for the door handle. But the second I stepped into the hallway, a shadow passed over me and I let out a squeak, dropping the clothes from my hands.

"Grandma Ann!" I said. "You scared me." I bent

down to pick up the clothes. When I stood up, her thin eyebrows were raised and she had the oddest expression on her face. A sinking feeling formed in my stomach. "I'm going to go shower now," I whispered quietly, and quickly padded to the bathroom, closing the door behind me.

Grandma Ann seemed sharp for an older woman and it didn't appear that she ever missed much. What had made her act so strangely just now?

I stood in front of the mirror and rubbed my hands over my face. I was still groggy from the night before. I'd stayed up later than normal, still living in the excitement of the fair. I grabbed Casey's brush and moved the bristles through my hair. A chunk of hair slid away from my shoulder and I gasped. I couldn't believe I'd made the mistake again of choosing a sleeveless shirt. This time it had been one of Casey's pajama tops.

I stood there, staring at myself. Grandma Ann couldn't have seen the distinctive mark on my shoulder. Could she? My heart began to race as I continued to brush my hair. My mind went back to a few minutes earlier when I dropped the clothes in the hallway. I'd been able to see Grandma Ann's face perfectly since the morning light shone brightly through the large oval window, opposite Casey's bedroom door.

Placing the brush on the counter, I brought my shaking hands up to my face. If she had spotted the birthmark, I was in so much trouble!

I took as long as I could in the shower and dressed for the day, hoping that Grandma Ann was in the kitchen so I'd be able to sneak back into Casey's room unnoticed. But when I walked into the hallway, I bumped into her again. I had a feeling she'd been standing there the whole time. I swallowed the lump in my throat.

"Can you come with me for a minute?" she asked, and without another word, she turned and headed down the hallway.

My stomach sank even more. Something wasn't right. I looked toward Casey's bedroom, desperately wanting to hide away. There wasn't a sound coming from the other rooms. Lucas and our mother were still asleep. I had no choice but to follow Grandma Ann and pretend that everything was okay.

When I reached the living room, Grandma Ann was sitting in the overstuffed armchair waiting for me. I hesitated in the doorway, a lump in my throat and a shiver of fear working its way down my spine.

She patted a spot on the sofa alongside her, indicating for me to sit.

I shuffled over to the sofa and tried my hardest to keep a blank expression on my face. Casey and I had made it through most of the weekend and I didn't want to ruin it only one day away from school.

Grandma Ann took a breath and leaned closer. "Do you have something you want to tell me?"

***

Book 3

The Truth

CHAPTER ONE
Ali

Grandma Ann's question echoed in my head. *Do you have something you want to tell me?*

I should have stayed in bed that morning. At least if I'd waited for Lucas and my mother to wake up, Grandma Ann wouldn't have confronted me. I had a feeling she knew I wasn't Casey. I had accidentally revealed the heart-shaped birthmark on my shoulder on the way to take a shower. Why hadn't I been more careful? My love for sleeveless shirts put me in this situation. I only had one more day before Casey and I swapped back and here I was about to ruin it.

Her eyes kept darting between my eyes and my shoulder. I'd put on a t-shirt with sleeves after my shower. With one slight lift of the fabric, I'd be found out.

My stomach churned, partly empty but mostly with nerves. If I told her the truth—that I was Ali, and Casey had been at my house all weekend—what would she say? Would she demand Casey come back to the house? Or would she be happy to meet her long-lost granddaughter? I'd had the best weekend with my real family, I didn't want that to go away just yet.

"Casey?" Grandma Ann asked.

I swallowed. "No, I don't have anything I want to tell you."

"Are you sure?" Grandma Ann asked firmly.

I'd already lied the entire weekend about my identity. It was different being face to face with an accusation, but I had to stick with the plan for one more day.

"Yes, I'm sure. Why do you think I have something to tell you?"

"I saw your shoulder this morning, *Casey*," she said. I

noticed the tone in how she said Casey's name. It was like she already knew I was a phony and wanted me to admit it.

I tried to pretend I had no idea what she was referring to. I lifted the sleeve off my shoulder—the one without the birthmark. "I really don't know what you're talking about. I think I should go—"

Grandma Ann reached her hand out, and my heart raced. Her cool fingertips brushed over my other arm and she moved my sleeve away from my shoulder, tucking it higher. The heart-shaped birthmark was in full view.

She sat back in her chair and looked at me. I breathed heavily as she stared. Her face was expressionless and unflinching.

"Did you somehow get a new birthmark, Casey?" she asked. "I've never noticed this before and I'm sure I would have been aware of such an unusual mark on my granddaughter. It's almost a perfect heart-shaped. There can't be too many people who have a birthmark that looks like that. Do you care to explain how it got there?"

She clasped her hands in her lap and watched me. Her expression was unreadable.

I avoided looking at her eyes. Instead, I focused on my hands that sat uselessly in my lap. My fingers weaved together and began to sweat. My chest tightened and my eyes started to water. I could keep lying, but what if Grandma Ann told my mother that she didn't think I was Casey. I could tell her it was a temporary tattoo or something, but what if she wanted me to prove it and try and wash it off?

I was digging myself deeper into a hole and now the only way out was to tell the truth. But then what would Casey say? Would she blame me for ruining the swap? Neither of us wanted to get into trouble. And I'd been the one to suggest the swap, to begin with. Maybe if I explained that this was all my fault, they wouldn't be mad at Casey for lying too. I wished I could go back to camp and think through this plan. Even if Casey hadn't been sick, I should have thought of how all of this would affect those around us.

Would Grandma Ann and my mother ground Casey for lying? Had I made the situation worse for her? Would Casey never want to talk to me again? If I admitted the truth, what would happen next? Would Grandma Ann force me to go back to my house? And how would I make the swap without my adopted mom finding out? Would it make her condition worse? I couldn't handle being responsible for hurting my mother and upsetting her when she was so ill.

I pressed my hands against either side of my head. All the scenarios that I'd thought of including more lies and made the situation worse. There was nothing else to do but tell the truth and hope for the best. I prayed that Casey wouldn't be mad at me. I'd just found my sister and I wanted her to trust me. She had to believe it was an honest mistake.

Taking a deep breath, I finally found the courage to look at my grandmother. "I've always had this birthmark. And the reason you've never seen it before is because you've never met me before this weekend. My name is Ali Jackson. And I'm your granddaughter."

Grandma Ann let out a long breath. She nodded gently and whispered, "I know."

The calm way in which she said those words was all I needed. She wasn't upset with me. I could see it in her expression and her reaction. Relief filled my body and I jumped up from my chair and wrapped my arms around her. She was my kind, understanding and caring grandmother, the grandmother I had craved for my entire life. I let go of all the tears I'd been holding in. She held onto me as I cried. I'd only met her a couple of days earlier but the bond between us was already intact. Hugging her seemed the most natural and wonderful thing to be doing, and the reassurance I felt right then meant more to me than words could express.

I'd hated lying to everyone. The swap was only so I could meet my real family. I didn't mean to hurt anyone's feelings. That was the last thing I ever intended to do.

She gently rubbed my back and held me tighter. When I was finally able to catch my breath, everything I'd been holding in came rushing out of me. "I knew I was adopted. I also knew I had a biological family somewhere. I've always known it. Deep inside, I was sure there was more. But every time I asked, my parents avoided talking about it. And it just seemed to make my mom upset, so I had to let it go."

More tears came, choking off the words still in my throat. I didn't tell her my adopted mother was sick. It was always in the back of my mind, but I didn't want Grandma Ann to feel bad for us.

She shuffled along the couch so I could sit next to her. But she held my hands in hers, keeping us close together.

"So, you were never told you had a twin? Your adopted parents kept that secret from you?"

I nodded. "I had no idea. It sounds strange, but I've always known that a part of me was missing. I could feel it."

Grandma Ann sighed, and I could see the tears

glistening in her eyes. She was just as affected as I was. "I'm sorry, Ali. I'm so sorry! We had no right to keep this a secret from you girls." She hugged me again and her words filled my ears. "We all have a lot to answer for."

"Why is everyone up so early?" Lucas asked, yawning widely as he entered the room.

We both turned to him but his half-lidded eyes barely noticed us as he focused on the television. Jumping onto the couch next to us, he spread himself out and grabbed the remote. "Space Frontier is on." He flipped through the channels until he found the cartoon. "I love this show! I'm never up this early to watch it."

Wrapping the throw rug that normally rested on the top of the couch around his little body, he ignored us, his attention solely on his favorite show. I noticed his eyes were closing again as if he were about to fall back to sleep.

He had no idea what had happened between Grandma Ann and me. And that was a good thing. I wasn't ready to include him or my mother in that conversation just yet.

Grandma Ann stood up and took my hand. She mouthed the word, "kitchen" and indicated with a jerk of her head that I should follow her.

When we reached the enclosed area of the kitchen, she pulled out a stool from under the bench top and patted the top of it. I climbed up and took a seat.

"I didn't want Lucas to hear our conversation," she said.

The volume of the television increased. Lucas was always turning the sound up louder, something Grandma Ann found annoying. But there was no way he could hear us now, which was a good thing.

"I think we could both use a nice hot drink." Grandma Ann filled the kettle and placed it on the stove top. She turned to me. "Would you like me to make you a hot chocolate?"

I shook my head. There was no reason to pretend to be Casey around her anymore; at least until Lucas or my mother was around. "Would it be okay if I had a cup of tea?"

Grandma Ann's eyebrows raised high up on her forehead in surprise. "Of course," she smiled. "I'm so used to making hot chocolate for Casey. I suppose I'll have to get used to making new things for you." She pulled out two tea bags and plopped them into empty mugs. "Do you like milk or sugar in your tea?"

"A cup of tea, Casey?" my mom's voice came from the doorway.

Grandma Ann and I jumped at her voice.

"I didn't know you drank tea," Mom said, coming into the room. Her hair was in a messy bun atop her head.

Grandma Ann and I stared at her as she opened the refrigerator door and grabbed the carton of milk. She turned around and looked at Grandma Ann then at me.

I wiped at my face, trying to brush away any remaining traces of tears from my outburst a few minutes earlier.

It was too late. Mom noticed and rushed over to me, placing her hand on my forehead. "Casey's what's wrong? You don't look well. Are you okay?"

CHAPTER TWO
Casey

"Ali!" The voice beside me and the gentle shaking of my shoulder woke me from a deep sleep. My eyes sprung open and I looked up at Ali's dad sitting beside me. The light on the bedside table was on but the rest of the room was dark. It was still the middle of the night.

"What's going on?" I asked, rubbing at my eyes. I glanced over at the clock on Ali's side table. It was almost one am.

I yawned and then noticed he was fully dressed, even though his hair was a mess.

He pulled the quilt away from my body and stood up. His hands were in fists by his side and his eyes were wide and very alert for that early in the morning. "You need to get up and get dressed. Mom had a bad night and we're taking her to the hospital. Right now!"

Oh my gosh! I knew she didn't feel well the night before but she promised she'd be fine. "What's wrong? Is she okay?"

"Meet me in the hallway in two minutes," he said without answering my question. Then he fled from the room. He left the door open and I stared at it as if it would be able to explain what the heck was happening.

Ali's mom obviously wasn't okay. I jumped out of bed and grabbed the first set of clothes I saw. It was the same outfit I'd worn yesterday. But I didn't care. This was serious and I didn't want to delay getting Ali's mom to the hospital. Her dad was the most disheveled I'd ever seen in the days since I'd met him. Even last night he didn't seem that concerned about us leaving the show. But now he looked almost frightened.

I grabbed a pair of sneakers I'd tossed across the room the day before. I wasn't sure what was about to happen or how long we'd be away from home, but I figured they were the best choice right then. Slipping the sneakers on, I ran out of the room.

When I reached the top of the stairs, I was out of breath. My heart thrummed wildly in my chest just like the rapid beat of a hummingbird's wings. The hallway was quite dark but I could make out two figures coming from the other end. Ali's dad was walking toward me, holding Ali's mom against him. When they were close enough, I could see she wore sweatpants and a sweatshirt but her teeth were chattering as if she were standing outside in the dead of winter. Her face was paler than I'd ever seen it. It almost glowed in the dim light of the hallway. She breathed heavily as if she couldn't quite catch her breath.

My stomach dropped. This was much more serious than I thought.

"Ali," he said. "Help me get her down the stairs."

My entire body was numb but I focused on my task. *Everything's going to be okay*, I said to myself, trying to calm my own nerves. *Everything is going to be okay.* I kept repeating the phrase, willing it to happen. Everything had to be.

Ali's mom did not speak. Instead, she breathed heavily through her teeth as if she were the one holding me up.

I swallowed my fear and tried to put on a brave face, but she was putting most of her weight on us. I struggled to hold onto the railing and her at the same time. She needed to get help quickly.

"Should we call an ambulance?" I asked. I had a bad feeling about her and I was sure paramedics would be able to give her the help she needed faster than we could. I also wasn't sure she'd be able to make it to the car.

"It will be much quicker if I drive," Ali's dad said. "It will take them the same amount of time to get here."

I didn't know how far we were from the hospital but it looked like this was something they'd done before. Almost as if it were routine. Surely "Ali" would have known about this, so I didn't ask any more questions.

I did not let go of her until we reached the car. She looked as if she were about to pass out while Ali's dad helped her with her seatbelt. I stood there, unsure of what to do. I had to get in touch with Ali. She needed to know what was going on.

ALI!

I patted the jacket I'd thrown on and realized in the rush to leave the house, I didn't grab her phone. I sucked in a breath and realized I'd left behind the most important thing. Picturing it sitting on her computer desk plugged into the charger, I looked back towards the house, desperate to run back inside and get it.

"Dad," I said, trying to hide my panic. "I need to go

back up there and get my phone, I'll be right back."

"Get in the car, Ali," he said sharply. "There's no time for phones. We have to go now!"

I stood there for a moment, stunned at his tone. But when he slammed the car door and raced to the driver's side, my body jumped into action and I did as I was told. I climbed into the back and buckled myself in. My hands were shaking as I shoved the belt into place. Staring at the window to Ali's room, I felt my stomach churn. I could not believe I'd left the most important thing behind.

Ali's dad climbed behind the wheel and turned on the engine, then quickly reversed out of the driveway. I held onto the door handle as he whipped the car out of the drive and sped down the street. It was early enough that there weren't any cars on the road but I'd never seen anyone drive so quickly. At least not when I was in the car. I knew this was serious but the way he was driving made it seem so much worse. I felt sick with fear.

The sight of Ali's phone lying on the desk in her bedroom, raced through my thoughts. I needed to contact her, but how!

I wrung my hands in my lap. What was I going to do? If I'd used my head for two seconds after getting up, I would have grabbed her phone and brought it with me. Then I'd be able to update her with any information we got along the way. But I'd been in panic mode ever since her dad woke me. Even if Ali was still asleep in my bed, I could send her a text to keep her updated. What if this was it for her mother? Ali would be completely oblivious to what was going on with her family. And it would be all my fault.

I had to find a way to contact Ali to let her know. But how? Maybe I could borrow Ali's dad's cell phone once we were at the hospital? I wondered if it was something Ali would do? But then I shoved that thought out of my head. I didn't care about being Ali right now, I needed to contact her right away, even with the risk of getting caught in a lie. I would want her to do that for me if someone in my family was in trouble. And knowing how close Ali was with her mother made my guilt worse.

The radio was off so Ali's mom's breathing was the only sound we heard in the car. It was more labored than when she was walking. This wasn't good. Everything about this situation was not good at all.

I blinked back tears and reached a hand forward to touch her shoulder. I squeezed it lightly, letting her know her daughter was here for her—even if in spirit.

O-M-G. What if something happened to Ali's mother and Ali wasn't with her. What was I going to do?

CHAPTER THREE
Ali

Everyone was tense and no one spoke. I glanced at Grandma Ann and she was stiff as a board. The only sound was the second-hand *ticking* from the clock on the wall. I felt a lump forming in my throat. The same pit of anxiety that I hadn't felt since earlier in the weekend erupted once more, and my stomach did a serious flip-flop. Heat flushed my cheeks and I began to feel quite ill. I had no idea what was going to happen next. Should we tell my mom about the impostor standing in as her daughter, Casey? Would she be upset? Grandma Ann's reaction had been unexpected. But had my luck already run out?

Before I could decide, Grandma Ann spoke. "Jackie," she said to my mother. "I need you to have an open mind about something."

My mom's forehead wrinkled. "What are you talking about?"

"This," Grandma Ann said, opening her hand out to me. "This isn't Casey. Her name is Ali."

My mom turned to me and her mouth slackened. Her look of shock wasn't helping me feel any better.

"What do you mean her name is Ali?" She directed the question to Grandma Ann but she was still looking at me, stunned. "Casey, I don't—" she stopped speaking as if she couldn't believe what was happening.

I couldn't either. There were many ways I had wanted to reveal myself to my mom, but this scenario wasn't one of them. I wasn't sure what to say either, so we all continued to stare at each other until she spoke again.

"How can that be?" she asked. "You look exactly like my Casey…" then realization registered on her face. She took a step closer to me. Her eyes moved across my face, inspecting me. She leaned over, her face close to mine. Her eyes squinted as if she was looking for differences between Casey and me. As identical twins, she wouldn't be able to find many differences even looking up close. With all the swaps we did at camp, Casey and I had looked at each other close enough to know that other than my birthmark, there weren't any physical differences between us.

She stood back up again. Her mouth opened and closed a few times. I glanced over at Grandma Ann who was waiting to see what else my mom had to say. My insides felt as if they were vibrating. I wasn't sure why I was so scared. The talk with Grandma Ann should have been a trial run for talking to my mom. But now that my secret was out with my real mother, I waited for her reaction at our ruse.

"You're Ali? You're Casey's twin? It's really you?" she asked. Her mouth was agape in shock. She stood frozen to the spot for a moment, trying to register and comprehend the sudden news. Then she reached forward and gently stroked my hair.

I looked up at her, my eyes wide and my heart still madly thumping. My mind raced. Her expression was a mix of emotions. Was she upset? What was going to happen next?

I didn't have to wait long. She choked out a sob and reached for me, wrapping her arms around me. I hugged her back, inhaling the scent of my real mother. My heart overflowed with love for her, even though I'd only just met her a couple of days earlier.

"I can't believe this," she said. She sniffled and stared at me once more. Then I began to cry too.

"I knew something was off," Grandma Ann said. "I'd never believed that Casey would like pumpkin, even if it was wrapped in bacon and drizzled with chocolate."

I laughed, smiling against my mom's shoulder. We'd hugged before but that was when I was pretending to be Casey. Now she was hugging me as her long-lost daughter. It was as real as I imagined it, and it felt so good to let out the secret.

We embraced for a few minutes before she took a step back. Wiping away her tears, she took a steadying breath. Then she looked at Grandma Ann before turning back to me. "I have to say I'm stunned. But I'm so happy to meet you!! There's one thing I have to ask though. If you're Ali, then where is Casey?"

The kettle let out a high-pitched whistle and Grandma Ann poured the hot water into the mugs. She placed one of the mugs in front of me. "I would assume she's at your home?"

"Yes, she is," I replied with a gulp. "She went there directly from camp. My parents think she's me."

"Oh my goodness," Mom exclaimed, grabbing the stool behind her to sit down on. "How did this come about? How long have you been pretending to be Casey?" She stared at me in shock as all the repercussions registered in her brain.

I took a deep breath, getting ready to reveal everything I'd been holding in since camp. "Only since

Friday. When we got to camp, Casey told me about the conversation with you, Grandma Ann. About how we were twins."

Grandma Ann and my mom shared a look, but I kept going, afraid I might stop talking altogether if I was interrupted by what they were thinking.

"From then on, we were inseparable. So many of our classmates commented on how we looked alike, but I never dreamed I'd have a sister. A twin! We thought it would be a fun game to swap places at camp and see if we could fool everyone. And we couldn't believe that it worked. Not one person, not even Brie, could tell us apart. Then I had the idea of the home swap. I wanted to meet my real family. We thought since we fooled everyone at camp that it would be easy enough. But I have this birthmark," I moved my sleeve aside, showing the heart-shaped mark on my shoulder, "that Grandma Ann saw this morning. It's the only difference between us."

I paused for breath and waited for their reaction.

"If I didn't discover your birthmark this morning, you would have kept pretending to be Casey?" Grandma Ann asked.

I shrunk back. "Yes. This was part of the plan."

My mouth went dry and I took a sip of the hot tea. It stung a little on the way down my throat, but I needed to do something while my mom and grandmother processed what I told them.

Mom touched the birthmark, her eyes still filled with tears.

Grandma Ann was the first to speak. "I'm very surprised to hear that it was your idea. Casey can be strong-willed and since she was so upset before leaving for camp, I thought this must be her way of getting payback. She can be quite stubborn."

I knew how upset Casey was with her family, but I didn't want to be the one to tell them that. It was up to her to mend the relationship between our mother and grandmother when she came back home.

"Well it was only an idea at first," I said. "And then the swap happened without any proper planning. Casey was sick the last morning of camp and since she was still pretending to be me, my parents ended up picking her up instead of me. I was so worried when I saw her drive away from camp in my parent's car. I wasn't sure what to do but since we'd both agreed to the swap, I figured I wouldn't tell anyone so we wouldn't get into trouble."

"She's sick?" Grandma Ann sputtered her sip of tea.

"What do you mean she's sick?" Mom interrupted. "And she had to leave camp early? Is she okay?" She was frowning then, a look of concern filling her features. "Have you been in contact with her since she was picked up at camp? Will she be okay at your house? Where is she anyway? And where do you even live?" She stood up from her chair and moved her hands through her hair, her excitement at meeting me was quickly fading. She was worried about her other daughter.

I didn't think about that when I explained my side of the story. How would my adopted mom feel if Casey explained the situation to her? Oh my gosh! I couldn't believe I'd been so reckless.

"No, she's—"

"Ali, I need to speak with Casey," Mom interrupted. "I want to check to make sure she's okay. This little game ends now. She has to come home right away." She reached for the phone on the bench top next to me. "Ali, what's your number? I need to speak with Casey."

CHAPTER FOUR
Casey

The closer we got to the hospital, the more frantic Ali's dad became. He didn't show it on his face but his erratic driving made my stomach flip-flop even more. I started to recognize the area and realized that Ali lived across town from me, in the wealthier suburbs. That was obvious by the size of her house but even if I tried to sneak out and get to her, it would have been a long walk.

The car skidded to a halt and the seatbelt pressed against my chest, taking my breath away.

I flinched as her dad cursed. It wasn't the first time. Any red light we encountered came with several curses under his breath. At least he tried to keep them under his breath. Mom and Grandma Ann never swore, at least not in front of me. Hearing the curse words was jarring to my ears.

He turned and looked at his wife. His eyes were filled

with concern for her, just as mine probably were. He patted her arm. "Hang on darling, we're almost there."

She shifted in the seat but said nothing. Her breathing became more and more ragged as we got closer to the hospital. Ali's dad had been right. If we'd waited for an ambulance I didn't think they would have made it in time to help her.

I forced back the tears welling in my eyes. I had to be strong for Ali.

Her dad lifted something from his pocket and placed it on the console between the two front seats.

My heart soared as I stared at the cell phone mere inches away from me. I wanted — more than anything — to lean forward and take it. I would only need to text Ali a quick message to let her know about her mother. We were still a few minutes away from the hospital. Her dad was distracted enough by getting us there that he wouldn't notice if I took it.

But what if he did catch me? He told "Ali" there was no time for phones and he was so frantic. Would I make him more upset if I were caught?

But there was no way that I could suddenly admit to Ali's parents that I wasn't their daughter.

I made my decision.

Reaching for the phone, I moved my hand tentatively towards the console. Keeping my eyes glued on Ali's dad, I edged ever so slowly in case he turned around or looked at his wife again. There were no red lights in sight so he concentrated on the road ahead.

My fingers hovered above the phone and I was just about to grab it when the screen lit up and a loud ringtone blared from the speakers.

Jumping back with fright, my heart thumped loudly in my chest.

He glanced down at the phone. Grabbing it in his hand, he reached back to hand it to me. "Ali, answer this for me."

I held it in my hands, staring at my perfect opportunity to get in touch with Ali. I silently thanked whoever was watching over me.

"Ali!" he said, breaking me out of my thoughts. "Answer the phone!"

I swiped at the screen and lifted the phone to my ear. "Hello?"

The line disconnected before I could finish answering. I looked down at the screen and realized the person had hung up.

"Who was it?" he asked.

The phone number hadn't been in his contact list or else a name would have shown up. Instead, it was just a phone number, one I didn't recognize.

"I don't know," I said, "they hung up."

"Don't worry about it," he said, refocusing his attention on the road.

Not wanting to lose the opportunity, I held the phone next to my leg and opened the messages app. I typed in my cell phone number and started to type a quick text to Ali. I wanted to reassure her that I would be in touch as soon as I could, without worrying her. I planned on deleting the message as soon as I sent it and I hoped Ali would be okay until I spoke with her later.

The car stopped again and I looked up, the message only half written. The bright lights from the hospital spilled into the car, illuminating everything. He'd found a vacant car park reserved for disabled drivers right at the entrance.

I glanced down at the phone, seeing my half-written message.

He turned towards me and I shoved the phone under my leg to hide it. "Let's go. You need to help your mom out of the car while I go to find a doctor."

I nodded, and he shot out of the car and sprinted to the entrance.

I got out too and shoved the phone into my back pocket. It was small enough to remain hidden but I covered my pocket with the back of my shirt just in case he saw it and wanted it back. I hoped he'd be too distracted to notice I had it.

When I opened the passenger side door, I saw that Ali's mom was slumped over and her eyes were closed. Her breathing had steadied somewhat but it was labored enough that another wave of worry spilled over me.

"Dad has gone to get a doctor," I said to her.

Her eyes fluttered open and she sat up, staring at the space in front of her. Had she been sleeping?

My hands began to tremble. This swap had gone too far. Ali should be here with her mother. But there was nothing else I could do. So I took a deep breath and leaned over, grabbing her arm.

"Let's get you out of there," I said.

It took her some time to move her legs out of the car but I patiently waited. I glanced over my shoulder a few times. What was taking the doctor so long?

"Ali," she said, "I'm so sorry. I don't think I have the strength."

"That's okay," I said reassuringly. "I'm here to help you. The doctor will be here very soon. You're going to be better in no time."

A sad smile crossed her lips and I sucked in a breath. *Don't you dare cry, Casey!*

Ali wasn't a robot, she had emotions, but she would be strong for her mother. I was certain of that. And I had to do the same.

I managed to get her standing before the sliding doors to the hospital opened again.

Ali's dad came out, rolling a wheelchair in front of him. An older nurse was at his side.

I smiled. At least Ali's mom could rest instead of attempting to walk further into the hospital. She definitely wasn't up for that.

"Grace," Ali's dad said, taking over. "There is a room waiting for you. Everything is going to be fine." I moved out of the way as he helped her into the wheelchair. He kissed the top of her head when she was settled in.

A familiar ringing sound made me jolt.

He turned to me. "I'll take my phone back. It's the office."

I stood there, unsure what to do.

"Ali," he said, holding his hand out between us. "My phone?"

I let out a breath and lifted the phone from my pocket. My heart pounded in my chest. What if he saw the half-written text message?

He pressed the red button to end the call and relief filled me. I'd find a way to get the phone back before he read it. I tried to remember exactly what I wrote but my mind went blank. It wasn't a good time for them to realize I wasn't their daughter but there was nothing else I could do at that point. Sure, they would be upset but maybe it would help Ali get back together with her family before something bad happened.

Ali's dad wheeled the chair toward the hospital. I closed the passenger side door and watched them all enter the hospital and head toward the emergency ward.

For some reason, I couldn't move. I wasn't supposed to be here. All of this was wrong. I wouldn't be able to forgive myself if something happened and Ali wasn't informed. I prayed that her mom would be okay. And I made a silent promise to somehow get in touch with Ali as soon as I could.

CHAPTER FIVE
Ali

Mom reached for the phone next to me, intending to call Casey. I didn't want to give her the house number in case my parents answered. It was still early and I didn't want to wake them. My adopted mother sometimes slept late for days after a treatment, so this phone call wouldn't be a welcome wake up.

I decided to give her my cell phone number, knowing Casey promised to keep it on her at all times.

Holding the phone in front of her, I watched as Mom pressed the green CALL button.

I swallowed and began to give her my cell number when Lucas burst into the room.

Pressing my lips closed, I wondered how much of the conversation he'd heard.

"I'm hungry!" he whined. He went to the cabinet and grabbed a box of cereal and a bowl.

He seemed unaware that anything was going on. None of us spoke while he got the carton of milk from the refrigerator and poured the liquid over his breakfast.

Mom hung up the phone and let her hand drop to her side. Calling Casey in front of Lucas would alert him to the conversation we'd had. And it appeared she wasn't ready to share with him that he had another sister who looked exactly like the other.

I noticed Mom and Grandma Ann sharing a look. I wasn't sure exactly what they were thinking but I had an idea.

When he turned around to go back into the refrigerator he noticed we were all looking at him. "What's going on?" he asked with his eyebrows furrowed. "Why is everyone so quiet?"

Mom placed the phone down next to me but didn't answer him.

She glanced at Grandma Ann and then back to me. I stared at the clock on the wall, the second hand appeared to be moving slower than usual.

Lucas rolled his eyes. "Whatever! You're all being weird. I gotta get back to my show before the commercials end." He left the room, balancing his cereal bowl and glass of juice in his hands.

"Please turn it down," Grandma Ann said to him as he disappeared around the corner.

"Yes, okay," he said from the other room. The sound was muffled under the blasting commercial for some action figure. I didn't even need to see the television to know what it was about. Even in the situation we were in, I smiled. Lucas was exactly the little brother I'd always wanted, although he had some quirks that annoyed Casey, she didn't know how lonely being an only child could be sometimes. At least in her house, there was never a dull moment.

The volume lowered significantly, but we could still hear every word of the cartoon as the show came back on.

The kitchen stood still.

It wasn't until my mom grabbed the phone again that my anxiety spiked once more. "Ali, I need your number."

After the interruption from Lucas, my fear suddenly ramped up again. "Please don't call."

"Ali, I have to see how Casey is. You told us she was sick—"

"She's fine," I interrupted, I had to stop her from ruining this. I didn't want Casey to be mad, and selfishly I wasn't ready to leave yet. I knew if our mom called, then this whole weekend would be over, and I wasn't sure when I'd see my real family again.

"We've been texting back and forth and she's fully recovered now. It was probably the twenty-four-hour flu or something. And she said she's having a really good time at my house. They saw *Wicked* last night."

Grandma Ann raised her eyebrows at this news and looked at my mom, who kept glancing at the phone then back up to me.

I needed to push my case further, even though I hated using my adopted mother's illness as an excuse. "To be honest, it's my adopted mom who I'm really worried about. She's very sick. And in the past, when I've asked about my birth parents, the conversations really upset her. I think if she finds out, she might be disappointed that I went behind her back and deceived her. I know it's not right, but we never planned for this to happen so quickly. I want to talk to my parents face to face about this. And I can't do that until tomorrow after school."

"Your mother is sick?" Grandma Ann asked, her eyes were filled with concern.

I nodded. I missed my mom more than I let on, but I only had one more day with my real family before I had to go back home. I'd never be in this mess to begin with if my adopted mother had been honest with me, but at the moment I didn't want to go back and argue that point with her. It wouldn't be fair in her current condition, and I'd already found my real family. It wouldn't make sense to stir up trouble now. At least when I saw her again I could explain how it was a coincidence that I met Casey at school. I wasn't sure I would even tell her about the swap. I wouldn't need to if I explained that I wanted to have a relationship with my sister. She'd have to understand. Right?

"Besides," I said. "Today is the last day of the swap and Casey will return home tomorrow after school."

"I don't know…" Mom said.

I stood up from the chair and wrung my hands together. "Please, don't call my parents. Let's just continue with the plan for today. I don't want the weekend to end yet. Or badly for that matter. It's been so unexpected and the best weekend of my life."

Mom took a deep breath and let it out slowly.

I took her hands and looked up into her eyes. "I wanted to get to know you." I looked to Grandma Ann. "And I wanted to get to know my family. My real family. Not just the people who adopted me. This has been the most special few days of my life. Casey is fine now. I promise. Just let me stay. Please.

I reached my hand out to Grandma Ann as tears welled in my eyes. My mother and grandmother both wrapped their arms around me and I closed my eyes, taking the moment in.

Inhaling the scent of them, I breathed it in. I hadn't lied. This had been the best weekend of my life so far. I hoped that I'd convinced them enough to let me stay. It was less than a day before Casey would return home. They had to give me one more day to get to know them. It was the least they could do after keeping me a secret for all these years.

Lucas's shuffling feet entering the kitchen interrupted the moment, but none of us moved from our spot.

I opened my eyes, wishing I could let him in on the secret. But that would be up to my mom to decide. I'd only known Lucas for a few days so I wasn't sure how he'd take the news. I hoped he wouldn't be as mad with our mom as Casey had been. We'd gotten along so well this weekend, maybe he would be happy he had a sister that he could have fun with, instead of one he argued with all the time.

He reached into the cabinet and grabbed a granola bar. "Why does everyone keep hugging each other today?"

Mom stepped away from me and wiped the tears from her eyes. That was when I made my decision. "Mom, I want to be honest with everyone."

Grandma Ann nodded. "I think that's for the best."

Mom took a deep breath and smiled at me. Her eyes were filled with tears but they were happy tears. We were a family united, once again.

And by telling Lucas, there would be no more secrets. It was everything Casey and I wanted.

"Lucas," Mom said, pulling me to her side, "we have something very important to tell you."

CHAPTER SIX
Casey

I caught up with Ali's parents and walked a few feet behind them as we made our way down the long corridor of the hospital. Her dad didn't turn around once. I noticed the phone-shaped bulge in his pocket and couldn't believe I'd lost my chance to contact Ali. I should have silenced it after that random phone call. It was the same number again that had called. He'd been distracted and didn't know I had the phone. I'd wrecked my chance and it was all my fault.

Letting out a frustrated sound under my breath, I sighed heavily. I was really messing this up for Ali.

I could hear her dad informing the nurse about what had happened the night before and I strained to listen to the details. Apparently, Ali's mom had barely slept and continuously had issues trying to breathe.

Rubbing my eyes sleepily, I stood alongside him, not believing this was really happening. How did I not see how bad all of this was? It wasn't my fault since I'd never been around someone who was sick. I should have asked Ali if there were any signs to look out for.

We slowed down in front of a set of double doors. Above the doors was a large sign for the Emergency Room. The nurse allowed Ali's dad and mom to go inside.

I started forward but she stepped in front of me and the doors closed behind her.

I looked up at the nurse. "Those are my parents."

She leaned down and put a hand on my shoulder. "Sweetie, you need to wait in the waiting room. Here, I'll take you."

I didn't like being spoken to as if I was Lucas's age. But I also wasn't sure if this was a routine for Ali. Her dad didn't say anything to me, so would Ali fight back and demand to be taken in with her parents? Surely, her dad would have brought me inside if I was allowed. I didn't have the energy to fight. He'd come to get "Ali" when it was necessary. I glanced at the doors again, unable to see into the window that sat high up on the door. With no other choice, I allowed the nurse to take me to the waiting room.

"If you need anything, let those nurses know." She pointed to a large desk in the center of the room where several women sat behind computers, and others were looking at medical charts.

"Okay," I said.

"We're going to take good care of your mom," she

offered a quick smile and then left. I watched her go to the desk and talk to one of the other nurses. They both glanced at me and then back to their work.

I didn't want them to feel bad for me, I wanted them to fix Ali's mom.

The emergency room was surprisingly busy for that time in the morning. I wasn't sure if that was normal since I'd never been to one. I counted myself lucky. How many times had Ali been there or at other emergency rooms? The thought made me shiver. I'd learned so much more about Ali in these past few days than I ever could have if she told me. She kept her mom close to her heart but now I really knew the struggle she went through on a daily basis. I couldn't believe I used to be jealous of her. Sure, she had nice clothes and a nice house but that meant nothing if her mother died.

I shook my head and the thoughts from my mind. Ali's mom was going to be fine. She had to be.

As I sat quietly on the couch in the far corner of the room, I tucked my legs up to my chest. Fighting to hold back my tears, I prayed that Ali's mom was okay. And I worried that Ali would find out too late that her mom was really ill. I wished that we'd had more time to make the swap. Maybe if I hadn't become sick or had informed Mrs. Halliday of our game when Ali's parents arrived, Ali would be here with her mother, giving her the support she needed. It's not like I could do anything from the waiting room but I'd feel better if Ali was going through this with me.

Watching the other families and individuals in the waiting room helped to distract me. Then, as I glanced around, I suddenly noticed a pay phone in the corner of the room. Without thinking, I shot up from my chair and headed over to it. Glancing down the hallway, I made sure that Ali's dad wasn't around to see me. I doubted Ali would have anyone to contact in this situation, but Casey did. When I was sure he wasn't going to catch me, I lifted the phone from the cradle. I was about to dial when I realized I had no money. The coin slot mocked me and I put the phone down, realizing that I was back to where I started.

Turning around, I realized that no one cared that a 12-year-old girl was wandering around the emergency room waiting area by herself. But maybe I could ask someone for a quarter?

There was a woman close to me who looked exhausted and worried. I didn't want to bother her. Apart from her, there was a dad who looked half asleep, nursing his little baby. I certainly couldn't bother him.

"Emergency Room," a nurse said from behind the desk. She was an older woman with gray hair. She was speaking into the phone. A FREE phone.

She would have to let me use the phone, right? I could tell her I needed to call my sister to let her know our mom was in the hospital. It wasn't a complete lie. And it would make me feel so much better to have spoken with Ali. It was the best plan I'd had since losing her dad's phone.

I stepped closer to the desk, not wanting to disturb the nurse's phone call. Forcing myself to wait as patiently as I could, I tapped my shoe on the floor. The conversation seemed to drag on.

When she was finally finished, she hung up the phone then glanced at me. Her eyes narrowed, then she turned away and continued on with her work.

She was about to get up and I saw my chance. "Excuse me!"

She scowled at me. "Can I help you?"

"I, um, need to use the phone to call—"

"Our phones aren't for personal use," she interrupted. "If you need to call someone, use the pay phone over there." She pointed to the payphone and began to walk away again.

"Wait!" I said.

She turned around again, clearly annoyed with me. I needed to convince her to let me use the phone. I had to.

"I don't have any change for that phone. My mom is very sick. She just went into the emergency room with my dad. I'm all alone out here and I need to call my sister to let her know."

She raised an eyebrow at me but didn't walk away. I was making progress. "Where is your sister?"

I couldn't tell her my sister was living a lie in my house. "She's in college. So, she won't know about this unless I call her. Our mom has cancer and she's been really sick through the night."

The tears filling my eyes weren't a lie. In the past few days, I'd taken a liking to Ali's mom and I realized I really didn't want anything bad to happen. Especially when everyone thought I was Ali. Ali needed to be with her mom and I would tell any lie to get her there.

The nurse pressed her lips together and her expression softened. She sat back down in her chair. "Oh dear, I didn't know." She looked around the room. "You have to make it quick." She handed me the phone over the

261

top of the desk. "What's the number?"

She dialed the number to my cell phone that I gave her. My body flooded with relief. "Thank you," I said, as the phone began to ring.

She smiled at me and I waited.

The phone rang several times before my voicemail came on. "Hi, you've reached Casey. Leave a message!"

I glanced over at the nurse who was within earshot. I couldn't explain to Ali what had happened over my voicemail. There was no way for her to call me back and I didn't want to scare her. She might be desperate enough to call her dad which would make everyone more upset than necessary.

"You can hang up," I said to the nurse.

She pressed the button and the line went dead. My insides swelled with frustration. Ali had promised to have my phone on her at all times.

Although, so had I!

CHAPTER SEVEN
Ali

Mom went over to Lucas and took his hand. He looked up at her, his eyes expectant. "What I'm about to tell you is very important. And I want you to know you can come to me with any questions you might have."

I wondered if she was going to give the whole story or some of it. I didn't know how I would handle it at his age. I sat back on the stool, waiting to see what happened.

"Lucas, this," she opened her hand to me, "is Ali. She's Casey's twin sister. They go to school together and switched places this weekend so she could meet her biological family."

Lucas opened his mouth in disbelief and looked at me, wide-eyed. I wasn't sure why I was so nervous. We'd spent the weekend together but that had been me pretending to be Casey. Now that the truth was out, my stomach fluttered with butterflies.

"When I was very young," she continued, sensing his astonishment, "I gave birth to both Casey and Ali. Due to some circumstances beyond my control, I had to give one of them up for adoption. Ali is that baby. Lucas, Ali is your other sister."

His mouth started to open in a big O-shape and then he rolled his eyes and laughed. He doubled over himself in a fit of giggles. "Yeah right, Mom. And I have a twin brother who is suddenly going to switch places with me, right?" He continued to laugh as he left the room.

We all watched him leave. For a young boy who loved cartoons, he certainly didn't have much of an imagination. Or maybe playing jokes between each other was something this family did? Either way, I was a little disappointed in the reaction. Maybe it would sink in for him in a little bit.

Grandma Ann shook her head. "He needs to be told the truth. We can't keep it from him any longer."

"I don't know what else to say," my mom said. "I did tell him the truth. Just give him some time. We can try again later."

"The more you put it off—"

"I know, Mother," my mom snapped at Grandma Ann.

It was the first time I saw her lose her temper. At least it wasn't directed at me. I knew from the conversation with Casey, that the twin issue was something that divided Grandma Ann and our mom. Grandma Ann had insisted we should have been told about each other a long time ago, but had left that final decision up to our mother.

Grandma Ann said nothing else while she sipped her tea.

Lucas came bounding back into the kitchen. He handed me Casey's phone. "I heard it ringing when I was in the bathroom."

I wanted to try and convince him that I wasn't Casey, but he bounced from the room before I had a chance. If Casey had called me, then I might be able to show him that I was Ali. But instead of my cell number, the screen showed the words, "No Caller ID". Who would be calling this early from a blocked number? It wouldn't be Casey. I'd added my number to the contact list when I first found her phone. And my home number wasn't blocked. It couldn't be from Casey. Could it? Without a caller ID or a number to call back on, I couldn't ring back and check. I had a strange sensation trickle down my spine. I had to be sure.

I quickly typed a text to Casey. *How's everything going and how's my mom? I got a missed call from a blocked number and wanted to make sure everything was okay. Call me as soon as you get this.*

The house phone rang from its place on the bench top

next to me, and I jumped. Maybe the blocked call had been Casey and she was trying the house phone now? Would she have called again that quickly? I'd only sent the text a few seconds ago. Was everything okay? Was my adopted mom okay?

Mom answered the phone quickly as if she were hoping it was Casey too. Both Grandma Ann and I listened to the conversation.

"Hello?" she said, then paused. She breathed a sigh and nodded, closing her eyes. "Yes, hello Meredith. Absolutely." She glanced at the clock.

I wasn't sure if I was relieved or more annoyed. I didn't know a Meredith. I looked down at Casey's phone but she still hadn't responded. I knew she liked to sleep late so I would probably hear from her later that morning when she woke up. I turned up the volume and flipped on the vibrate option as well. I wasn't going to miss another call or text.

Mom hung up the house phone.

"Who was that?" Grandma Ann asked.

"That was Matt's mother, Meredith. She's having car trouble and Matt needs a lift to the game this morning. She's panicked that Matt is going to miss the game. So we'll have to swing by there on the way."

Grandma Ann glanced at the clock. "The game starts in about an hour. We'd all better get moving or Lucas will be late."

"I'll get some breakfast together," Mom said, grabbing the cereal box and some bowls from the cabinet. "It's going to be a quick meal this morning. I hope you like cereal, Ali."

Hearing my name coming from my real mom was amazing. I nodded. "Cereal is fine."

Grandma Ann finished off her tea and placed the mug in the sink. She grabbed a banana from a bowl full of fruit and peeled it. Then she placed the banana on a cutting board to slice it.

"Do you want sliced bananas in your cereal?" Grandma Ann asked me.

I wrinkled my nose. "On the side, please."

She smiled and stopped chopping when she reached the halfway point of the banana.

I watched them perform what looked like a routine for a few seconds. A burning question built up in my mind and I couldn't hold it in any longer.

"So," I said, wanting to get their attention.

Grandma Ann glanced over her shoulder at me. "Yes?"

"Is it okay for me to stay another night?"

Mom turned around and smiled at me. "Yes, darling, just for one more night. But from here on out, we must be honest with each other. No more secrecy. And that means talking to your adopted parents as well. We should probably schedule something for later this week. Maybe a meet-and-greet of some sort. I'd really like to meet the people who took such good care of you all these years."

"They're really great," I said, meaning it. Aside from all the lies, they'd given me everything I ever wanted. For a second, I thought of how it would have been if I'd stayed with my real mom and Casey. There was no turning back time, but I would hate if I'd never had my adopted parents in my life. They were so special to me.

I jumped off the stool, beaming. I could stay with my real family, as myself! And I could spare my adopted parents the shock for at least one more night. I wanted to speak to my adopted mom in person, so this was going to work out perfectly.

"As soon as you've eaten, Ali," Grandma Ann said, "can you please help Lucas get organized. His equipment is in his bedroom and his uniform is hanging in his cupboard."

There was nothing else I wanted to do more.

"Sure!" I quickly gobbled down my cereal and headed into the living room.

Lucas was still bundled under the throw rug watching his show.

"Lucas," I said, crossing the room. "Your game starts soon. We're picking up Matt on the way, so Grandma Ann wanted me to help you get ready."

His eyes flicked from the screen to me. "I don't need help getting ready." Then his attention went back to the television.

Why wasn't he getting up? Surely as his older sister, I had some authority? If he still thought I was Casey, then I guessed he'd probably ignore me. They didn't get along at all. But throughout this weekend, I felt as if I'd broken through that barrier. Lucas wanted to include "Casey" but it appeared the real Casey didn't have the time or patience for him. I could change that. Since my secret was revealed, I could start fresh with Lucas and be the supportive big sister he wanted.

The first thing I needed to do was get his attention. I took the remote from its place on the armrest of the couch and pressed the POWER button. Lucas jumped up as if he were on a trampoline.

"Why'd you do that?" he asked in an annoyed tone.

I stood my ground and firmly said, "Grandma Ann asked me to get you ready."

"Since when do you do what she says?" he asked.

I went forward with the plan of convincing him I was Ali and not Casey. "I only met Grandma Ann this weekend."

He rolled his eyes. "Are you all still playing this prank on me? It's not very good."

"It's not a prank," I said.

"Yeah, okay," he said, not believing me. He got up from the couch and left the room.

I stood there. Why didn't he believe us? If my adopted mom told me I had a twin, I would believe her right away. I supposed Lucas was too young to understand. Maybe he didn't want another sister. I sighed. I hoped he wouldn't be too upset when he found out the truth. I thought we'd had lots of fun together, especially at the fair.

I promised myself I'd be the best sister I could, until he actually believed the real story. And then when he realized I was a good person, he wouldn't be too disappointed.

CHAPTER EIGHT
Casey

I decided to try once more and asked the nurse to dial my house number, saying it was my sister's landline at "college". Her annoyance with me returned, and I stared at a small chip in the desk while she dialed. Her glare could melt an icicle. Maybe if I didn't make eye contact with her, she would quit making that face at me. I wasn't the type to beg for anything. I learned a long time ago that I had to fend for myself. But this was a life and death situation! Explaining that to the nurse would take way longer than necessary.

Why hadn't Ali picked up my cell phone? My phone charger was right next to my bed. So even if she was sleeping she should have at least heard it vibrate or ring. My home phone didn't even ring. My ears were filled with a busy signal sound. What if Ali saw my call and was trying to call her cell phone? As much as I accused her of not answering my phone, I'd been the one to leave her phone at the house in our rush to the hospital. I was as much to blame for this mess as she was. I couldn't believe what an awful day we were all having!

"It's busy," I said to the nurse.

She held out her hand for the receiver. I grasped tightly to the phone and tried to think if there was another number I could call. Calling my mom or Grandma Ann's cell phone wasn't an option. I needed to get to Ali or at the very least, Lucas. What I wouldn't give to be snuggled up in my own bed with my annoying brother in the next room! I didn't want to be in Ali's shoes anymore. This was all too much and our game wasn't fun anymore.

"I need the phone back," the nurse said. "I need to make my own important phone calls."

I reluctantly handed the phone back to her.

"You should take a seat. I'm sure someone will come out and get you soon."

"Thank you," I said. I went back to my seat and glanced at the emergency room doors. No one had gone in or come out in the time I was trying to call Ali. My worry came back in full force and I really hoped that Ali's mom was okay.

I tried to distract myself by reading a magazine from the stack on the table next to me, but the words blurred together and I could barely comprehend what I was reading. My mind was focused on Ali and her mom. I put the magazine down and thought of how I got into this mess, to begin with.

Switching places with Ali at camp had been fun. And being with Jake—even if it was as Ali—had made this year at camp the best ever. The smile disappeared from my face when I thought of the consequences and how they were too much for me. I wished I would have told Ali that I wanted to sleep in my own cabin that night. I had sort of felt a little unwell at the campfire, but with Jake by my side, he was all I could think about. At least when I woke up sick the next morning I would have been Casey instead of Ali. Or we should have at least swapped back before I went to the nurse. Then *her* parents would have never been contacted.

As much as I loved Ali's house, I wished we would have thought out the plan better. We could have switched when we were both well and fully prepared. I wondered what else Ali had done in my shoes. I hoped she was having some fun. Once I was able to get a hold of her, her fun would be over.

The thoughts raced around and around inside my head. And all I could think of were the negatives; how everything had gone so wrong. But I couldn't blame Ali. As much as it had been her idea for the swap. I was also to blame since I agreed to it in the first place.

I closed my eyes against the churning in my stomach.

How had we not thought of these things? Especially with the condition of Ali's mom!

Thinking about it some more, I wasn't completely to blame and neither was Ali. If Mom and Grandma Ann had been honest with me then none of this would have happened in the first place. I shouldn't be feeling so guilty when it was Mom and Grandma Ann's fault for lying all these years. If anything bad happened, they would be the ones to blame, not me or Ali.

I had so much nervous energy that I jumped up from my chair and began to walk across the room. I noticed the cranky nurse at the desk watching me, but I didn't care. I hadn't been this upset with my family since I left for camp. I dwelled on my anger for a little bit while I wandered around the space. I passed several vending machines and my stomach growled. I looked through the glass at the yummy cookies and candy. I wished I had some money. At least then I'd be able to eat as well as try the pay phone again. I'd try until my fingers hurt. The nurse was so mean and unhelpful, I didn't dare ask to use her phone again.

There wasn't even a clock in the room to know how much time had passed since we'd arrived. The television mounted in the corner of the room turned on. I hadn't realized it was there before. I glanced at the cranky nurse who held a remote pointed in that direction and she flipped through the channels until she got to a news station. And even though it wasn't my ideal station, I silently thanked her for the distraction. I took a deep breath and settled into my chair, praying that Ali's mom would survive until Ali got home.

I tried to be distracted by the television. But my eyes continued to glance back at the double doors. I hoped Ali's dad would come out to give me an update sometime soon.

CHAPTER NINE
Ali

After the breakfast dishes had been done, we all headed to the car. Lucas seemed surprised that I was coming with them.

"Why wouldn't I?" I said, patting him on the head. He'd traded his favorite yellow cap for a white one with blue stripes. I imagined it wouldn't be so white after the game.

"You never come to my games," he said pointedly.

I looked at Grandma Ann and she shrugged. Casey never went to her own brother's baseball games? It was one of those things I'd always imagined doing if I ever had a sibling. As much as my parents supported me, I thought having another kid in the house would make us that much closer.

"But I'm really happy you're coming, Casey!" he said, wrapping his arms around me.

I hugged him back. Before I could correct him on my name, he jumped into the back seat and I followed. "I'm really good at batting. I'm usually number four which means I'm the best. Coach always practices more with me since he says I have potential, I guess that means I'm good. I'm not afraid of the ball like some of the others. I run right up to it, even if it's a line drive."

He continued on, his excitement making me smile. This wasn't the right time to convince him of the truth about me and Casey. I didn't want to upset him before his game by bringing it all up again. I'd wait until later that day. Hopefully, his team would win so he'd be in a good mood.

We picked up Lucas's friend, Matt, on the way. He was standing in the driveway waiting for us and I could see instantly that he was a cute little kid, just like Lucas. He looked familiar and I wondered if I'd seen him somewhere before. Maybe at the fair.

When I moved over to give him my seat, he seemed nervous, almost surprised that "Casey" was there too. As much as I love Casey, we were totally different when it came to siblings. But I supposed me missing out on having a little brother made me that way. I could see how Lucas's endless energy could be annoying, but I wasn't ready to feel that way just yet.

Lucas and Matt talked about the game. Since we were around other people, I needed to pretend to be Casey again. And if she never went to Lucas's games then she wouldn't feel the need to interrupt or be included in their conversation.

When we arrived at the field, Lucas and Matt grabbed their things and raced off toward their side of the field, where there were more kids in the same uniforms. Grandma Ann led the way up the bleachers to a spot in the middle. We sat down and waited for the start of the game.

"How come Casey never comes to the games?" I asked in a low voice. I didn't want anyone else to hear me.

"She and Lucas don't get along that well," Grandma Ann said. "And it gives everyone a break from the fighting between them if we let her stay at home. She tends to hold grudges."

I couldn't imagine my twin doing that, but I guessed I had more to learn about her than I thought.

"I've never been to a little league game before," I admitted excitedly. Since I didn't have a younger sibling to watch, I'd never had a reason to.

"They are very long games," Mom admitted, "but Lucas really loves it."

Several people stood up a few rows down to let a family move past them. My mouth dropped open when I realized it was Jake, and who I assumed were his parents. I turned around and tried to hide behind my hair. Why was he here? Was one of these kids his little brother?

Panic rose in my stomach. Oh no! If he sees me, he'll think I'm Casey. And that would be so awkward now that Grandma Ann and my mom know I'm really Ali and not Casey. What had I done? I should have stayed at home the way Casey always did. Though I was sure she'd change her mind about going to the game if she knew Jake would be there.

Jake and his parents settled in their seats. I moved my body behind the large man sitting directly in front of me so I could avoid Jake. Deep down, I didn't really want to avoid him. What I really wanted was to go down there and sit and talk with him while the game was on. It was all so frustrating.

The game started and I couldn't help splitting my attention between it and Jake. He turned his head every so often and I caught sight of his adorable profile and cute smile. My stomach churned, but this time it wasn't nerves.

I glanced at Grandma Ann and my mom, who didn't appear to notice how strange I was acting. I wouldn't want to draw Jake's attention up to where I was sitting. If only this game didn't move so slowly…

"Strike three!" the referee called from home plate.

The families on the other side of the field cheered as one of the kids on Lucas's team dropped his bat, defeated.

"No way was that a strike!" someone yelled from behind me. "I think you need to get some glasses, ref. That was way outside!"

Everyone turned around to the father who was yelling at the top of his lungs at the referee. The ref looked up at him and waved a yellow card in warning. I had no idea of what the yellow card meant, but it was obviously not good, and I guessed that it was best not to upset the referee.

The man's face and neck flushed bright red because the ref had called him out. I suspected the boy was his son.

I turned back around towards the ref to see what he planned to do, but instead locked eyes with Jake. He'd been looking up at the yelling parent sitting a few seats behind me.

His mouth split open into a beaming smile. My heart fluttered. He waved at me and stood up.

I waved back and opened my mouth as if I'd just noticed him too.

My smile faltered when I realized he was climbing the bleachers toward me.

Oh no! My whole body froze as I watched him get closer. What was I going to do? I had to pretend I was Casey but what would Grandma Ann and my mom think?

"Casey!" Jake said. He was still smiling.

Grandma Ann moved over, giving him room to sit.

"Are you here to watch your little brother?"

"Yeah," I said. "L-Lucas." My mouth wasn't cooperating with my brain.

"Hi, Mrs. Wrigley," Jake said politely. Then he introduced himself to Grandma Ann.

My mom and Grandma Ann were polite but their straight-lipped expressions told me they weren't happy that I continued to lie about who I was. My palms began to sweat. Guilt pooled in my stomach.

"It's nice to see a friend here," he said, bumping my arm. He was completely unaware of the frowns coming from my grandmother and my mom.

Even though I wanted to talk with him while the rest of the game went on, I wanted our conversation to end so that my mom and Grandma Ann wouldn't look so upset with me. I wondered if Mom was now thinking about how I'd acted at the mall when we bumped into Jake. I wanted to explain to her that Casey actually did have a crush on him.

I could see where she might not understand. Casey

276

and I had lied to her. Now she saw me lying to one of our classmates.

"This is a coincidence. I didn't know your brother was on the same team as Matt."

Matt? The kid we picked up? That's why he appeared so familiar! He was Jake's little brother. That was such a coincidence. It appeared that they'd sorted out their car problems after all.

"Yeah," I said, not looking at him. I tried to be standoffish and focus on the game. But Jake didn't even seem to notice.

"I never come to these games," Jake admitted. He scooted closer to me, and the battling feelings inside of me intensified. "What are the chances I'd run into you?"

"Crazy!" I shook my head in disbelief. Considering Casey never came to the games either, it was quite bizarre that he and I would both end up there on the same day. For some reason, the idea of Casey being there instead of me, created a swirling feeling of jealousy inside me. It was so wrong of me to feel that way, but I couldn't help it.

"It's nice to talk to someone in my class instead of my parents," he said. "They really get into the game. Not as much as that other guy." He hooked his thumb in the direction of the parent who'd been yelling.

I stifled a laugh in my hand. "He was a little over the top," I admitted.

"A little? We felt his spit from down there."

This time I didn't hold back. I laughed out loud at that. With Jake's warm and friendly personality and his handsome smile, it was hard to remain standoffish with him. He made me feel so comfortable and for a moment I almost forgot I was playing Casey again. It was hard to not have feelings for Jake. I consoled myself by knowing that he thought he was with Casey. And he genuinely wanted to make her—me—laugh. Technically, I wasn't doing anything wrong. Just like at camp, Casey would be encouraging this so that she could pick up where I left off and continue getting closer to Jake when we swapped places at school the following day.

And Jake would have no idea that we'd swapped! This is what Casey would want so I continued to talk with him as Casey probably would have.

Jake sat with me for the remainder of the game.

I tried to ignore the pointed glances from my mom. I wished I could have sent her telepathic messages so she knew this is what Casey would have wanted. But instead, her questioning looks and raised eyebrows only made those feelings of guilt return and worsen.

CHAPTER TEN
Casey

The local news station repeated their cycle of stories two times before the emergency room doors opened. I felt more informed about our local area but what I really wanted to know was the condition of Ali's mom.

I jumped from my seat when I saw her dad come through the doors. I ran over to him and he wrapped me in a tight hug.

"Ali, I'm so sorry it took so long," he apologized.

I shook my head, tears almost spilling from my eyes. "How is she? What happened?" I needed her to be okay. She had to be!

"She's resting now," he said.

"Oh, thank goodness!"

"She had a relapse and the doctors were able to give her another treatment before she got worse," he explained.

My jaw dropped. How much worse could it have been? She was barely able to breathe the whole ride to the hospital. I shivered, unable to imagine what "worse" meant for the doctors.

"Does she have to stay here overnight?" I asked. "Or can she come home with us?" I wondered if we were supposed to stay overnight with her. I hoped not because I desperately wanted to get back to the house so I could get in touch with Ali.

"I told the doctors she will be much more comfortable at home," Ali's dad explained. "They agreed as long as she continued to respond to the treatment. Which is why I took so long in there. She had to be monitored and I didn't want to leave her side. I hope you were okay out here." He looked somewhat ashamed for leaving his young daughter out in the waiting room by herself for so long.

I'd been okay; just worried about Ali's mom and getting in touch with Ali. But now that we were headed home soon, I would be able to contact her. My shoulders finally relaxed.

"I was fine," I assured him. "Can I see her?" I wanted to see for myself that she was doing okay. And I desperately wanted to get out of that waiting room with the cranky nurse and the boring news.

We headed through the emergency room doors and down a long hallway. There were other patients being treated in the rooms. One guy's head was bandaged and I saw a big red stain blotting the gauze. From then on, I tried to keep my eyes focused in front of me. I didn't want to risk seeing something worse from the other patients.

Ali's mom was in the last room in the hallway. Her eyes were closed when we arrived, and for a minute I thought she was sleeping.

I watched the steady movement of her breathing. She was such a beautiful person inside and out. She didn't deserve to have this happen to her. I realized how brave Ali had been through this ordeal. She was so good at hiding it.

"Grace," Ali's dad murmured quietly, to see if she was awake.

Her eyes fluttered opened and she gave us a weak smile. Her skin was paler than it had been that morning. I swallowed and entered the room. I went to her side and she reached her hand to me.

"My brave girl," she said in a small voice.

I wasn't nearly as brave as the real Ali or her mother. But I wasn't about to tell her that her real daughter was miles away right then.

"How are you feeling?" I was unsure what else to say.

"I feel better than I did this morning. And I can't wait to get back home with you two."

I smiled and she squeezed my hand.

The nurse took her vitals and it appeared everything

was good, at least as good as they could be. Ali's dad brought a chair over for me so I could sit. We were going to be there for a little while longer it seemed, and I certainly didn't want to be anywhere else but there.

We ended up being in the emergency room for another couple of hours. Ali's dad brought me some breakfast from the cafeteria and I felt much better. The mood in the room had greatly improved in the time we were together. I forgot all my worries from the waiting room and was happy to be included. Ali was so lucky to be a part of that tight-knit family. Her parents were so different to my mom and Grandma Ann. I wasn't sure why they were never able to have kids but I was happy they were able to care for my sister. They were perfect, and I was so happy to have met them.

By the time we packed up and left the hospital, Ali's mom was in better shape than I'd seen her all weekend. She was back to the sweet woman that had been doting on me when I was sick. Ali's dad didn't discuss the details of the relapse and I hoped that it wasn't my illness that hurt her somehow. There were a lot of things that were wrong with the swap. If I'd had something to do with her getting sick, I'd never forgive myself. I was prepared to help her in any way possible, at least until it was time for me and Ali to swap back.

On the way home, Ali's parents chatted about his work. It was as though we hadn't spent half of the night before and the majority of that day in the emergency room at all. I supposed spending time in the hospital was normal for them.

When we neared the house, I felt anxious about getting to Ali's phone. I imagined there were hundreds of missed calls and possibly a zillion texts from her. I could not get back to her bedroom quickly enough. I hoped Ali wasn't freaking out because I hadn't been in contact. What if she thought something was wrong and her and our mom were waiting at Ali's doorstep when we got there.

I held my breath as we turned into their street and passed through the front gate. But to my relief, my twin wasn't anywhere in sight. I needed to get to that phone in a hurry, or I'd go crazy.

Ali's dad pulled into the driveway. I expected to help Ali's mom to her bed, but surprisingly, she didn't need help getting out of the car. We all walked side by side into the house.

"I feel fine," she insisted, after Ali's dad told her she should go upstairs to rest.

"The doctor said you must rest," he reminded her.

She gave in. "Oh alright. I am a little tired, I guess."

By the time we got to the top of the stairs, she was a little out of breath, but nothing like that morning. She didn't even need assistance from the banister.

When we got to her bedroom, I sat on the side of her bed for a moment. I knew she needed to sleep, but I didn't want to leave her side just yet. She went into the bathroom and changed into a new set of pajamas. They were beautiful and silky. Now I knew where Ali got her style from.

I helped her into bed. Ali's dad kissed her on the cheek. She closed her eyes and seemed to fall immediately asleep. When I turned one last time to check on her, I could see that a contented smile remained on her lips. She was clearly happy to be at home.

A wave of exhaustion came over me too and I wanted nothing more than to put my head on the pillow and fall asleep as well. But I had something important to do first.

"I'm going to go to my office for a little while, while Mom rests," Ali's dad said. "If you need me, just come down, I'll have the door open. I have to catch up on a heap of work, so you'll be on your own for the afternoon. I'm going to check on Mom soon but please keep an ear out while you're upstairs."

"Okay," I replied.

He left the bedroom ajar. The house was so big I was sure he could have left it wide open and it wouldn't disturb Ali's mom at all.

After kissing the top of my head, he went down the stairs. I waited until he was all the way down before I sprinted to Ali's room.

Once inside, I closed the door and locked it. Quickly crossing the room, I pulled the charger from Ali's phone and turned the screen on, expecting the worst.

I let out a relieved sigh when I only saw two message bubbles on the screen. It wasn't ideal but I'd take that over the millions I'd seen in my head earlier.

Ali had texted me that morning asking about her mother.

Shoot!

Did she somehow know what happened?

There was also a missed call from her. I clicked on the voicemail, expecting the worst.

"Casey, its Ali. Please text or call me. I've been waiting to hear back from you. Is everything okay?"

I checked the timestamp of the call and it had come hours earlier. I hoped she wasn't going to be mad at me for forgetting her phone, and for not leaving a message earlier. But I had good news to share so I hoped she'd forgive me.

I unlocked the door to the bedroom, in case Ali's parents needed me, and then went into Ali's private bathroom. I turned on the shower as background noise. Leaning against the edge of the sink, I took a deep breath and pressed the screen to return Ali's phone call.

CHAPTER ELEVEN
Ali

The rest of the game went by too quickly. My heart was torn between my growing feelings for Jake and my loyalty to Casey. It didn't help that my mom was obviously listening to everything we said.

When the game was over, all the families stood at the same time to collect their kids and head home. It was the first time that Grandma Ann and my mom left me alone with Jake. I wasn't sure how Casey would say goodbye. It was obvious that Jake wasn't ready to go either. He glanced at his parents but was in no rush to go just yet.

"So, I guess I'll see you at school tomorrow?" he grinned.

"Yeah, I guess so," I smiled back.

A part of me was sad that tomorrow he would see me, but I

would be Ali again. He would remember our conversations at the mall, during the fireworks, and during the game, but think that each one had been with Casey.

His smile widened and the butterflies in my stomach did a crazy dance. "I'd better get moving. They're waiting for me and we're going out for pizza."

"Have fun," I replied.

"Bye!"

"Bye." I watched him leave and when he paused to take one last look in my direction, my heart fluttered once more.

He smiled again and waved.

"Casey!" my mom called, from the other end of the bleachers, snapping me out of my Jake-daze. I sighed heavily and went down to meet her.

There wasn't any time to explain to her or Grandma Ann about Jake. Lucas came running over to us and recounted the entire game as if we hadn't been there to watch it. To be honest, I'd hardly taken notice of any of it after Jake sat down next to me.

I listened to Lucas and acted impressed, all the while brushing off the conversation with Jake as if it were something normal for Casey. Mom hadn't met him prior to the day at the mall and Grandma Ann hadn't either, so they wouldn't know if it was out of character for Casey. I created multiple situations in my head in case they confronted me about it.

When we got home, Lucas took off toward the bathroom to clean up and Mom told him he could watch a movie before dinner.

I went straight to Casey's room and closed the door. I laid on the bed and checked Casey's cell phone again. There wasn't a single message from her. I hoped everything was okay. I mean, if it wasn't okay, she would call me, right?

285

I stared up at the ceiling, imagining I was looking at the stars stuck on my own ceiling. I thought of Jake and smiled. Gosh, he was so cute! And he was so funny. Now that I was alone, I allowed myself a little time to think of him. I knew it was wrong to have a crush on Jake, knowing how much Casey liked him, but I couldn't help it. We got along so well together. Even before I knew Casey was my twin, he'd been welcoming to me and so nice. I wondered if Casey would understand if he preferred me over her.

I shook my head and sat up. No. I would not do that to Casey. It was totally wrong, even if he was the cutest and nicest boy I'd ever met. Being a good sister was so important to me. And tomorrow we'd be back to our normal lives and Casey would be able to be with Jake as we'd planned.

Suddenly Casey's cell phone began to ring. My name filled the screen and I grabbed it as quick as I could to turn the ringer off. I glanced at the door. Would my mom want to know if Casey was calling?

I picked up the phone and put my hand over the speaker. "Casey? Is everything okay? How's Mom?"

"Ali?" Casey said, "Your mom is fine."

I let out a huge sigh. "Good. How come you didn't pick up the phone earlier? Someone called here and hung up and I thought the worst."

"That was me. I didn't want to leave a message," she said. "Ali, listen to me. I have to tell you something."

That didn't sound good. "What is it?" She said my mom was okay so it couldn't be that.

"This morning, your dad woke me up to take your mom to the hospital."

I sucked in a breath. "You said she was okay."

"She is okay. Now she's okay. He made me leave the house so quickly that I forgot your phone. I'm so sorry for doing that. I tried to call you from the hospital but I didn't want to leave a message in case Lucas got to the phone first. If you haven't noticed, he's quite nosy."

I nodded. She was definitely right about that.

"What happened, though? Why did she need to go to the hospital?"

"Your dad said she had a relapse or something. The doctors were able to give her treatment and we're home now. She's resting and we're keeping an eye on her. Please don't worry."

Casey sounded distraught but I didn't want to upset her with my own worry. There was nothing I could do at that point. I couldn't sneak out under Grandma Ann's watchful eye. And if my parents found out about the swap that would be sure to make my mother's condition worse. I didn't want her to suffer any more than she had to.

"Do you want to come home?" Casey asked as if she were reading my mind. "I can't go anywhere since I'm sure your dad wants to stay at home with your mom. But maybe I could borrow your bike and meet somewhere? Do you have a bike?"

"It's fine," I said. "If Mom's okay, let's continue as planned and do the swap tomorrow. It's the best way."

"Okay," Casey agreed. "But I normally take the bus in the morning. How do you get to school?"

"My mom or dad takes me," I said. "What time do you get there? We should do the swap before our first class."

"There is a bathroom on the second floor that no one uses. It's all the way down the hall close to the stairwell. I promise to keep your phone on me and I can text you when I arrive. I'm always there at least fifteen minutes before the first bell."

"That sounds good. We're going to have to swap everything — our bags and clothes — so I'll hurry there when I get off the bus."

"I can't wait to see you again," Casey said. "I had a lot of fun being you but I'm ready to get back to my life."

"Me too."

Casey giggled from the other end, and I smiled. It was

a relief to talk to her again. I truly missed her as well, and I hoped that we'd be able to reveal that we were sisters to everyone soon. I didn't like lying to everyone anymore.

"So where have you been all day, anyway? And what have you been up to?"

I hesitated. "I, um, went to Lucas's baseball game."

"Ugh. Was it super boring? I hate going to those."

"It was okay," I said. Jake was bound to say something to Casey tomorrow about the game and I didn't want her to be caught off-guard. "Oh and guess who was there?"

"Who?"

"Jake Hanley."

"Seriously?"

"Yeah, he, um, sat with us during the game. Don't worry, I pretended to be you."

"Oh my gosh! Tell me everything."

I told Casey everything Jake and I had talked about. Bringing up the details of our conversation made me smile. It was a good thing Casey couldn't see my face. I didn't mention the fair or the fireworks at that moment. I would talk to her about that tomorrow at school.

Casey went on about how awesome it was that Jake thought I was her and she'd be able to use that to get closer to him. I bit my lip and tried to be happy for her.

After a few minutes of her gushing, she told me she had to go. "I won't let this phone out of my sight. Text me later."

"Okay, bye Casey." I hung up the phone. My stomach began to growl. I knew a confrontation with Grandma Anna and my mom was inevitable but I was hungry. I turned toward the door and froze.

Lucas stood in the open doorway and was staring at me.

When had the door opened? I didn't hear him come in. "Lucas?" Had he heard the conversation between me and

Casey? If so, what had he heard? I tried to think of everything we'd talked about, but my mind went just as blank as his expression.

He blinked a few times before he spoke. "Where's my sister?" His bottom lip trembled as if he were about to cry.

"Oh, no, Lucas come here." I took a step toward him and his eyes widened as if I was someone to be scared of. I couldn't imagine what he was thinking while he listened to my phone conversation. Casey was right in saying that he was nosy.

"Please sit with me on the bed. I can explain everything."

He slowly moved toward the bed and sat on the edge. I sat down, far enough away that I wouldn't make him uneasy.

"This is what our mom and Grandma Ann were trying to explain before. My name is Ali. Mom had twins when Casey was born and had to give one up for adoption. That was me. I moved here recently and Casey and I met at school. And when we went to camp together last week, we thought it would be fun for me to meet my real family. But we made the swap without telling anyone. Grandma Ann figured it out this morning and we wanted to tell you. But you didn't believe us."

He continued to stare at me wide-eyed. I had to ease his mind about his sister somehow.

"Casey is fine. She's at my house with my parents. We're going to switch back at school tomorrow. I really wanted to meet all of you. I'm so sorry for lying, Lucas."

When I was finished talking, Lucas did something unexpected. He launched himself at me and wrapped his arms around my neck in a big hug.

"This is so cool! I have two sisters! Twin sisters!"

I laughed. I was so happy he wasn't upset with me.

He let go of me and jumped off the bed. "I'm going to call Matt and tell him. This is the coolest thing ever!"

I smiled and nodded. But as Lucas ran out of the room, I remembered that Matt was Jake's little brother.

I gasped and ran after him. He was almost to the kitchen before I caught him. "Lucas, you can't tell Matt about this."

His eyebrows furrowed. "Why not?"

I had to stop him before Jake found out about Casey and me. That would ruin everything. "We're going to tell my parents about this first. I don't want them to find out from anyone other than me." And I needed to delay Jake finding out until Casey and I were back in our own lives. I didn't intend to ever tell Jake about the swap.

"Okay," he agreed slowly. The disappointment was clear on his face.

"How about we watch a movie together and you can ask me any questions you want."

He threw his fist in the air. "Yeah!"

Lucas and I watched the first Harry Potter movie together. He wanted to eventually watch all of them with his "new sister". Even though I'd seen all of them before, this was special for him and I didn't want to disappoint him.

During dinner, he asked Mom questions about Casey and me and how it came to be that we were separated at birth. Even though I knew most of the story, I listened intently in case there was something I'd missed. I was sure she'd have to do this again when Casey got home but I had a feeling she wouldn't mind. Casey always talked about how our mom was a workaholic, but I'd barely seen her working at all over the weekend. Maybe things would start to turn around after all of this. At least I hoped so.

After dinner, Lucas insisted on watching another Harry Potter movie, which made it difficult for Mom or Grandma Ann to question me about Jake. Thinking of Jake during the movie made my stomach twist. And not in a good way. Now that Lucas knew about our secret, I didn't want him to ruin this for Casey and me.

And when I finally went to bed that night, the panic increased. Would I be able to trust Lucas with a secret this big? If he told Matt and then Jake found out, all of this would have been for nothing. For not only me but Casey too.

CHAPTER TWELVE
Ali

Even though I was exhausted, I must have finally drifted to sleep in the early hours of Monday morning. When Casey's alarm went off, I sat up, my eyelids heavy and my body still wanting hours more sleep. All night I'd tossed and turned, imagining Jake confronting Casey and me about our swap. My imagination ran wild after that, making my brain work on overdrive and keeping me awake. I wondered how I'd manage to stay awake through school.

The one thing that kept me moving was the excitement of seeing Casey again. We'd talked on the phone but I wanted more details of what she'd been up to that weekend. And I suspected she wanted the same. I wondered if Brie had contacted her about the fireworks. That would save me from having to go into it all.

I hoped our psychic connection wouldn't reveal my crush on Jake. I had to work on hiding that from her and myself. It wasn't right that I had a crush on a boy that Casey had liked before me, even though I'd been the one to spend the majority of time around him. I shook away the thoughts. This was going to be harder than I imagined.

I was the last to shower and change that morning. I chose the most Casey-looking outfit to wear. I knew she liked to be comfortable and I hoped that she wasn't sick and tired of my preppy clothes.

By the time I got to the kitchen, I only had fifteen minutes to spare before Lucas and I needed to leave for the bus. It wasn't enough time! I wasn't sure what to say to my mom and Grandma Ann, but I hoped we'd be able to see each other soon. I wanted to hang out with them more as myself, rather than pretending to be Casey.

Grandma Ann made Belgium waffles from scratch.

They were delicious! I hadn't had a waffle in forever and it was a special treat before I had to leave. As much as I wanted to swap back to my life, I didn't know when I was going to see them again. I had to be careful when telling my parents about Casey. I wasn't even sure I'd mention the swap at all, especially since my mom was going to the hospital more and more lately.

I had a feeling the treatment wasn't working as it was supposed to and I wasn't sure how she'd react when I told her a stranger had pretended to be her daughter for an entire weekend. Although, if they heard about the swap from my real mom, Grandma Ann or Lucas, they would be more hurt than if I had just been honest with them.

My panic began again at the thought of the mess we'd created. Deep down I knew I had to tell her everything. It was the right thing to do. She would never forgive me if she found out.

Lucas jumped up from his chair, and his fork clattered to the floor. "We have to go, Ali, or we'll miss the bus. I mean, *Casey*." He laughed uncontrollably and left the room.

I hoped he didn't say that on the bus! Casey and I were so close to swapping back, I didn't want anything to ruin it. And answering questions from Lucas's friends if he spilled the beans, wasn't something I wanted to do at all.

Mom and Grandma Ann stood up from the table at the same time as I did. We stood awkwardly for a moment until Mom opened her arms to me. I rushed to hug her and could not stop the tears from forming in my eyes.

"Thank you for letting me stay," I said, "this was the best weekend of my life."

She laughed. "The best? You don't have to say that."

I stepped back and looked up at her. She was teary as well. "Yes, I mean it! I've been wanting to know my real family for so long. And my wish has finally come true. You're more than I ever expected."

Mom and Grandma Ann shared a look. Then Grandma Ann hugged me too. "We're so happy to have met you, Ali. You've turned into such a lovely girl."

I really hoped this wasn't our final goodbye. I couldn't bear it. "Can I come back again soon?"

"Of course!" Mom exclaimed. "Now that we've finally met, we want to see you as much as possible, Ali. As long as it's okay with your parents that is."

I nodded. I would make sure my mom was feeling well enough when I got home today and then tell her. If not, I'd have to wait and until she was feeling better. Now that I'd met my real family, there wasn't too much of a rush. I could warm her up to the idea.

They gave me one more hug each before I had to leave for the bus. Scooping up Casey's backpack, I threaded my arms through the straps then gave my biological family one more wave before I headed off.

Lucas was already at the bus stop when I arrived. He was talking to a group of friends and I sucked in a breath. I expected them to rush over to me and ask questions about my twin. But surprisingly they didn't. I crossed my fingers he'd be able to keep his mouth shut. Even I wanted to tell everyone about being Casey's twin sister, but I knew this wasn't the right time.

As their focus moved to the school bus approaching us, I touched Lucas's shoulder and dropped down to his level.

"What is it, *Casey*?" he said with a wide grin.

I wished he'd stop doing that. "Lucas, remember this twin thing is a secret. You can't tell anyone, even if they promise not to say anything."

"I know! I know! Geez, you're really acting like Casey now."

I still didn't trust him completely. "This is very important. I want to speak with Casey first before we tell everyone."

"I can keep a secret!" he looked offended that I would suggest otherwise.

His adorable bubbly-self turned frustrated as he stalked off toward the bus.

"Lucas!" I called after him. But he ignored me.

He would have to get over it. I needed to make sure our secret was safe from my parents and Jake. At least until I spoke with Casey. I wondered if she had done the same thing I had and told my parents about the swap. I doubted it. She knew how delicate my mom's condition was, and wouldn't risk hurting her on purpose. Casey was a much better person than me. She at least could keep a secret. I was the one to ruin the swap with one stupid outfit.

On the bus, I sat alone in a seat behind Lucas, making sure he kept his promise. He chatted on with his friend about some cartoon show he liked and completely ignored me.

Good. Casey and Lucas were great at ignoring each other as big sisters and little brothers supposedly did. While I was okay with that for the moment, I wasn't sure I'd be that type of sister to him once we revealed our secret. I'd always wanted a brother and I would work hard to keep our relationship strong.

I stared out the window and sighed. I didn't realize how much I missed my own life and my parents. It had been over a week since I'd seen them before leaving for camp. I couldn't wait to see them both, especially my mom. Casey might have downplayed the situation since she didn't know the highs and lows of my mother's illness. But I'd be able to tell right away how well she was.

Going to the hospital must have scared Casey. It had scared me the first few times, but the move here had been the best option for her health. She'd seemed better than she had before. And I hoped that would continue for a long time. I had to believe it would. I didn't want to think about the alternative. I didn't want to even imagine my life without my mother. Sure, she hadn't been honest about where I came from, but there were more important things than that. And I would be there for her as much as I could.

When we arrived at school, I was the first off the bus. I didn't care who saw me running across the campus and into the front doors. If anything, the others would think it was Casey. A burst of energy flew through me as I entered the building and took the stairs two at a time to the second floor. I hoped that Casey was already in the bathroom, waiting for me. We only had a short amount of time before the first period and I wanted to get as much information from her as I could before we swapped for the day. We wouldn't be able to discuss much during the school day and my dad was always on time to pick me up. Any delay in getting outside might make him think something was wrong. And I wasn't ready to answer those questions yet. Not until I was able to see Mom again.

My heart was racing by the time I got to the second-floor bathroom. I took a deep breath and opened the door, prepared to get back to my life. And oh how it had changed!

CHAPTER THIRTEEN
Casey

After the phone call with Ali, I felt so much better about our situation. My goal for the day had been to contact Ali and I had done that. I could finally relax. By the time I got into the shower, I expected all the hot water to be gone, but it wasn't. In my house, we had to take quick showers so the next person could have enough hot water.

After the shower, I changed into another one of Ali's expensive outfits. I knew we were stuck home for the day while Ali's mom rested, so I went with a comfortable pair of mauve leggings and a purple shirt to match. Even though the weather was warm, I was careful to pick a shirt with sleeves so that no one would notice I was missing the heart-shaped birthmark that Ali had on her shoulder. The house was air-conditioned anyway, so I didn't have to worry about feeling hot.

I made myself a big turkey sandwich for lunch. I thought about going in the office to see if Ali's dad wanted one, but I didn't want to disturb his work. I had no idea what he did but for someone to call him numerous times early that morning, I knew it was important.

Instead, after lunch, I settled into the living room couch and watched several movies. After each one, I went upstairs to check on Ali's mom, who was sound asleep for most of the day.

Around dinner time, Ali's dad reheated some leftovers that were in the fridge. We sat at the table together and ate. He asked me how I was fitting in at school. I was honest and told him I — Ali — was making a bunch of friends. I should have felt jealous but I was happy for my twin. Brie was my best friend and I was comfortable just hanging out with her, rather than a big crowd. But Ali had walked into our school and everyone had wanted to be her friend. I realized that she was the type to make friends easily, and everyone wanted to be around her.

Ali's dad was so happy to hear that. I loved seeing the smile spread across his face. It was actually the first time I saw a genuine smile from him. I wanted him to know that his real daughter had settled in well to her new school after moving all the way across the country.

He heated up some soup for Ali's mom and took it up to her. I didn't want to interrupt their time together so I stayed downstairs. After that, I didn't see either of them until the next morning.

I went to bed early but I couldn't fall asleep right away. Instead, I plugged Ali's headphones into her cell phone and listened to Hailee Steinfeld, until her voice sounded distant and faded away...

The next morning, I woke up early. I'd set the alarm on Ali's phone to give me enough time to prepare. My entire body buzzed with excitement as I got ready for the day.

It took a while, but I picked the most Ali-like outfit for school that day and packed an extra one in Ali's backpack in case she didn't like the one I'd chosen. My own style was totally different to hers but I wanted to be sure that I was dressed the way that she would normally be. Considering the fact that everyone thought Ali had to leave camp early as she was so sick, I was sure she'd have a lot of attention on her when we got back.

When I went down for breakfast, Ali's mom and dad were already in the kitchen. I didn't expect to see her mom out of bed that early in the morning.

She had showered and changed into jeans and a t-shirt. She looked like a normal mom. I doubted anyone would have guessed she was ill or had been in the hospital the day before. To me, she looked radiant.

Ali's dad was sipping coffee and reading the newspaper at the table.

"What can I get you this morning, Ali?" her mom asked.

"Oh I can make something," I said, going for the refrigerator.

By their silence, I knew I had messed up. Ali's mom had brought me food the whole time which I'd assumed was because I was sick. I was thrown off by making myself lunch the day before. But I guessed Ali's parents usually made her meals.

I had to cover myself. "I mean, I wasn't sure how you were feeling…Mom. I can make myself something if you're not up to it."

She waved her hand dismissively. "I don't need to be resting anymore. I feel fine, Ali. How about some pancakes? I have chocolate chips!"

"That sounds great," I said, and settled into a chair.

I watched her prepare the pancakes and took note of the cheerful way she moved around the kitchen. I could see why Ali had called her mom her best friend. When she was

299

well, her cheerfulness was contagious. I couldn't help but smile while watching her.

After eating three whole pancakes, my stomach was bursting. But they were better than any restaurant. She was an amazing cook! I wondered how soon we'd reveal our swap to our parents. I wanted to sleep over at Ali's house with her as much as I could, so I could enjoy more of her family's company and cooking. I'd much rather spend my time here in this quiet house than go home to Lucas running around the place like a maniac.

"We should get going, Ali," Ali's dad said, suddenly breaking into my thoughts. "You don't want to be late."

He hugged Ali's mom and kissed her on the cheek. "Call me if you need anything, Grace. I'm going to stop by here for my lunch hour."

"You don't have to, Chris. I'm fine."

He squeezed her hand. "I know. It's more for me."

After putting Ali's jacket on, I went over to her mom and gave her the tightest hug I could muster. Tears sprang to my eyes and I had to quickly wipe them away.

"Oh, Ali, that's quite a hug. I'll see you this afternoon."

"This weekend went by too fast," I said to her.

She kissed the top of my head. "Well let's plan something fun next weekend to make up for you being sick." I had a feeling she meant for *her* being sick, but I didn't say anything.

"That sounds perfect," I said, knowing it was going to be Ali doing something special. I hoped that would make up for the weekend she had with my family. They'd probably bored her to death. I hoped our mom didn't ignore her the whole time but I wouldn't be surprised if she had. Though Ali seemed happy enough to be there. It was probably because it was something different. I was sure she'd be ecstatic to get home and have some well-cooked meals that didn't involve a microwave.

I got into the car with Ali's dad and reality sunk in as we pulled out of the driveway. I hoped we'd be able to include Ali's parents in the secret soon. I wanted to see them again, especially her mom. I prayed that she'd be okay and the treatment would be successful. I hoped more than anything that Ali and her mom would have many more years together.

I was still a little scared about what had happened this weekend. And I knew it wasn't the last time Ali's mom would end up in a hospital. But I hoped the next time would be just for a checkup rather than an emergency. She had begun to feel like my family and I wanted her to survive, more than anything.

Ali's dad was quiet for the entire ride to school. I assumed that was normal, or perhaps he had too much on his mind. It was a nice change not having to pretend to be Ali for a little while though. Besides, I was about to get back to my life and what a better time to start than now?

When we arrived at school, Ali's dad drove me right up to the front entrance. I unbuckled my seatbelt and gave him a hug. It was a little awkward but I wanted to show how much I appreciated him and everything he'd done this weekend, even if I was pretending to be his daughter.

"Love you, sweetheart," he said, chuckling. I wasn't sure Ali was so affectionate with her parents, but I was really going to miss them. They had made this weekend so much better than I'd ever anticipated. It was so good to see where Ali came from and get a break from my own family. As much as both families had lied, my mom was more to blame since she was our birth mother and the one who had separated Ali and me at birth. I wasn't sure what I was going to go home to that afternoon, but I would hold onto the memories I'd experienced with Ali's parents to get me through it.

"Love you," I replied and got out of the car.

Closing the door behind me, I waved to him as he

drove off. We'd arrived early enough that there were no buses in front of the school, only a few kids hanging out on the front steps.

I hurried into the building and headed for the second-floor bathroom. At least I'd have a little time to collect myself before Ali arrived.

I couldn't believe we had done it! The swap had gone off without a hitch. And Ali had also managed to build a relationship with Jake in the process. I couldn't wait to hear more about it. Maybe Jake would talk to me today like I always dreamed he would. Maybe we had inside jokes now! I smiled so hard my cheeks hurt.

The bathroom was empty as I'd expected. I stood in front of the mirror and unbraided my hair, fully prepared to become "Casey" again and get my life back to normal.

Although, it wasn't really normal now, was it? Now I had a twin and soon enough everyone would know. That was a little scary, but I finally felt complete. The thing that was always missing inside of me, now felt whole.

The bathroom door opened and I turned, coming face to face with my twin. This time was nothing like when I first met her. I felt closer to her than ever and I was excited for our future together.

CHAPTER FOURTEEN
Ali

The door hadn't even closed before Casey rushed over to me and wrapped me in a tight embrace. I laughed and hugged her back. The relief of seeing her in front of me was so overwhelming that tears sprang from my eyes. "I really missed you!" I said.

"Me too!"

We swayed back and forth a few times before we let go of each other.

Casey took a step back and her eyes were glassy too. "I can't believe we did it!" she laughed. "And I totally forgot how alike we look. I mean, duh, we're twins but being away from you for a few days made me start to forget."

"I know," I said, having the same thoughts. Our psychic connection was stronger now than ever. I could almost feel her excitement inside of myself. My heart felt full again.

"I almost don't want to switch back, have I mentioned how much I love your wardrobe?"

"You can borrow anything you want, anytime. I have more than enough." I knew my wardrobe was a little over the top but I didn't mind sharing at all, especially not with my twin.

"We don't have much time," Casey said, glancing at my cell phone. "We should probably swap everything now so we're ready for class."

"Yes, you're right," I said. "Let's do this!"

We went into separate stalls and undressed.

"How's my mom this morning?" I asked. Along with worrying all night about Lucas not being able to keep our secret, my worry had spread to my mom and her health. We hadn't had an emergency room visit for some time so I

304

hoped she wasn't getting too much worse.

"She was actually great," Casey said, passing my clothes under the stall. "She even made me breakfast this morning."

I smiled. If Mom was able to make breakfast, then I knew she was feeling better. Anytime she wasn't feeling well, the smell of food would make her ill. "That's so good!"

"I'm sorry again for forgetting your phone yesterday," Casey apologized. "I was so stressed when I couldn't contact you!"

I handed over her clothes. I had a lot more to feel guilty about than she did. "It's okay, Casey. I'm sorry you had to go through all of that at the hospital. That must've been really scary for you!"

Casey sighed. "I was just glad that your mom was okay. But I felt awful the whole time because I couldn't contact you. And there was this really mean nurse who was so horrible to me."

"Ugh, I know. Some of the nurses in the ER are terrible. But most of them are nice." I knew many good nurses. I doubted Dad would deal with anyone who was less than nice to my mother. My heart ached to see my parents again. I only had a little more than eight hours until that would happen. And if Mom was feeling well, I could tell them both about Casey.

Speaking of telling parents…I had to tell Casey about her family knowing about me.

Casey and I came out of our stalls at the same time. I stood in front of the mirror and braided my hair.

It felt good to be back in my own life.

Then I turned to Casey. "Casey, I have something else to tell you."

"Is it about Jake?" she asked with a smile.

I inhaled sharply. "No, it's not." If I could help it, I'd never tell her about my crush on Jake.

Casey raised her eyebrows. "Then what is it?"

I took a deep breath. "I didn't want to tell you yesterday because I wasn't sure what you'd say...but your family knows about me. About the swap."

Casey whipped around to look at me. "What???"

"When I went to take a shower yesterday morning, Grandma Ann saw my birthmark. I'm so sorry Casey, I kept forgetting about it."

Casey blinked a few times. "Oh my gosh! What did she say?"

"She was actually really nice about it. Then we told Mom and Lucas."

"You told *Lucas*?" Casey said loudly. She rubbed her eyes in disbelief. Her face was masked in shock. "His best friend is Jake's brother. Ali, I can't believe you did that. He's going to ruin this!"

"No, he won't," I tried to assure her. "I told him it had to stay a secret!"

Casey sighed in desperation. "Ali, I know you meant well, but Lucas *cannot* keep a secret!"

We said nothing for a minute or so. My stomach twisted with guilt. Maybe I should have kept it quiet. But it had been our mom's idea to tell Lucas. "Mom wanted to include him. It wasn't my idea. She wanted to be more honest."

Casey sputtered. "She wanted to be more honest? She's been lying our whole lives!"

I could see that Casey was still angry with our mother. I hadn't spent my whole life with her but this weekend made me think she wanted to change.

"Casey, I know you're still upset with her. But I think after your argument with Grandma Ann, our mom really wants to change. She spent the whole time with me this weekend. And she thought I was you. She was open to questions and everything. I think you should give her a chance."

Casey shook her head. "You've known her for a few days. She's lied to me my whole life. This is different. I appreciate you trying to defend her but I can't forgive her that easily."

"My parents lied too," I said softly. I knew it wasn't the same, but I wanted Casey to know she wasn't alone.

"I know," she said. I sensed her calming down.

"Is there anything else about this weekend I should know about?" Casey asked.

Jake's face came to the front of my mind. "No," I said

quickly.

"So when do you want to tell your parents about us?" she asked. "Do you want to do it together or separately?"

I hadn't thought about that. Maybe it would be better to have Casey there with me. Then they would be able to see for themselves that we were twins. I didn't think my parents would be as upset if Casey were there too. Seeing Casey and me together might make them understand how much I needed my twin in my life.

"Maybe we should do it together," I said. "I'm not sure I want to go through this on my own again." Even though Grandma Ann was understanding, I doubted my parents would be the same right away. If I had Casey with me, then I would have more confidence to stand up to them.

Casey moved her fingers through her hair, moving her wavy hair over her shoulders. We looked at each other in the mirror and smiled the same smile.

The door to the bathroom opened and I turned to see who it was, just as Casey said, "I can't believe I doubted we were twins when I first saw you."

My eyes bulged. Casey didn't see that someone had entered the room!

"You two are twins?" Ronnie asked, folding her arms in front of her.

She and Holly had come into the bathroom together and they both opened their mouths in surprise.

Casey jumped and then looked at me. My mind went blank. I thought no one ever used this bathroom. That's what Casey had said. Or maybe today was our unlucky day.

Casey and I looked at each other, then we looked at Ronnie and Holly.

I had to think quickly on my feet. "You misheard, Ronnie," I said, "she said we're *like* twins. You know, because we look alike."

"That's not what you said," Holly said.

"Ali's right," Casey said. "It's what I meant. How

would we be twins? We have different parents. I mean it is a coincidence that we look alike but that doesn't mean anything."

Casey was rambling, but it seemed to work. The girls quickly lost interest and turned to the mirrors to fix their hair. They started talking among themselves about the fair on the weekend, while Casey and I slipped out the door.

The first morning bell rang as we entered the hallway.

"Wow! That was close!" Casey exclaimed.

"I know. I really don't want anyone to know about us being sisters until I tell my parents. I'm not sure how they'd find out from any of the kids at school but I'd feel better if I told them in case they do hear it from someone else."

"I totally get that," Casey said. "I promise not to say anything to anyone. Let me know if you want me to come with you to talk to them, though. Like I said, I had such a great time with them this weekend. They really are lovely people. And they're such great cooks!"

I smiled. I was so lucky to have them in my life. But I was luckier to have a twin sister and a little brother now as well. I wished we could go home early and I could get this over with. But that wasn't possible. I'd have to wait.

CHAPTER FIFTEEN
Casey

Ali and I went into Mrs. Halliday's class. Brie was already there and I wanted to run over and tell her everything. But at the risk of someone hearing or thinking something suspicious was going on, I couldn't.

We arrived at my desk and Ali said a quick goodbye before heading to hers at the back of the room.

Brie leaned over close to me. "Casey?"

"Yes," I said.

She narrowed her eyes. "The real Casey?"

I giggled. "Yes, of course!"

"Well, you can't blame me for asking," she laughed.

I smiled at her. "I know."

"So, tell me everything that happened this weekend," she demanded. "How are you feeling by the way?"

"I'm better now—"

"Hey Casey," Jake said from the other side of me. I hadn't noticed him come into my aisle.

I smiled up at him. "H-hey Jake." I glanced back at Ali and she gave me a thumbs up. She hadn't told me exactly what she and Jake had chatted about at Lucas's game so I felt really unprepared. He'd never approached me before. She must have said something he liked.

"I had a good time with you yesterday," he said.

"M-me too?" His eyes drew me in and my mind went blank.

His eyebrows furrowed. "Are you okay?"

"Yes, I'm fine. How are you?" Wow, I was really

messing this up!

Even Brie looked uncomfortable.

Mrs. Halliday stood up from her desk and closed the door. "Everyone to their seats."

Jake looked back at me. "I guess I'll see you later, then."

"Bye," I said but he was already gone.

Tears pricked at my eyes. I couldn't believe I didn't ask Ali about anything she and Jake had talked about. I hadn't been prepared to see Ali's parents but I did better than just then with Jake.

Jake turned in his seat and began talking to Ali.

"That was, um, awkward," Brie said as Mrs. Halliday took attendance.

"It was so bad!" I said, brushing my hair away from my face in frustration.

"I guess Ali did a good job of making Jake like her, er, you at the fireworks."

My head whipped in her direction. "The fireworks? What fireworks?"

"At the fair. Ali didn't tell you about the fair on Saturday night?"

I chewed on my lower lip and glanced back at Ali who was smiling and talking to Jake. I'd totally forgotten about the fair. I supposed I was so wrapped up in telling Ali about the musical that I never asked her about that night. But she'd told me about everything else. Was she hiding something from me?

I couldn't believe that she would. We were sisters after all and she knew how much I liked Jake.

I pushed those thoughts out of my head. Ali would never do that to me. She probably just forgot since it most likely wasn't a big deal. I'd ask her about it later.

Mrs. Halliday started class so I couldn't ask Brie anything else.

I tried to pay attention as much as I could to the

lesson, but my mind wandered to what might have happened between Ali and Jake over the weekend. She'd obviously worked hard to get Jake to like me or else he wouldn't have approached me before class.

It was my fault that I acted like I normally did around him, shy and awkward. I made a promise to work harder at being normal in front of him. In between classes, I would ask Ali what they talked about so when I saw him again, I could pretend I hadn't been such a dork earlier.

I felt a little better, knowing that I had a chance to make things better.

When class ended, I went to the back of the room and asked Ali to come to my locker with me. In my rush to get into the building that morning, I'd forgotten my book for Miss Tucker's history class. Brie tagged along with us.

"What did you and Jake talk about?" Ali asked.

I groaned. "It was awful. I was a total dork. I couldn't think of anything to say to him."

"I'm sure he didn't think anything about it," Ali said. "Casey!"

Ali turned around and I continued to roll the combination to my locker.

"Casey!" Brie hissed in my ear.

I turned around and came face to face with Jake.

My eyes widened.

Jake's eyes darted between Ali and me.

Ali was smiling at him as if he had called her name.

I bumped Ali in the arm and she moved out of the way and went to talk with Brie.

"What's up?" I asked casually. I hoped he couldn't see my hands shaking.

Jake shoved his hands in his pockets. "Did I say something wrong earlier?"

I shook my head. "No, why do you ask?"

He scratched his chin and glanced over his shoulder at Ali. "You seem different all of a sudden," he said.

"Almost like a different person."

"Sorry," I said quickly. "I'm a little off today, I guess. I didn't get much sleep." A total lie. I'd slept better in Ali's bed than I ever had in my entire life.

"Oh, okay," he said. "Well, I just wanted to make sure you were okay. Like I said, I had a good time at the game yesterday. Hopefully, I'll see you at the next one too."

I glanced at Ali. Had she promised to go to the next game? "S-sure," I stammered.

He gave me a quick smile and left us.

I blew out a big breath. That was close! I did much better than this morning but I still had to be more confident. Ali and I had some serious catching up to do.

I moved next to her, "Hey, Ali," I said.

She didn't move. She was distracted with something down the hall.

I touched her shoulder. "Ali." She jumped as if I'd shocked her.

"Are you okay?" I asked. "You zoned out for a second."

"Sorry, Casey! I can't believe I responded to your name. I've been doing it all weekend. I guess it was a force of habit."

"It's fine," I laughed. "I can't believe I ignored my own name! But we'd better get ourselves back on track before there are more mess-ups."

The swap had become more complicated than I realized. I really needed to pay close attention for the rest of the day until my brain went back to Casey-mode.

"I have to go to the bathroom before class," Ali said. "Too much tea this morning, I guess."

She left and I finished up in my locker.

"Something is off with her," Brie said.

"What do you mean?"

"You didn't see her staring at Jake when he left?"

"No."

314

"And during the whole conversation you had with him, she looked so uncomfortable."

"She messed up. She was probably embarrassed."

"Are you sure about that?"

"Absolutely," I said. But Brie had raised the same questions that I had in the back of my mind. I decided to ignore them. I reminded myself Ali wouldn't do anything to hurt me. We were sisters. That meant something.

There were only two other close-calls that morning. During our history lesson, Ali started to answer a question after Miss Tucker called my name. When Miss Tucker corrected her, the rest of our classmates laughed. Ali brushed it off, but it was still awkward. Although, no one seemed to ask any questions about it.

And during gym, when Ali's name was called to go to a certain team, I moved in that direction until Brie stopped me. Thankfully, Mr. Pavoni had called my name immediately afterward, so no one noticed.

We had to pair off within our groups to warm up for the activity. This week we were doing relay races. Since Jake was on our team, I wanted to ask him to be my partner but he'd already asked Ali before I got to him.

Ali looked at me when he asked her and I moved next to Brie as if that was the plan all along. My stomach felt uncomfortable. Why did Jake ask her when he clearly wanted to hang out with me earlier? I thought back to the conversation and wondered if I'd actually said something wrong.

I felt like I had the first day Ali appeared in my life. She and Jake seemed to be getting on as well as they did back then. This wasn't supposed to happen! One of the reasons for the swap, which had been *her* idea, to begin with, was for her to help me with Jake. And now we were back to the beginning.

After class, Mr. Pavoni asked Brie and me to help

clean up the orange cones that were used. It gave me an opportunity to tell my best friend how I was feeling.

"Did you see how he was looking at Ali throughout the whole gym class?" I asked Brie.

Brie stacked several cones and handed them to me. I was in charge of the blue mesh bag that held all the equipment.

"Like I said before, something is going on with her," Brie said. "And Saturday night, she and Jake were very close at the fireworks. At first, I thought she was doing it for you, but now I'm not so sure. I know she's your sister and everything, Casey, but you might want to talk to her about all of this."

I started to believe her. My instinct was to be close to my sister but if she was interested in Jake, even though she knew how much I liked him, I wanted to know. Even though it hurt to think that might be the case.

For the rest of the day, I watched Ali and Jake interact. He and a few of his friends sat with us at lunch.

Jake talked to everyone, but I noticed he kept looking at Ali. She was doing the same. I didn't think they noticed me watching, but each time they glanced at each other, my stomach hurt even more. I didn't bother eating anything since I'd suddenly lost my appetite.

How could Ali do this to me? First, she had a great time with my family and now she was going to steal my crush away from me? It was totally unfair!

I wasn't able to be alone with her at any point to ask what was going on. But I also wasn't sure what I would say. I didn't want to appear jealous, but that's exactly what I was and I really hated that feeling.

I thought I'd be able to talk to her after school, but Ali wanted to leave straight away. I asked her to text me and let me know about the "big conversation" with her parents. Maybe she would want to have me over and I'd be able to ask her about Jake. Ali said goodbye to us, anxious to get home. I understood that. I knew she missed her mom and would want to check on her.

As Brie and I finished up at our lockers, Holly rushed over to us.

"I have some juicy gossip!"

I tried not to roll my eyes in front of her. Holly was a gossip queen and most of the time it had nothing to do with me.

"We have to get to our buses, Holly," Brie said.

"I'll be quick," Holly said. "I wasn't going to tell you but I figured since you weren't interested in Jake, you wouldn't be mad if I told you about him."

I froze. *When did I say I wasn't interested in Jake?* "What do you mean?"

"The last night of camp," Holly explained, "you two laughed when I mentioned you liked Jake, so I know you're not interested in him. Anyway, I have the best gossip!"

I turned to Brie and her cheeks began to flush.

"Guess what!" Holly said, trying to draw out the suspense. "Ronnie just overheard Jake Hanley asking Ali if she wants to go out with him!"

"What???" I asked, astonished. It was my turn to

flush red. I was unable to help my shocked reaction.

Holly's mouth popped open. "You said — you said you didn't like him."

I grabbed Brie's arm and I dragged her down the hallway. Holly called after us but I didn't bother to respond.

I rushed into the bathroom and dropped my backpack. "Did Ali tell Holly I didn't like Jake? Is this some sort of prank?"

"It wasn't like that," Brie said. "Holly mentioned something about Jake liking Ali and since Ali was sitting with me, we thought it was funny since she was supposed to be you. I don't know why we did that. But Holly needs to mind her own business. Even if you did stop liking Jake, she shouldn't keep putting that in your face."

My chest tightened. I tried to breathe through it but I couldn't. This was all messed up. I couldn't believe my sister could hurt me like this. I wasn't sure there was an explanation in the world to allow me to forgive her.

***

Look out for Twins Book 4
Available NOW!

If you love the Twins series and would like to read on, you can also purchase the next 3 books as a collection. This is much cheaper than buying each book individually.

Twins – Part 2: Books 4, 5 & 6

***

Thank you so much for reading this book. I hope that you really enjoyed it. If you did, would you mind leaving a review. I'd be so grateful!
Katrina x

Remember to subscribe to our website
Best Selling Books For Kids
so we can notify you as soon as we release a new book.

Like us on Facebook www.facebook.com/JuliaJonesDiary/

And follow us on Instagram
@katrinakahler
@freebooksforkids

The following series are also available as a collection, which is much cheaper than buying each book in the series individually.
Just search the titles on Amazon or on your favorite book retailer website…

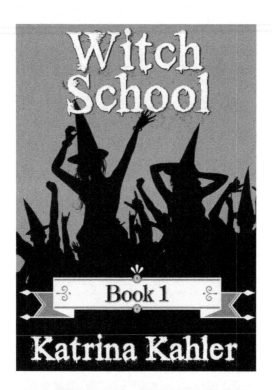

Made in the USA
Middletown, DE
02 November 2018